HARD RIDE

A.M. ARTHUR

carina
press

**carina
press®**

Recycling programs
for this product may
not exist in your area.

ISBN-13: 978-1-335-45948-0

Hard Ride

Copyright © 2020 by A.M. Arthur

This edition published by arrangement with Harlequin Books S.A.

For questions and comments about the quality of this book,
please contact us at CustomerService@Harlequin.com.

Carina Press
22 Adelaide St. West, 40th Floor
Toronto, Ontario M5H 4E3, Canada
www.CarinaPress.com

Printed in U.S.A.

HARD RIDE

Chapter One

Derrick Massey leaned his shoulder against the porch post and gazed out at the dark shapes of Clean Slate Ranch, barely lit by the tiny thumbnail of a moon somewhere in the night sky. He was probably the only person on the ranch still awake, and that suited him just fine. For all that today had been about joy, love and friendship, Derrick was grateful to finally be alone so he could grump over everyone else's good fortune.

This was the second time Derrick had traveled from the San Francisco suburb he lived in to the working dude ranch that was Clean Slate for a wedding. The first had been about a year and a half ago, when his little brother Conrad married Sophie Bentley here on the land. Today (or yesterday, since it was technically Sunday now), he'd watched two gay couples get married and profess their love and commitment.

And then Sophie had promptly gone into labor.

Derrick snickered softly at the memory of Conrad's panic and excitement. Their whole family—Conrad and Sophie, Sophie's big brother, Wes, and his partner, Mack, Sophie's parents, and Derrick had all ended up at the county hospital yesterday afternoon. But Derrick, Wes, Mack and Mr. Bentley had been sent back to

Clean Slate to get some sleep when the nurse told them Sophie's progress was very slow and the baby was unlikely to be born before mid-morning Sunday.

For as much as Wes complained about leaving his sister, he'd fallen asleep in the car.

Derrick couldn't sleep, though. Hell, he wasn't even tired, which surprised him since it was past three in the morning and he wasn't usually a night owl. But he was agitated by his own jealousy over the double wedding and the new baby. Seemed like everyone around him was pairing off, getting hitched and settling down, and Derrick...wasn't. And his confidence had taken a few big hits in the last two years.

A light came on in a second-floor window of the main house. The ranch owner lived there with his foreman and the ranch's cook. Derrick watched, but the light shut back off quickly. Someone up for a bathroom break, maybe.

Restless and bored, he stepped off the porch of the guesthouse and wandered down well-trodden paths. This one branched in two directions. One went to the row of small, two-man cabins behind the guesthouse where the ranch hands lived. The other path led to the big barn, and Derrick went that way.

The last time he'd been inside the barn, he'd embarrassed the hell out of himself by kissing one of the ranch hands before verifying they were both on the same page. They hadn't been, and Derrick had been very politely turned down. He and Colt had remained friends, though, and yesterday Colt had married his longtime love, Avery.

I really am happy for them.

Jealous of them, too. Intensely.

The barn was quiet, with a few dim lights giving the long corridor a gentle nighttime glow. One of the horses nickered softly. Derrick watched the nameplates on the stall doors until he found Valentine. He'd ridden her during his vacation here two years ago. He laughed at himself, because Derrick had thought Colt asking if he wanted to "visit Valentine" was code for hooking up.

"Wishful thinking, girl," he said to the horse, who blinked big brown eyes at him. "You wanna be my Valentine?" Cheesy but whatever. He was alone. As usual.

His little brother was married and having his first kid. His brother-in-law, Wes, was happily settled down and living with his partner here on the ranch lands. Every single person he worked with was either married, engaged or making new baby announcements. Not that Derrick was jonesing to raise a litter of kids, or to even get married, but a long-term boyfriend or girlfriend he trusted would be nice.

Except trust…yeah. Derrick no longer trusted easily. Hadn't for a lot of years. Not since his first serious girlfriend in college cheated on him and gave him a case of the clap, courtesy of the dude she was fucking on the side. And while that had been nearly a decade ago, Derrick seemed to have developed a neon sign on his forehead that said "Cheat on Me," because it had happened two other times before he gave up on dating.

Pump-and-dumps scratched an itch and didn't break his heart afterward. Except for Robin, yet another ranch cowboy Derrick had gotten involved with. But that had been Derrick projecting and seeing more into their frequent hookups than had ever been there for Robin, who was happily in love with *his* own boyfriend, Shawn.

Seeing them together at the weddings had hurt more

than it should have. But Derrick and Robin had been hooking up regularly for about a year, and their sexual chemistry had been off the charts. The fact that they rarely had anything in common to talk about after the sex was over should have been a big clue to Derrick not to get attached. But he had. And when Robin officially said he was off the market and their arrangement was over, Derrick had hidden his hurt. Derrick hadn't had a clue Robin had been dating Shawn for weeks, and the omission, deliberate or not, had dinged his honesty button hard.

No more cowboys for me. Nope.

"No more," he whispered to Valentine. "Maybe I'll give one of those dating apps a try. What do you think, girl?"

Across the way, another horse nickered. He glanced over his shoulder at the nameplate. Zodiac. Sophie had ridden her during their vacation, and she'd looked so tiny up on that horse. Well, she had been to begin with, and Derrick had teased her throughout her pregnancy about falling over if she wasn't careful. She'd simply blow a raspberry at him and go back to work, and she had worked all the way up to this Friday.

And sure, she was about two weeks early but incredibly healthy, and the nurses kept assuring their family she was doing great. Derrick wanted to text Conrad and see if there were any updates, but Conrad would wonder why Derrick wasn't asleep and his brother had enough to stress about. Derrick's niece or nephew would be along soon.

The barn was peaceful at night, so he wandered and visited with the horses until boredom set in. He explored a bit more, his bravery increased by the silent buildings and quiet land, broken only by the occasional rustle of air through the trees. On the other side of the main house was a big, barnlike building that Wes once told him was a garage for employees to park their personal vehicles in, so they didn't have cars parked all over, ruining the aesthetic of the ranch.

Two big barn doors probably opened to let cars in and out, and Derrick found a regular door a few yards down. It wasn't locked, so he went inside. Sure enough, a handful of cars were parked in various spots, including Robin's familiar red convertible. Because Saturday was the one night a week the ranch didn't have paying guests, a lot of the employees went into the cities for fun and entertainment. It had certainly been Derrick's favorite night of the week for a while, and he had many fond memories of that convertible…

A muffled clang from the rear of the building caught his attention. Derrick wandered closer, curious. The back wall had several doors and light shined from beneath the one farthest to the left.

Someone besides him was awake.

Were they allowed to be here this late? Not that Derrick exactly had permission, but no one had expressly said the garage was off-limits. What if they were stealing from the Garrett family?

Derrick approached the room on silent feet, glad he'd put on his sneakers in favor of the dressier shoes he'd worn for the wedding. The closer he got, the more distinct sounds filtered through the shut door. Grunting. Metal grinding. Some thumping. Was there some sort of machine shop in that room? And who was using it at zero-dark-thirty?

Derrick knocked sharply, then twisted the knob.

Pulled it open. The glare of an overhead florescent light made his eyes water for a few seconds before clearing. The simple, white drywall reflected the light and showed off a home gym. A treadmill, a heavy bag and speed bag, a set of free weights and a bench, and a stationary bike.

A man glared at him from the bench and put the set of weights he'd been using on the ground. Tall, familiar, with very muscled arms displayed nicely by his white, sleeveless tee. Muscles covered in tattoos and the tan skin of someone used to working outdoors. Thick, wavy brown hair and eyes that, even from a distance, were bright blue. The glare slipped away, and Derrick tried to remember the guy's name but failed.

"Wedding party," the man said in a gruff tone that tickled down Derrick's spine. "The brother-in-law. Sorry, I can't remember your name."

"Derrick Massey, man. Sorry if I startled you."

"Slater." He didn't give Derrick anything else to indicate if that was a first, last or nickname. Slater simply reached out and snagged a water bottle off the floor. Squeezed some into his mouth. "I heard Wes's sister went into labor up at the ghost town. Congrats."

"Thank you." Derrick wasn't sure how gossipy this crew was, but Robin had frequently said the ranch hands were like a family. "Looks to be a long labor, so some of us were sent back to get some sleep."

"You don't look to be doing a very good job of it."

Derrick laughed. "Busted."

Slater tipped his water bottle in Derrick's direction. "I'd ask if you came here to work out and wear yourself out, but most people don't work a treadmill in black jeans and a button-up shirt."

"I was exploring the place and heard you in here. I didn't know the ranch had a gym."

"It's something a few of us have pitched in on over the years." Slater stood and stretched, and no, Derrick did not stare when that tee's hem slipped up and showed off washboard abs.

Holy moly, this guy's smoking hot.

And unlikely interested in unwinding Derrick's favorite way. The odds of everyone who worked here swinging his way were impossible. Right?

Except Slater caught him staring and winked. "The ranch is a physical job but some of us like to get some gym time in, too, and this is more practical than driving all the way to San Jose to find a good one."

"Makes sense," Derrick replied. "So you lift?"

"Depends on my mood." Slater crossed his arms and shifted his weight, which cocked his hips ever so slightly. "Sometimes I'm in the mood for lifting some weights, getting an upper-body burn. Other times I want to run on the treadmill, get some leg action going. You?"

"I'm a big fan of diversity in exercise." He wasn't completely sure if Slater was flirting or not, so Derrick played along. No more cowboy flings for him, but this was more fun that staring at the sky by himself. "Switching it up keeps things interesting."

"Agreed. Sometimes I almost feel bad for the folks who only like one or the other." Slater's expression was mild but something twinkled in his eyes. A subtle teasing Derrick played along with.

"You figure you'll ever pick one over the other? Settle down?"

Slater shrugged. "Doubt it. Tried that once and it blew up in my face like a phosphorus grenade. You?"

"Same." Good. He liked knowing Slater wasn't looking to date. Maybe Derrick could scratch his cowboy itch one more time before he left the ranch tomorrow. One last hookup for nostalgia's sake. "I'm a big fan of testing out new equipment, too. Seeing what's out there."

Slater's expression became more intent, and that blue gaze very blatantly cruised up and down Derrick's body. "See anything in here you're curious to test out, Derrick?" The heat in Slater's eyes when they met Derrick's sent blood rushing to his dick and arousal burning in his gut. The front of Slater's sweatpants rose, tenting with what looked like a very nice package.

"Could be," Derrick hedged. "So long as we're both in it for the exercise and not because of any particular…model color?" Back in the heyday of his using hookup apps to find "dates," he'd gotten so many private messages asking if the whole "do all black guys have huge dicks" rumor was true that he'd eventually deleted his profile.

"Don't care much about the outside as long as I'm attracted to it in some way," Slater replied. "And since I'm running out of exercise metaphors, I think you're hot as hell, rumor is you're bi, and I am very much in the mood to get my dick sucked."

Derrick laughed. While flirting was fun for a while, he preferred blunt people who got down to business. Probably why he liked Colt and Robin so much. "Then we are absolutely on the same page. And if you're up for more than just swapping blow jobs, I've got stuff in my wallet."

Slater considered him for a beat. "Club fan?"

"You only live once." And Derrick was only a few

short weeks away from turning thirty. While his clubbing days were nowhere near over, some nights his body told him that his habit of going out every weekend was no longer the best idea in the world. "I like to be prepared."

"You got a preference?"

For a split second, Derrick thought he meant being with men versus women—and then his brain caught up to positions. "Nah, I'm vers. You?"

"I top but I'm open to new things." Slater jacked his thumb at a pile of blue mats in the corner of the room. "You wrestle ever?"

"Tried my hand at it in high school but the first time I sprang a boner during practice, I quit." He'd been picked on mercilessly for that until he finally hit the growth spurt that shot him from a skinny five-seven to his current six feet. Then the bullies had backed off. "Why?"

"Take your pants and shirt off. Let's exercise a bit before we get down to the fun." Slater whipped off his sleeveless tee, showing off swaths of sunkissed skin and more tattoos on his chest and back. Derrick had never been with a guy with so much ink, and he was fascinated by all the different images. Words and cartoon characters, animals and a sunset.

They made Derrick wonder why Slater had chosen some of those particular tattoos as he shucked his own clothes, leaving himself in boxer-briefs and a white undershirt. He palmed his erection as he watched Slater lay down four of the blue mats in an empty corner of the room. Not a lot of space but they were kind of crowded by the other equipment.

"Let me guess," Derrick asked. "You were a high-school wrestler who got a wrestling scholarship to a great school, but an injury forced you to quit and work with horses for a living?"

Slater laughed so hard he doubled over. "Man, you are not even close to my backstory. I learned how to wrestle from a guy I met in Basic Training." He stood straight and went perfectly still, expression flat, as if shocked he'd admitted such a thing.

And the confession intrigued Derrick. He'd flirted with the Armed Forces before getting a hard-on for charity work after a childhood neighbor's house burned down, leaving a family of six with nothing. "How long were you in the Army?"

"About six months. Wasn't a good fit. Discharged." His tone indicated the conversation was over. Slater cracked his knuckles. "You still into this?"

"Definitely." Slater definitely struck him as a guy with a lot of secrets and stories worth hearing. But this was a fling, not a date. Derrick strode toward the mats. "How do we start? Neutral or referee's position?"

"I think neutral works for our purposes here."

Derrick wasn't entirely sure what their purposes were, other than getting hot and sweaty before they fucked. And he was down for that. Slater prowled the mats before stopping at one corner. Derrick came at him from the opposite corner, and they both leaned in. Put their hands in the proper places. It left their faces very close together, and Derrick caught a hint of something sweet on Slater's breath.

"So who's the ref here?" Derrick asked.

"Me." Slater whistled, and in a whip-fast move, had Derrick on his ass, shoulders down in a perfect pin.

Derrick blinked up at him, stunned and slightly

winded already. "Can I get a do-over if I say I wasn't ready?"

"Nope. But how about we do best of five?"

"Yeah, okay."

On his third straight hit to the mat, Derrick knew he'd lost but he wasn't about to give in just yet. Playing around with Slater was too much fun. He rolled fast, pushing Slater onto his back so he could straddle him and press their groins together. Slater made a show of struggling, but he pretty much allowed Derrick to clasp his hands above his head on the mat. They were well matched in height and bulk, and Derrick liked that. He preferred guys who were close to his size, versus super big or really small.

Derrick thrust their groins together, pleased by the soft moan Slater released as their hard dicks rubbed and pressed. Nowhere near enough to get off but it felt great, and Derrick hadn't played around like this in a long time. Quick fucks meant no chance of getting attached. He had no desire to get attached to Slater but he also had no plans to sleep anytime soon. This was way more fun than waiting for news about Sophie.

"This doesn't count as a pin," Slater said with a hard upward thrust of his own hips. "Three in a row means I win."

"Yeah? What's your prize, then, Mr. Winner?"

In a sudden display of dexterity, Slater hooked a leg between them and shoved at Derrick's chest, knocking Derrick backward onto his ass. Slater rolled with him and expertly reversed their position so Derrick was flat on his back, half off one of the mats.

"Damn," Derrick said with a smirk. "You sure you aren't a pro wrestler?"

"Learned how to fight and defend myself after spectacularly fucking up my life." A fine sheen of sweat had broken out over Slater's face, giving him a slightly dangerous edge that heated Derrick's blood even more. He groped the side of Derrick's butt. "I'm thinking I wanna take this ass for a ride."

"Horse ride? I'm not very good but—oh, fuck."

Slater squeezed Derrick's dick through the thin fabric of his boxer-briefs, tight enough the hold bordered on painful. But Slater never tipped over that edge, only kept Derrick teetering on the precipice of too much. Then he slithered down the length of Derrick's body, yanked his underwear down and off, and sucked on the head of his cock. Derrick moaned, a little surprised by the intense heat of Slater's mouth. The way he worked the foreskin back with his lips instead of his hand, testing and playing, and holy crap, it was incredible.

Derrick wanted to grab Slater's head and shove deeper inside, to get more of that wonderful heat around his dick, but Slater was watching him with so much intensity—so much "let me drive, just enjoy" in his eyes—that Derrick submitted. For now. Submission was not his thing but he could let Slater be in charge for a little while. Something told him it would be worth it in the end.

Slater sucked him and played with his balls, keeping eye contact almost the entire time. As if not quite trusting Derrick. Derrick didn't take it personally. They were basically strangers acting on chemistry and instinct. And Slater knew what the fuck he was doing, edging Derrick close to release before Derrick warned him off. He wasn't a fan of being fucked if he'd already come, and he really wanted Slater to fuck him.

"Get your stuff," Slater said.

He was naked and kneeling on the mats when Derrick returned with the condom and two lube packets he kept in his wallet. He didn't always fuck (or get fucked by) his hookups but he liked being prepared for when the desire struck. And it was striking like lightning all over the place with Slater. Seeing the well-built, tatted-up cowboy kneeling naked, his lips spit-shiny and cock straining for attention, put a strange feeling deep in Derrick's gut.

More than lust, more than horniness…he wasn't sure how to describe it beyond…need? A desperate need not only to come, but to come with this man in particular, and to make him come in return.

"Stand up," Derrick said. Slater did but turned his head when Derrick went in for a kiss.

"I don't kiss one-offs." Slater quirked an eyebrow, as if daring Derrick to make a fuss or force a kiss.

"Cool." Derrick slid to his knees and gripped Slater's hot cock by the root. "Can I kiss this?"

"Please do."

Derrick leaned in and inhaled the man's scent, delighting in just the right amount of sweat and musk, and his mouth watered for a taste. He licked into the slit and stole a bit a precome. He enjoyed tasting his partner, discovering their unique essence. Working them delirious with mouth, fingers and tongue.

"You gonna suck it or propose to it?" Slater drawled.

He looked up the length of Slater's inked torso. "Why? You got a ring you want me to put on it? I'm fond of black rubber myself."

Slater's lips twitched. "Maybe. Don't have it on me,

though, so how about you get to sucking before I take over and just fuck your brains out."

"I dare you." The words slipped out, and he'd only meant to tease. But Slater's half smile went feral and he tackled Derrick to the mats. They rolled and wrestled, naked bodies rubbing. Slater nipped at his bicep and throat and even one ass cheek, and Derrick hadn't realized how much little bites like that turned him the fuck on. It was one of the most erotic things he'd ever done in his life, and they somehow ended up in a sixty-nine, with Slater on top.

Slater pushed his cock into Derrick's mouth, and Derrick opened for him. Relaxed his jaw and throat to take Slater's length, while Slater jacked Derrick's dick slowly. Teasing strokes while he thrust steadily against Derrick's tongue. Derrick wasn't sure how Slater got hold of the lube packets, but a slick finger rubbed between his cheeks. Derrick spread his legs, giving Slater room to push that finger into his ass.

It had been a while since he'd been fucked, and the sudden intrusion made Derrick shout around his mouthful of cock. The slight burn faded quickly, though, especially when Slater went right for Derrick's prostate. That first press against his gland nearly made Derrick bite down.

"Fuck, you're tight," Slater said. "Sure you've done this before?"

Since he couldn't currently speak, Derrick pinched Slater's ass hard. Slater laughed and kept working his ass with that wicked finger. Two burned in the very best way, and Slater seemed in no hurry to get to the main event. Even after Slater pulled his cock out of Derrick's mouth and rolled Derrick onto his hands and knees, Slater kept fingering him. Pulling and stretching, stuffing him full of lube. Teasing his prostate. Tugging on his balls until Derrick was a panting, broken mess.

"Fucking fuck me already," Derrick snarled, annoyed he'd been reduced to begging but also so desperate to come he'd have eaten his own shoe if that was the only way he could. "Come on."

"Not so cocky now, are you, Tiger?"

"You keep messing around, this tiger's gonna bite you."

"Promise?" Slater circled his rim once more with a single finger, then withdrew. Derrick listened with silent gratitude as Slater opened the condom and put it on. The sticky sound of more lube. A hand gripped Derrick's left hip and blunt pressure against his hole became the entire focus of Derrick's world.

Hot, steady pressure, and so fucking slow when Derrick had expected a quick, brutal penetration. But Slater took his time, working his not-insignificant girth into Derrick's ass half an inch at a time, in small nudges and pulls, driving Derrick kind of insane until Slater's pubes finally tickled his bare ass.

Firmly seated now, Slater draped his chest over Derrick's back and bit his shoulder. Derrick clenched at the sudden sting, and Slater did it again. "Damn, you feel good," Slater whispered, hot breath right by his ear. "Could stay like this all night, with you so tight around me."

Derrick wasn't usually much for games like this, but something about Slater made him want to play. To tease and poke the bear. And in some other ways…to submit. He didn't do much, simply relaxed his shoulders a fraction and let his head hang lower, but it was

enough. Slater seemed to recognize that Derrick was
giving in and accepting what Slater had to offer, and it
shifted things between them.

Slater pulled out completely, then shoved his way
back inside. Derrick shouted and held on, hands sliding on one of the rubber mats as Slater let loose and
fucked him exactly like Derrick had asked. Hard slams
of hips to ass that made Derrick's own dick smack up
against his abs on each thrust. Slater wrapped his arms
around Derrick's waist and pulled him up so they were
both kneeling, Slater still pistoning into Derrick's ass,
the penetration even deeper like this. It kept Slater's
cock from hitting Derrick's prostate, the bastard, but it
also prolonged Derrick's orgasm. He clutched at Slater's ass, unsure if he was encouraging him or not, but
he needed to hold on.

He didn't know how long it lasted. Minutes. Hours.
Slater turned him onto his back and fucked him with
his body bent nearly in half, until Derrick's sweaty body
slid across the mat with each brutal thrust, and Slater
lost traction. Being turned over the weight bench and
fucked made Derrick lose his mind a little bit, and he
started cussing at Slater. Alternately swearing at him
and begging to come, and he had no shame in it, because
Slater had reduced him to nothing more than ass, cock
and balls, and the ocean of pleasure rising to meet him.

"Fuck, close," Slater panted. "Yeah. Fuck!" He
pushed deep inside and stilled, forehead pressed between Derrick's shoulder blades, breath fanning across
his damp skin. "Oh, fuck, yeah."

He reached around and fisted Derrick's dick, and it
only took a few tugs before that ocean crashed down
on him, drowning Derrick in his release. Derrick rode

it out, struggling simply to breathe. Vaguely aware of Slater pulling out and easing Derrick onto his back on the floor, they lay side by side for a while, simply breathing. Derrick couldn't find two brain cells to rub together for a long time, his legs still occasionally twitching with aftershocks of the most powerful orgasm of his life.

And he'd had *a lot* of orgasms.

"Think you'll be able to sleep now?" Slater asked.

"Guh." Not his finest response ever. "Could sleep for a week after that. Damn."

"You're welcome." Somehow Slater rolled easily to his feet and put his shorts on.

Derrick was barely able to sit upright on the mat by the time Slater was dressed, had his water bottle in hand, and was striding toward the gym door. "Dude?"

Slater paused at the door and looked over his shoulder. "Take it easy, Tiger. Maybe I'll see you around sometime." And with that, Slater strode out the door.

Chapter Two

Derrick hadn't expected a goodbye hug or anything, but the way Slater had simply dismissed him…well, it kind of hurt. Especially after the sex had been so incredibly mind-blowing. That kind of chemistry didn't come along every day, and the last time Derrick had felt it, he'd allowed himself to fall in love. And get cheated on. Again. So maybe Slater walking out the door was a good thing. It stated exactly what last night had been, which was sex. Nothing else.

The best sex of his life, which kept Derrick from really falling asleep in his bunk for the few hours he managed to relax until dawn. With a new crop of paying guests arriving at the guesthouse a little after ten, their group of wedding guests needed to be gone by eight thirty so Patrice could get the place cleaned up and ready. When Derrick had stayed here before two years ago, he hadn't given much thought to how carefully the employees here kept the ranch going behind the scenes.

He was sharing the room with two of Colt's brothers. Brand snored away in his own bunk, and Rem slept as silent as the dead, while Derrick couldn't get comfortable in his—which had nothing to do with his sore backside. He had no regrets about the rough sex. Only how it had ended.

As the rising sun brightened the room, he eagerly rolled out of bed and into the small shared bathroom to shower and dress for the day. He hadn't packed much, since they'd only been here for one night, and while Brand used the bathroom, Derrick packed up his stuff. The elder Bentleys, plus Sophie and Conrad, were using the guest rooms at Mack and Wes's cabin, and while Derrick could have crashed on their couch, he liked staying at the ranch.

And it had given him a spectacular encounter last night (this morning?) hadn't it?

Downstairs, the living area and dining room were abuzz with baby chatter, and Derrick assured everyone who asked he hadn't heard anything new yet. As far as he knew, Sophie was still in labor, Conrad was still hovering, and Mrs. Bentley was still holding her own baby girl's hand every step of the way.

Mack and Wes were there, and Mr. Bentley spent most of breakfast checking his phone between bites of pancakes, even though it never dinged or sent an alert. Derrick did the same, though, eager to head back to the hospital to see the newest addition to the extended Massey family.

Slater was one of the last people to enter the kitchen for food, and he didn't give Derrick a second glance. Derrick pushed down a wave of hurt, because fuck him. It had been sex, nothing else, and Slater didn't owe him anything. Not even a "good morning" wave. If Slater wanted to pretend they didn't know each other, fine.

Derrick swallowed his final bite of pancake and was considering another piece of bacon for fun when Wes's phone pinged. He checked the message and then let out an ear-piercing squeal. "Sophie's in active labor, let's go!"

A loud cheer went up around the crowded kitchen and, by extension, the dining room where some of the lingering wedding guests were eating. Derrick managed to put his plate in the dishwasher bin and follow Wes, Mack and Mr. Bentley out of the guesthouse. Wes and Mack had driven down to the ranch in Mack's truck, but they had more room in Mr. Bentley's car, so their quartet piled in. Wes and his dad up front, Mack and Derrick in the back.

Wes was glued to his phone the entire drive to the regional medical center, and when text updates stopped coming through, it could only mean the newest Massey was almost here. Derrick wanted to burst with excitement. While most of their cousins had four or more siblings, Derrick and Conrad were their parents' only kids, because their mom had an emergency hysterectomy after Conrad was born. Derrick liked the idea of kids of his own, but it wasn't a deal-breaker, and he hadn't grown up craving a wife and passel of kids like Conrad. He could totally be the cool uncle, though.

And niece/nephew number one was almost here.

Derrick tried not to fidget too much during the drive, because his butt was still a tad tender from the hard pounding he'd gotten only a few hours ago. Mack shot him curious looks but didn't ask any direct questions, and thank God for discreet sort-of-brothers-in-law like him. Mack and Wes weren't married, but they were beyond committed and he made Wes happy, so Mack was family.

Mr. Bentley was just pulling into a spot in the visitors' parking lot when Wes announced to the car, "It's a girl! Five pounds, ten ounces, eighteen inches."

"That's a small baby," Mr. Bentley said. "But Sophie's not that big herself."

"She got a name yet?" Mack asked.

"Not yet that Mom texted," Wes replied. "Oh, my God, I have a niece!"

Derrick laughed, because he had a niece, too. A perfect little girl he intended to spoil rotten every chance he got. He shared a quick hug and backslap with Mack in the car, and then proper hugs with Wes and Mr. Bentley once they all got out. Their group wasn't allowed in the delivery room, but Leta Bentley came out to hug everyone while Sophie and the baby were settled in a proper room for a few hours.

"She was such a champ," Mrs. Bentley said with tears in her eyes. "Put off the epidural as long as she could but it's not easy to go without."

Wes kissed his mom's cheek. "I cannot wait to see the little podling," he said.

"Podling?" Mack parroted.

"Sweet pea? Mini-me? Cutie-pie? I dunno, I'll come up with the perfect nickname when I actually meet the kid."

"We all can't wait to meet her," Derrick said. He had a little competition going with Wes for who got to be the favorite uncle, and he was up for the challenge.

Derrick and Conrad's parents, Robert and Sharon, arrived a few minutes later with balloons and a stuffed fish that Wes got a good giggle out of. "Sophie said the nursey has a nautical theme," Mom said after sharing a bunch of hugs.

Dad clapped Derrick on the shoulder. "When are we going to get you to settle down like your brother?"

"Never," Wes teased. "He's too picky."

"It's not my fault I have high standards," Derrick retorted. He and Wes had gotten along immediately the first time they met, and Derrick considered the highstrung flirt every bit as much a brother to him as Conrad.

A nurse finally said they could see the new parents, and Derrick tried not to bounce on his toes. Mrs. Bentley hung back a bit because she'd seen the baby, but the rest of their group swarmed the bed where Sophie sat with Conrad beside her, cradling the swaddled bundle.

"Everyone," Conrad said with a huge grin, "meet Mia Ebony Massey."

Wes squealed and kissed Sophie's temple. "I love the name Mia, oh, my God. She's gorgeous."

Derrick was tall enough that he could peek over Mr. Bentley's shoulder and get a look at the baby. She had amber skin and a button nose and the thickest eyelashes he'd ever seen. She wore a little cap over her head and her eyes were closed, and she was just the most precious thing ever.

"She came out with a full head of hair, too," Conrad preened. "Just like I did."

Mom laughed. "Yes, you did. Your brother was practically bald until he was two."

"How did I not know that?" Wes asked.

Derrick swatted his shoulder. "Who cares how much hair I had? This is about little Mia and who gets to hold her next."

Conrad stood and offered the baby to Mr. Bentley— she was his first grandchild after all, so Derrick wasn't too jealous—and the free space on the bed gave Wes room to properly hug his sister. They whispered a bit, and Wes kissed her cheek again. "You did good, sis."

All the grandparents got to hold Mia first, and finally it was Derrick's turn. Mia was awake and her big, dark eyes adorably cross-eyed. Derrick's heart turned over hard, and he silently vowed he'd protect this precious angel with his life. "Hello there, Miss Mia. You are going to be so spoiled by your Uncle Derrick."

She spit bubbles at him.

Derrick reluctantly turned Mia over to Wes, who was so nervous he had to sit in one of the visitor chairs first. Mack crouched next to him and they both admired the baby. Conrad returned to sit with Sophie. Mom and Dad held each other, just like the Bentleys. And Derrick…stood there. The only person in the room without someone by their side to share in this beautiful moment.

And it really sucked.

He pushed the dour thoughts away and concentrated on his family until a nurse said it was time for Sophie to try breastfeeding, so everyone except Conrad cleared out. In the waiting room, their group discussed how long to stay, versus going home. The Bentleys needed to get their and Conrad/Sophie's stuff from Mack's cabin, and Derrick's bag was still back at the ranch. In the end, they agreed Sophie needed to rest, and there would be plenty of time to dote over Mia once they got her home.

Mr. Bentley drove Derrick, Mack and Wes back to the main ranch and dropped Derrick off so he could get his bag and say goodbye to Valentine. Derrick would drive Mack's pickup to the cabin in a bit.

Derrick collected his overnight bag first, which had been stored in the kitchen, then chatted with Patrice for a few minutes. Derrick showed her some photos of Mia on his phone. "Such a precious little thing," Patrice cooed. "You tell her parents I said congratulations, all right?"

"I will, thank you, ma'am." Derrick accepted a quick hug from the older lady and then went outside to store his bag in the car trunk. Since Derrick had ridden into the town of Garrett with Conrad and Sophie yesterday, he'd probably hitch a ride home with his parents. Even though he'd moved out of his hometown and closer to San Francisco, they still lived somewhat nearby so it wouldn't be totally out of their way.

He'd parked near the main house, which gave him a good view of the barn's entrance, and he spotted a familiar backside disappearing into it. Slater was probably getting horses ready for this afternoon's riding demo and Derrick hated interrupting his workday. But he had to say something to the man.

It was important to him to at least say goodbye, even if he didn't understand why.

Derrick strolled casually toward the barn and entered its cool gloom. Hay and horse and dung assaulted his nose, and he sneezed twice, unused to the strong odors.

A deep chuckle prickled across his skin. "Now there's a city boy for you," Slater said from a few stalls down. "Sneezing over some straw."

"I only work in the city. I grew up in a small town. I'm just not used to barns." He had no need to defend his body's reactions but he didn't like the idea of Slater assuming he was some soft city boy. "Came in to say goodbye to Valentine. She's the horse I rode when I was on vacation here two years ago."

Slater leaned his hip against a stall door and folded

his arms, his expression difficult to discern. The barn wasn't dark, exactly, but the dim bulbs every couple of yards didn't produce much artificial light. "I'd say I remember, except I was on vacation myself that week and off the ranch."

"Yeah." Oh, yeah, Derrick would have remembered the guy from that week, and he'd only gotten a brief glimpse of Slater at Sophie and Conrad's wedding. "Do anything fun on your vacation?" *Or anyone?*

Slater quirked an eyebrow. "Got to spend time with someone I don't get to see very often." He jacked the thumb over his shoulder. "Your horse is down there."

"I know." Derrick resisted the urge to growl as he strode past Slater to Valentine's stall. He rubbed her forehead and nose, wishing he had a treat for her.

"Here." Slater handed him a sugar cube. "Guess you don't have time for a ride, seeing as you've got a new baby to spoil rotten."

Unsure what sort of ride Slater had in mind, Derrick shook his head. "No time. I have to pick Mr. Bentley up soon so we can get back to the hospital." He let Valentine take the cube off his palm, then chanced meeting Slater's eyes. Those bright blue depths simmered with a familiar mix of interest and wariness. "Don't suppose you ever make it into San Francisco on Saturday nights?"

"Clubbing hasn't been for me in a very long time."

"Not a dancer?"

"Not a lot of things." A kind of sadness flickered across Slater's face, and Derrick didn't like that.

He wanted to get things back to light and flirty. "Maybe I'll book myself for another week here as a guest this summer. We can go on…another hard ride?"

Slater smirked. "Maybe." That was it.

"Well, uh, I guess I should be heading out. It was nice working out with you last night, Slater."

"Same. You take care of your niece, you hear me? Babies are precious gifts." On that odd choice of words, Slater pretended to tip a hat at him and strode away.

Derrick watched him walk toward the corral at the other end of the barn, uncertain about leaving their conversation like that. But Slater hadn't offered to exchange numbers, so even if he was interested in another booty call, he obviously wasn't interested in being friends.

Oh, well. They'd had great sex and that was exactly what Derrick had been looking for. A smoking-hot one-off. Time to put the broody cowboy out of his mind and get on with his life.

Slater sat on his bunk long after his roommate, Hugo, had gone to sleep Sunday night, unable to find enough peace to do the same. He'd been upset and running on so many negative emotions since getting his mail yesterday, and the offending envelope lay on his lap. Opened. The card tucked back inside. He fingered the rough edge where he'd torn the paper, then traced his finger over the name printed carefully over the Clean Slate Ranch address.

Kendall Stamos.

He barely remembered who Kendall was most days, because that part of his life was so long ago. Slater was a nickname given to him in prison, because some guy thought he looked like the dude from *Saved by the Bell*. Slater never saw the resemblance, but it had stuck long after. Become almost a character he played, unsure who he truly was anymore. But once in a while, he got a letter that reminded him he'd been Kendall once, and he still had people who knew and loved that guy.

The guy he'd been before prison.

The return address simply said "R. Stamos."

Rachel. God, I miss you, baby.

He hadn't seen her in two months, not since his last vacation week rotation. His boss, Arthur Garrett, made sure all his horsemen got a reasonable amount of vacation time during the work year by rotating them out, so one guy was always on vacation for a week while everyone else worked the ranch. And that didn't count the week of Thanksgiving, and the month or so around Christmas and New Year's when the ranch was closed to guests. Sometimes hands traded weeks, especially if they had specific plans. Slater rarely had plans, and he coveted every week he got to spend with his little girl.

Although *little girl* was relative since the envelope in his lap contained an invitation to her high school graduation. Rachel was now the same age he'd been when he and her mom got pregnant. How had so much time passed? Somehow, he was thirty-five with a graduating seventeen-year-old, and it was such a mind-fuck he didn't know what to do. Hell, his roommate was only a few years older than his own kid.

A kid I barely know, and that's my own fault.

His thoughts swirled back to today's early morning news of Sophie Massey giving birth to a little girl of her own. Derrick's first niece. Slater didn't know the Masseys or Bentleys at all, but he sent frequent, silent prayers to the deities above for Derrick's niece to have a long, safe life. He'd said as much to Derrick in the barn a few hours ago, and Slater had almost said too much.

The only person at Clean Slate who knew about Rachel was Arthur, because Rachel was Kendall's daughter. Here, he was Slater. And Slater was tired. Bone tired. Yes, he liked his job, and he liked his coworkers, but he was stuck. Mired down in familiarity and routines. Sometimes he fantasized about packing a bag, getting on his motorcycle and just…riding. Leaving California, maybe going east.

He had, after all, completely met the terms of his parole and was now a free man. He could go anywhere in the damned world he wanted. Except Rachel was up north in Sacramento County, and he couldn't imagine leaving her behind completely. Especially not when she would be eighteen in July and able to see him whenever she wanted, no longer bound by the court's visitation order. He silently cursed his ex again for how she'd manipulated the court into reducing his role in Rachel's life to supervised visitation. At least his own father and stepmother had full legal custody, and Rachel wasn't living with her hot mess of a mother.

Although, in some ways, that had also been Slater's own damned fault for getting his dumb ass sent to prison in the first place.

In his bunk, Hugo let out a rough snore and twisted around in bed. Slater watched the kid until he settled. Hugo could talk at length about horses, farming and ranching, but he hated talking about his own personal life—which was fine by Slater, because he wasn't much for sharing, either. But Slater suspected the kid had nightmares once in a while, like just now. But Hugo also seemed friendly with Shawn Mathews and Miles Arlington, two guys closer to Hugo's age who worked up at Mack's ghost town. Maybe he talked to them about his shit.

Slater tucked the graduation invitation into a small box he kept under his bunk, where he stored the infrequent card or letter he got from Rachel. Then he stretched out and tried to sleep. But sleep didn't come, and he gave up after an hour. Headed to the garage and the workout room.

He eyeballed the mats he hadn't put away, and the used condom still laying in a dried-out heap on the floor. Sundays were usually too hectic with arriving guests and the weekly welcome barbecue for folks to use the room. He grabbed a paper towel from the dispenser over the utility sink in the corner and scraped up the mess. Put the mats back where they belonged.

Fuck, but Derrick has a fine, fine ass.

A fine ass, a great body, and hot damn, he'd been responsive to getting fucked. Slater liked to be rough when he knew the guy could handle it, and Derrick had definitely handled it. Almost seemed to crave it. Too bad they'd both agreed it was a one-off. He wouldn't have minded another go at Derrick's ass.

Oh, well. Slater shoved all thoughts of Derrick out of his mind, got the tape and boxing gloves, and took his inability to sleep out on the heavy bag.

Two weeks passed, nudging April closer to May. Slater found a few hours of sleep most nights after a good workout, then woke with the rising sun, dressed and out of the cabin before Hugo even stirred. He liked going on morning walks before breakfast was served up at the guesthouse, so he headed east toward the guest trails. Patrice's terrifying rooster call would go off any moment and wake the guests, so he was unlikely to run into any of them this morning. A long walk alone was something he'd taken for granted before going to prison. Now, he didn't take the outdoors for granted, ever. It was part of the reason he enjoyed doing the overnight camping trips with the guests. Sleeping outside, under the stars in open country?

Heaven, after five years in hell.

He was scheduled to go out with tonight's guests, so after breakfast he headed to the main office to check for signups. It was only nine and guests had until ten to sign up, but there were four names on it already. Cool. They offered the trips Monday, Wednesday and Friday evenings, so it was rare that all the guests decided to sign up on one night. The last time Slater recalled that happening was a few years ago when an eighteen-person wedding party booked the entire guesthouse for the week.

Slater had been somewhat new to Clean Slate at the time, and that experience had been…interesting.

He and Reyes were leading tonight's trip, and by ten they had three additional campers. The guests practiced riding in the corral, and after lunch they got on their way. Reyes rode lead on Mischief, a palomino with a scar on her forehead from an infected insect bite that made her look like she was always quirking an eyebrow at you and planning something. Slater rode on the chuck wagon, which was being led by Hot Coffee. Hot Coffee was Reyes's personal horse, but she was great with the chuck wagon, and with being ridden bareback for part of the trip.

They could store extra saddle equipment in the chuck wagon, but Slater had learned to ride bareback a few months ago, and he enjoyed how much freer he felt than riding on a saddle. And Hot Coffee seemed to like him.

The chuck wagon followed behind all the riders so he could keep an eye on them. They had two kids on this trip, both about five or six, and they each wore a safety helmet because they were on a horse solo. Their parents watched them like hawks. The other guests along were a young gay couple named Zack and Pike, who'd heard about how inclusive Clean Slate was and had decided to check it out with Pike's mom for her birthday.

They took a break halfway to the campsite to give riders a chance to stretch. The horses drank in a nearby creek. Then they kept going to the site, which had a dedicated fire pit and a rail for the horses. After getting the animals un-tacked and settled with feed bags, Slater unpacked the wagon while Reyes helped the campers rustle up firewood. They ate beef stew and biscuits and bullshitted for a while. Played poker for toothpicks. Gazed at the stars.

They had a good group, and Slater found himself envious of both happy couples. When everyone turned in, Slater took first watch, and when Reyes relieved him halfway through the night, he actually fell into a deep sleep. He always slept better out under the stars. In the morning, they left the chuck wagon behind and took a short trip up to the mountain summit. It had an amazing view of the vast valley below, where they often saw herds of deer in the distance and all kinds of birds swooping in the sky.

The gorgeous sight was slightly marred by orange safety flags pushed into the ground about three feet from the edge of the cliff. They'd had a lot of rain back in February and early March, and some flash flooding had ripped through the valley, making some of the cliffs soft and unstable. The flags were simply a reminder not to get too close to what could be dangerous ground.

Everyone dismounted. Reyes told the "legend" of Wes's horse spooking while on vacation and discovering Bentley Ghost Town to the north—free publicity for his husband's saloon and all that. Afterward the guests were free to wander for a bit. Slater had a little too much coffee at breakfast, and he wandered into a copse of scrub trees to take a whiz.

As he returned, a small figure too close to the edge of the cliff caught his eye. One of the boys. Sam? Where the hell were his parents? Slater started to look for them, but Sam's entire body wobbled. One of his feet had sunk into the ground, and the little boy was panicking.

Shit.

"Don't move!" Slater bolted toward the boy. Less than twenty feet had never felt more like a mile, and no one else was closer. The ground started to give way, and Sam lunged in his direction with a wail. Slater grabbed the outstretched hand and yanked Sam forward, away from the crumbling cliff edge.

The momentum sent Sam rolling to safety, but it left Slater off-balance. His feet gave out as the ground was suddenly not there, and he flailed as his body started sliding. Reyes screamed his name, and a strong hand clasped his wrist. Kept Slater from falling any farther down the rocky, pitted slope. But Slater couldn't find purchase with his feet on the soft, soaked land, and Reyes was starting to lose ground, too.

"Hold my ankles but don't come closer," Reyes shouted. "The entire edge could go."

Slater stared into his friend's terrified eyes, and a strange kind of peace washed over him. He'd saved

Sam's life, and he was okay with that. He wouldn't take Reyes down, too. Couldn't make Miles a widower after being married only two weeks.

The ground shifted again. Slater released his hold on Reyes's wrist.

"What are you doing?" Reyes asked with a kind of desperation Slater had never heard from the man before.

"Not getting you killed, too." With his free hand, Slater lunged up and squeezed a pressure point on Reyes's wrist. Reyes hollered a protest as his fingers spasmed. He released Slater.

And Slater fell.

Chapter Three

"Slater! Fuck!"

Reyes Caldero had been truly terrified only a handful of times in his life. He'd been terrified as a sixteen-year-old while watching his former gang buddies torment and torture a neighborhood gay kid, scared of being found out himself. He'd been terrified after crashing through the floor of a burning building and being trapped, forced to watch a fellow fireman burn to death, assuming he'd die the same way. He'd been terrified one night last fall when he and Robin had investigated a distant gunshot on ranch lands and found a bloody, shaken Miles on the ground with his stalker ex-boyfriend unconscious beside him.

This was a new sort of terror, because he'd just watched a man he considered a friend begin a long, tumbling descent down the slope of the mountain. On purpose. Slater had disappeared from view pretty quickly, but dust continued to rise, hinting at his path. He didn't scream, didn't shout, didn't make a sound.

Behind him, both the little boys and their mother were crying. The father, Frank, and the tall blond—Zack?—had been holding Reyes by the ankles. The young redheaded guy was desperately searching for a cell signal, despite Reyes telling them at the start of the trip there was no WiFi out here. The redhead's mother clung to his arm, worry all over her face.

Reyes scooted away from the edge on his stomach and then raced over to Mischief and grabbed his walkie. "Judson, you copy? I've got a 911 out at the summit. Judson!" He took a few deep breaths as he waited for a response, because panicking in front of the tourists was a bad look.

"Copy, Reyes, what's going on?" Judson replied.

"I need at least three horsemen up here to collect the guests and get them home. Then I need Search and Rescue as soon as possible." Reyes swallowed hard so he didn't vomit. "Someone got too close to the soft cliff, and Slater went over pulling them back."

"Christ Almighty. Let me get on all that. Stand by, okay?"

"Yeah."

Reyes turned and jumped a mile, surprised to see Frank right behind him. "I am so sorry," Frank said, obviously distraught and near tears. "He saved my boy's life."

"It's not your fault." Reyes forced the words out, because why hadn't Sam's parents been paying better attention? "Help's on the way, you just see to your family."

Frank returned to his wife and sons. The gay couple approached Reyes with equally shocked expressions. "Can we do anything?" Zack asked. "I'm a SEAL, man. I've got rescue experience."

Reyes's first instinct was to say yes, please, to the SEAL. But his job was to protect the guests, not put them in danger. "You just sit tight and wait. You're a guest and I can't risk you getting hurt. We've got more men on the way, and they'll get here a lot quicker at a gallop and take you all back to the ranch. Search and Rescue is being notified." All Reyes wanted to do was fling himself up onto Hot Coffee and find a way down into that valley. He was pretty sure he could get in about a mile or so east, where the land sloped down, but he had a responsibility to the seven people in his care. He needed backup first.

Judson called back on the walkie. "I've got Robin, Ernie and Hugo saddling up and heading out as soon as they can," he said. "Search and Rescue will be out with a chopper to get down into that valley. How are the guests?"

"Upset but coping." Reyes didn't know what else to say. He needed to hear Miles's soothing voice, to have his husband tell him everything would be okay. That they'd find Slater caught in a bush, cut up but alive. That Reyes hadn't just allowed a man to fall to his death. "Who knows?"

"Only a handful of people so far. None of the guests. Don't need a panic or for folks to think the trips aren't safe."

The last thing the ranch needed was bad publicity over an accident, but it had been one of the ranch's staff that was hurt, not a guest. Hell, Slater was a goddamn hero for saving that kid's life. "I hear that, Judson. What about Arthur?"

"Hell no, he's down at the rescue today, and I don't want him notified until we actually know something about Slater."

"Right." Reyes completely agreed with that decision. Arthur had had two heart attacks last year, was turning eighty this year, and his health was delicate some days.

The last thing he needed was the stress of worrying and wondering if Slater was alive. Hell, Reyes wasn't sure he'd manage this stress himself without exploding.

While they waited for backup, Reyes shouted Slater's name a few times to no response, other than his own voice echoing over the vast valley below. He kept rubbing his right wrist, still able to feel Slater's hand in his, then the sharp pressure that made Reyes inexplicably let go of the man. Maybe Slater had done it to keep Reyes from going over, too, but damn it, that had been Reyes's decision. Not Slater's.

Too much time passed before his walkie crackled. "Reyes? You there?"

Miles. Reyes pressed the talk button. "*Mi alma*, what are you doing there?"

"Judson called me. I think he could hear how stressed you are in your voice. How are you?"

Reyes turned away from the guests. "Barely holding it together."

"I can't imagine. Do you think…?"

"I don't know. I'm trying to have faith he's alive down there somewhere, but it's a long way down." He shivered once.

"I know. I love you, and I know you did everything you could."

I'm not so sure about that.

"As soon as backup gets here," Reyes said instead, "I'm going to go look for him. I won't be back for a few hours yet. Please don't pace and worry over me."

"I'll worry over you anyway. I can't—" He coughed hard. "Do you believe he's alive?"

"I have to believe that or I'll go crazy. I was holding on to him, Miles. I couldn't…" Reyes wasn't sure what he'd do if Slater's name ended up on the list of people he'd failed to save in his lifetime. "I have to believe he's alive."

"Then I believe it, too, my soul."

Reyes closed his stinging eyes and rubbed at them. "I'll make sure you're updated, okay?"

"Okay. See you later."

"Yeah."

He hated ending the conversation, but Reyes was also stretched thin. Thankfully, the small family had calmed down, and the other trio was sitting quietly together near their horses. Eventually, the thundering noise of hoofbeats rose in the distance, and three familiar faces on horseback appeared.

Reyes told Ernie and Hugo to get the guests and chuck wagon back to the ranch, and then he enlisted Robin to ride with him. Now that he knew more about Robin's history with horses and riding, he trusted the man to keep up. He'd already saddled Hot Coffee with the equipment from the chuck wagon, and they took off to the east at a gallop. The land did slope down, as he'd hoped, and they found a way to get into the valley itself.

Reyes wished he'd grabbed the shotgun from the chuck wagon, but too late now. They rode fast, over rocky terrain and around bushes and trees, moving west again, closer to the place where Slater had gone over. Being in a valley made walkie reception difficult, but they made it back to the summit at roughly the same time Reyes heard the whir of a helicopter in the distance.

They'd been leading guests to the summit for years and had exact coordinates for emergency crews to use. Horses were a bit trickier. He and Robin dismounted and tied their horses to nearby trees, in case they reacted poorly to the chopper noise. Slater was nowhere at the bottom of the slope, which suggested he'd gotten caught up somewhere above. As much as Reyes wanted to start climbing the damned mountain himself, he deferred to the authorities.

Twenty minutes of searching finally led to a shout of "We found him!" from one of the teams scouring the side of the mountain. The resulting urgency told Reyes that Slater was still alive. He and Robin hung back with their horses as the helicopter lowered a body-sized basket to a site roughly thirty feet up, where a big bunch of bushes and trees dotted the side of the mountain. A few minutes later, a body rose toward the waiting chopper.

"They've got him," Robin said.

"Yeah." Reyes watched the basket disappear inside the chopper and the vehicle flew away with its patient. They wouldn't be acting so quickly if Slater was dead, right?

More than any other question, as he and Robin led their horses back toward Clean Slate, was who did they call? Slater never talked about his past, about any family he might have. Who was Reyes supposed to tell about today's accident, other than his brothers at the ranch? Reyes didn't have a clue.

And deep, deep down, that hurt. A lot.

Eating dinner at Sophie and Conrad's apartment had become something of a tradition in the last year or so, and Derrick enjoyed spending time with his brother and sister-in-law. And now he had his little niece Mia to dote on for several hours a week, and he'd begun to crave Mia time.

Derrick had missed seeing Sophie at work for the last three weeks and looked forward to these evening visits, bringing with him treats for Mom, toys for Mia, and usually a six-pack for Dad.

Conrad wasn't a frequent beer drinker, though, and the six-packs were starting to add up. He accepted the new pack graciously as he welcomed Derrick into their place. After their engagement, Sophie had moved from her parents' house into Conrad's one-bedroom apartment, and it worked for them for now while Mia was still an infant. But they were looking for a bigger, affordable place now, since they tended to lease out quickly in the Bay Area.

"Hey, sorry, man," Conrad said. "Delivery should be here soon. I got home too late to cook, Mia has been fussy about breastfeeding, and Sophie's been distracted with Wes for the last two days."

"Why?" Derrick asked. "Wes having some kind of crisis?"

Conrad shut the door and crossed the small living space to the galley kitchen. "Not personally, no. Remember that summit we saw the morning after our camping trip?"

"Sure." He'd never forget the view.

"Apparently one of the ranch hands went over the side saving a kid and he tumbled almost to the bottom."

Derrick nearly fell over from that shocking statement. "What? Who was it? Are they okay?"

"Guy named Slater. The name's familiar but I don't remember him."

It was a good thing Derrick had given Conrad the six-pack, or he'd have dropped it. His heart started pounding. "Shit, really? Is he alive?"

"Yeah, he's alive." Conrad put the six-pack in the small pantry, then pulled two cold beers from the fridge. "Wes called a little while ago with an update. Apparently, he's got a small skull fracture, busted his right ankle all to hell and has all kinds of cuts and bruises, but by some freaking miracle, the guy is alive. Fell down a freaking mountain and survived."

Derrick took the beer from his brother but didn't drink. He couldn't wrap his brain around the idea that the hot guy who'd fucked him senseless three weeks ago had nearly died. "Jesus."

"Yeah. With the ghost town closed these last two days, Mack, Wes and some of the other guys have been spending a lot of time with Slater at the hospital."

"I bet." Derrick would have been there, too, if he'd had a clue Slater was hurt.

Wouldn't he? No one knew he and Slater had fucked, so how would Derrick have explained his presence at the hospital? "Wait, you said he has a skull fracture?"

Conrad nodded and gave Derrick a funny look, probably confused by Derrick's intense interest in this subject. "I'm sure Sophie can give you more details. She's feeding Mia in the bedroom but she'll be out in a bit."

"Right." Derrick finally sipped his beer but didn't really taste it. His thoughts were full of Slater and all the healing he had ahead of him. And the fact that the guy had saved a kid's life. How many times did people get to do truly heroic shit like that?

Their delivery arrived before Sophie emerged from the bedroom, sans Mia, and her finger-over-lips signal meant Mia was down for a nap. Sophie looked exhausted but she still tore into the container of chicken carbonara Conrad had ordered for her. Derrick wasn't a picky eater, and he accepted a chicken Parmesan sandwich and side of seasoned fries. The food was from a local place with good prices.

Ever since Sophie gave birth, Conrad had made liberal use of his phone's delivery service app.

"Conrad told me about Slater," Derrick said after a few minutes of eating. It hadn't come out quite as casually as he'd hoped, but Sophie didn't notice.

"Yeah, it's such a shame." Sophie speared a piece of chicken. "His ankle is really busted up and will need at least one surgery to repair the damage but even that doesn't guarantee he'll walk normally again."

That completely sucked ass for someone with an active job. "What about his head injury?"

"The swelling is going down, and the doctors are optimistic the fracture will heal on its own. But he's having some issues with hand-to-eye coordination, writing and a bit with remembering words. It's all stuff that can be relearned with physical therapy, at least, according to Wes."

"It sucks to lose his independence, though, with that ankle busted up. Slater doesn't strike me as the kind of guy who's used to leaning on others."

Conrad put his fork down and grabbed his beer, sharp eyes missing nothing. "I didn't know you and Slater were friends."

"I wouldn't say we're friends, but we had a conversation the other weekend. Neither one of us could sleep, and we ran into each other both not sleeping." *And then we fucked, and it was crazy-intense, and I need to know the guy will be okay.*

"So all you did was talk and not sleep?"

Derrick shrugged, because why lie? "We might have hooked up in the garage."

Conrad groaned. "When are you going to grow up and stop being such a horn dog?"

"Hey, I'm older than you."

"Exactly. I've got a wife and a kid, dude."

"Please, don't start." Derrick took several long pulls to drain his beer. "I'm going to get earfuls of it all summer long at every damned wedding I've RSVP'd for, just because I'm the oldest, unattached cousin in the family." He stormed over to the fridge and grabbed a second beer.

"Hey, leave him alone," Sophie said to Conrad. "Do you know how many times your mom has asked if I know any nice girls Derrick can date in the last six months alone?"

"No, but I can guess," Conrad replied. "Sorry, brother, I'm not picking on you. Just…you seem to have a type going on with that ranch. First Colt, then Robin. Now Slater?"

Derrick returned to the table and picked at a fry. "Maybe I do have a type. Dunno. We both made it very clear it was a one-time thing. I would like to visit him, though, make sure he's okay. Would that be weird?"

"Not at all, it's sweet," Sophie said. "Call Wes—no, bad idea. Call Miles. I'll give you his number. He and Reyes can coordinate a visit without spreading your personal gossip around. Which I'm sure Slater would appreciate, too."

"I know he would. Thanks, Soph."

"You're welcome. He must have been a good lay if you're still thinking about him."

Derrick rolled his eyes. "You're as bad as your

brother sometimes." Wes was a relentless gossip whose tact button was often stuck in the off position. Sophie could be a lot more discreet, she was only grilling him about this now because it was the three of them.

"That wasn't a no."

"Ugh, eat. I need quality Mia time before I go. Gotta be in early to finish a new batch of Dream Boxes that are going out at noon."

"Ooh, which one?"

"The children's T-shirt project."

"That's my favorite."

The nonprofit Derrick worked for—and Sophie was on maternity leave from—had various branches that worked with corporations and small businesses, in order to give back to the community, and Derrick oversaw the Dream Boxes branch. Dream Boxes were craft projects that companies could buy, assemble as volunteer hours or teambuilding exercises, and then have sent back so they were distributed to qualified charity organizations.

The T-shirt box came with blank shirts in children's sizes, fabric markers, stencils, ribbons, scissors and supplies for the volunteers to decorate shirts and to also make homemade cards to send to the charity receiving the gifts. Quantities sent depended on the number of volunteers, who decorated the shirts with the stencils (or freehand, if they happened to be artistic). The homemade gifts were a favorite of the kids who went through some of the local Bay Area shelters. Derrick liked working for Dream Boxes. It gave big businesses a corporate write-off while also getting their employees to give back to the community with a little creativity and two hours of their time.

And a chunk of the cost to the sponsor went right

back into the parent nonprofit to pay their workers and keep their projects funded. Derrick enjoyed his coworkers and the nonprofit at large, but sometimes he got itchy feet. Wondered what else he could do with his small-business degree and experience.

Not tonight, though. By the time they'd finished eating and cleaned up the kitchen table, Mia's familiar cry came over the baby monitor. The apartment was small enough that they really didn't need it, but it had been a baby shower gift and the signal was strong enough that if Sophie needed to run down to the basement laundry while Mia was napping, she'd hear if the baby woke.

Derrick fetched his niece from her crib. Tiny hands waved in the air, and her plump cheeks were streaked with tears. "None of that, princess, no tears." He carefully lifted her up, still amazed at how small she was. She'd gained a bit of weight since birth but had a lot to go.

She wrapped strong fingers around his index and gummed him. He patted her behind but the diaper felt okay. No obvious stinkiness. Probably just tired of napping and ready for another go at Mommy's boob. He sat in the rocking chair with her and simply studied her perfect face and big, round eyes.

Kids were great when they belonged to other people, and Derrick had never longed to be a father the way Conrad had. Their parents had been terrific examples of loving, supportive parents, and they had a great extended family. Most of them quietly ignored the fact that Derrick was bi, but he also didn't bring dates, male or female, to any family functions anymore. Not after the first two disastrous relationships he'd been in. Too bad he couldn't find someone to pose as his girlfriend or boyfriend for a few months this summer—just so he could get through the weddings without all the questions.

Even better if it was a guy. Maybe it would hammer home to a few of his relatives that him liking men wasn't a phase or Derrick acting out, but that he was bisexual and genuinely attracted to men.

Like I'm attracted to Slater.

Their chemistry was undeniable, and Derrick didn't usually have so much trouble forgetting a hookup. But Slater had a long recovery ahead of him, and they weren't even really friends, so if Derrick did go the "fake relationship" route, he'd have to find someone else willing to play along.

"Nah, what do I need a girlfriend for?" Derrick said to Mia. "I've got you, princess. I will spoil you rotten. Only the very best of everything for you. Toys, schools, colleges, you name it."

"Setting rules for my kid?" Conrad asked from the doorway.

"Yup."

"Do I get a say?"

"Maybe." He studied his brother, who watched Mia with so much love in his eyes that it made Derrick's heart hurt a little bit. "You did good, bro. You take care of my best girl, you hear me?"

"I will. Promise. They're my whole life."

"Good."

One day Derrick hoped to look at someone else with that kind of love and devotion in his eyes. Maybe it wouldn't happen this year, maybe not next year. But eventually.

He hoped.

Chapter Four

Slater only knew it was Friday because his phone told him so. His habit of leaving it behind at the ranch during overnights was the only reason it hadn't ended up crushed to bits during his long descent down the summit four days ago. Four? Three? Whatever. He was sick of this hospital and wanted to go home, but his stupid fucking ankle was scheduled for surgery today. And he had to stay at least one more damned day after that.

He vaguely remembered what might have been the slam against the rock that first damaged his ankle, but most of the fall was a blur because he'd banged his head pretty early on. Coming to an abrupt stop in a cluster of brush had knocked him out briefly, but when he came to he hadn't been able to move. Everything had hurt—even his fucking hair had hurt—and he'd waited for death to claim him.

Instead, rescue workers had claimed him, and he'd ended up here. Very much not dead.

Not that Slater wanted to die. But in that moment on the cliff, knowing he could take Reyes with him, he hadn't been afraid of it.

The first time he'd seen Reyes in the hospital, the man had been beside himself with worry and gratitude,

and he'd assured Slater his expenses would be covered
by the ranch's insurance. Slater hadn't cared about that.
He just wanted to be sure Reyes didn't feel guilty about
the fall; it hadn't been his fault. Sure, Slater had slurred
his words a little, and he'd momentarily forgotten how
to say "forgiven" but that was all his stupid head injury's fault.

TBI. Three small letters with one huge meaning.

He couldn't remember the meaning in that moment,
but he did know it.

Thankfully, he was in between visitors. He wasn't
given breakfast and wouldn't get lunch, because of the
damned surgery later, and he was pissy as a spring bear
when he was hungry. Miles and Reyes had visited him
every day, often bringing him boxes of Cracker Jack,
and Slater had no idea how they'd known it was his favorite snack food. He pulled his last box out from behind his pillow and started munching, despite orders
not to eat. He had a mighty bruise on the left side of his
jaw that made eating the crunchy stuff somewhat painful, but everything else throbbed anyway, so whatever.

Other guys had been by to visit, but he was fuzzy
on who. Definitely Judson. Maybe Hugo and Arthur.
Hadn't Patrice come by with a loaf of homemade banana bread?

Sure, they cared, but all Slater could think about
was how much of a burden he'd become to his coworkers. Instead of the independent adult he'd been since
he was a teenager, now he couldn't walk without assistance, and he fucking forgot words! He hated that
beyond anything else, but the only thing the doctors
would say was "it'll take time."

Slater didn't have that much time. Rachel graduated in…seven weeks? Give or take? He had to be up near Sacramento to see her walk the stage. Get her diploma. After being mostly absent in her life for the last decade, he owed his daughter that much and more. But his right ankle was damaged, and he'd never be recovered enough by then to ride his bike to the ceremony. Hell, he didn't know how he'd manage getting around Clean Slate with his foot in a cast and on crutches. How he'd shower in that small tub. Manage his own laundry when the machines were in the guesthouse basement.

Sure, the others would volunteer to help, but Slater was no mooch. He didn't take from others without thought for their feelings, not like Rachel's mom.

Someone knocked and Slater suppressed a groan. It could be another nurse poking at him as much as an unwanted visitor. "What?" he yelled. The door was half-open, and he waited.

Derrick Massey surprised the shit out of Slater by walking into the room with a plastic bag in one hand, the other dangling loosely by his side. "What are you doing here?" Slater asked without thinking.

"Sophie and Conrad told me what happened." Derrick stooped his shoulders and angled his head low, as if self-conscious of being there. He also wore a tentative smile that was…oddly cute. "I needed to see you for myself. For someone who tumbled over the side of a mountain, you…look good."

"Liar." While Slater used the bathroom with a nurse's assistance, he'd never bothered looking at himself in the mirror. He felt every cut, bruise and scrape vividly when he spoke or even smiled. He was a mess and they all knew it. "I feel like shit, so I must look like shit, but at least I'm alive, right?"

"You sound disappointed." Derrick stopped an arm's reach from the foot of the bed. "You got a death wish?"

"Nah. Don't have much of a life wish, but I don't want to die. I also didn't want to take Reyes down the mountain with me. I made a choice. Destroyed my ankle. Busted my head. But I'm alive. Gonna try to stay that way."

"Good."

Slater held his snack up. "Cracker Jack?"

"No, I'm good. I, uh, wasn't sure how bored you were." Derrick fished a magazine out of his plastic bag and tossed it onto Slater's lap.

Slater picked it up. A professional wrestling magazine. He started laughing but that just made his bruised ribs hurt, and he cursed Derrick for the amusement. "Bastard."

Derrick snorted. "I couldn't help myself. Look, I know we aren't friends. We aren't really anything besides acquaintances who banged once, but I'm glad you're semi-okay. I mean, not-dead is better than anything else, right?"

"We'll see." He stared down the length of his battered body to where his right ankle was immobilized. "If they can't fix that mess so I can walk again, being not-dead probably isn't worth it. Hard to mount and ride a horse with a bum foot."

"You could get another job with a bum foot."

Slater snorted but left the comment alone. There weren't very many companies willing to employ an ex-con, especially one with a bum foot. But Slater couldn't think that far ahead yet. He was too terrified of having surgery in a few hours. He'd never gone under the knife before. "We'll see, won't we?"

"I bet you're pretty tired of people calling you a hero, huh?"

"Little bit. Wasn't about to let a six-year-old die."

Derrick took four steps closer, his hand resting on the blanket by Slater's leg. "Rumor is you made Reyes let you go so he didn't go over, too."

Slater looked at the opposite side of the bed, beyond exhausted of defending that decision. The first time he'd seen Reyes after the fall and been halfway conscious, Reyes had alternated between berating Slater for his hero complex and thanking Slater for being so brave. And Reyes had babbled a little, drifting in and out of Spanish, until Miles got the man to calm down and think clearly.

"I wasn't gonna take another man down with me," Slater said. "The cliff was crumbling, and he would have died a fool, instead of living to love his husband."

"Maybe, but he strikes me as a loyal fool."

Slater grunted, way too at ease bantering with this man. "Why are you still here? I'm alive, you saw it with your own two eyes, and I appreciate the magazine. Now you can go. Shouldn't you be at work, anyway?"

Instead of annoyed, Derrick seemed amused. "You this grumpy with everyone who tries to be your friend?"

"Yup. Especially when every single part of my body hurts, even with painkillers on a steady drip. I went over a cliff, Derrick." *And I finally thought I'd give my family the peace they deserve.*

Derrick took another step closer, too damned observant, his eyebrows slanted in a deep V. "You sorry you lived?"

Instead of answering the question Derrick had already asked him once, Slater simply held his dark, sad gaze until Derrick looked away first. Derrick spotted his phone on the mobile tray and grabbed it. Slater didn't even try protesting, fully aware Derrick was adding his cell information to the contacts list. As much as Slater wanted to delete it the moment Derrick left the room…he wouldn't. Couldn't.

A strange part of him that enjoyed Derrick's company didn't want this to be their final goodbye. Slater had survived his fall, by some miracle. Maybe being friends with Derrick was part of his second chance at life.

"I've never had surgery before," Slater said without thinking.

Derrick returned the cell to the table and eased onto the side of the bed by Slater's hip. His expression was so clear and supportive that Slater didn't mind he'd let such a stupid thing slip out of his mouth. "They putting you under?"

"No, doc said they'd do a local, so I'll be awake but won't feel it." That was the part that worried Slater the most. He'd heard stories of people who'd woken up in the middle of surgery. What if he started to feel them installing steel rods, or whatever the surgeon said they'd be doing?

"If it helps at all," Derrick said, "I had my wisdom teeth removed a few years ago. All four. I was scared to be put under but it wasn't so bad. Counted back from a hundred, got to ninety-four, and then the surgeon was telling me he was all done."

"Sounds perfect. Maybe I can beg them to just knock me out." Slater tossed another piece of popcorn in his mouth. "Probably won't with my head injury, though."

"If you're having surgery, you probably shouldn't be eating that."

"I know." With a grumpy sigh, Slater stuffed the box back under his pillow. "Contraband from a friend."

"So when are they springing you from this joint?"

"Day after tomorrow." There was another reason the hospital had kept him this long. One of his organs had been bruised and they'd needed to monitor his…blood pressure? Reyes would remember. Slater had given his consent for all his medical stuff to be shared with the man, so at least one of them could keep it all in his head.

"You gonna go stay with family?"

Slater snorted so hard his nose ached afterward. "Hell no."

"Not close to anyone?"

"That's an understatement." One Slater was not unpacking with Derrick right now, thank you very much. "Besides, they're not close by and my insurance is through the ranch. Can't risk losing the therapy I'll need to walk right again if I move away."

And think right again, thanks to my busted-ass head.

"So you're going to recover at the ranch?"

"Don't have much of a choice. Why? You offering me your guest room?"

Derrick didn't respond right away, and Slater studied the man harder. He was definitely considering something, which made Slater nervous. Sure, Derrick was practically an in-law to the ranch itself, thanks to his relationship with Wes, and Wes's with Mack, but he had no reason to be so invested in Slater's recovery. Unless he thought Slater was suicidal or something and wanted to keep an eye on him.

"I'm not sorry I lived," Slater said, answering Derrick's earlier question. Unsure why he needed to reassure the guy. "I don't like being so uncertain about my future, that's all."

"I get that. And this is going to sound really bizarre, but I have a proposal for you."

"I only accept white gold and twenty-four-carat diamonds for all engagements."

Derrick chuckled, a deep, comforting sound. "Not that kind of proposal. Although between my insurance and the ranch's, you'd probably have way better options for physical therapists if I did marry you."

Slater blinked hard at the completely casual way Derrick said that. "You are a very strange man, do you know this?"

"What can I say? I think outside the box, which is probably why Wes and I get along so well. And it helps with my day job."

"Which is what exactly?"

"I work for a nonprofit called Open Hearts, Open Hands, which works with various corporations, local businesses and outreach centers to provide funding and assistance for other, smaller entities like shelters, community gardens, food banks, etcetera."

"Wow. Sounds complicated."

"It can be and it won't make me rich, but it's good work."

"So am I another assistance program for you? Help the injured cowboy to earn brownie points with your bosses?"

Derrick narrowed his eyes, a bit of temper peeking through. "No, this is because I like you, and I want to help if I can. Pay it forward, you know?" He seemed to debate how much more to admit. "My parents hit a rough patch when Conrad and I were kids. Money disappeared and so did food. Without the generosity of friends and strangers, and a local food bank, we wouldn't have gotten through it. So if I'm in a position to help, I help."

"Out of the kindness of your heart?" Slater wasn't buying it. No one invited a near-stranger into their home for the karma points.

"Not completely, no."

"Thought so."

"Look, I'm the oldest of seventeen cousins on both sides of my family, and I'm also the last single one. I've been getting crap about it for years, but it's gotten worse now that the last cousin is engaged, and I have to go to five weddings over the course of the spring and summer, and I need a fake boyfriend so my relatives will stop meddling."

Fake boyfriend? Is he serious?

Slater had recently slammed his head into the side of a mountain, so he needed to be sure he'd heard that correctly. "You want me to pose as your fake boyfriend in exchange for recovering in your spare room?"

Derrick's face shifted into discomfort, and Slater imagined the guy would be blushing if he was able. "My place only has one bedroom, but my couch is a futon."

Annoyance heated Slater's skin. "I'm not a house-boy, Derrick."

"Oh, hell, man, that's not even where I was going with all this. Just because we fucked once doesn't mean we ever do again. That's not part of the terms and conditions of living with me. And it will give you a stable place to recover, plus a lot more choices of physical therapists being closer to the city."

"And give you a fake boyfriend for five weddings?"

"Yes. You aren't someone my family knows, so when the wedding season is over and we—" he made air quotes "—'break up,' it won't be a huge deal. You should be recovered and able to return to work by then, and I'll go back to being happily single. No sex, no housekeeping, and I don't expect you do more than chip in for groceries. No expectations other than friendship and mutual respect."

Slater stared at Derrick, unable to puzzle the guy out with his generous—if truly bizarre—offer. And equally unsure what Slater wanted.

Derrick hadn't been sure what to expect when he walked into Slater's hospital room, and he hoped he'd kept his shock off his face. Almost every visible inch of skin on the man was either bruised, scraped or otherwise marked. He had bandages on his hands and neck, and the side of his head, probably the site of the fracture. One black eye. The skin on his nose looked raw and swollen. His right leg was propped up and suspended in something to keep it immobile.

Slater was a mess, so his actual level of alertness surprised Derrick a bit. As had the Cracker Jack, but the man was alive and eager to get out of the hospital. And Derrick had mad respect for how honest Slater had been with him about his feelings and fears. Maybe they were barely friends, but Derrick cared about the guy and wanted him to fully recover.

The whole "live with me and be my fake boyfriend" had been completely off the cuff, but he didn't take it back. Not even when Slater continued to stare at him like Derrick was insane for the offer he'd just made. It *was* a little insane and completely un-thought-through, but the more Derrick considered it, the more he liked it.

Besides, Derrick rented one of four apartments converted from an old, two-story house that had a single interior foyer which was treated like a common room, so Slater wouldn't be alone all day, every day, unless he chose to be. Derrick wasn't looking forward to the lying aspect of this plan, but it would be nice to have someone else around to have dinner with and shit. Cohabiting wasn't dating, wasn't trusting with his heart, and wouldn't shatter his trust by repeatedly cheating on him.

Even if Slater hooked up while he was living with Derrick, it wasn't cheating at all, because they weren't a couple.

"Let's say I'm crazy enough to agree to this insane plan of yours," Slater finally said. "Are you really going to lie to your brother and parents about us being fake boyfriends?"

"I don't know. Me and Conrad are pretty close, and we have a hard time lying to each other. If he's around us for any period of time, he'll probably figure it out." Unless his brother saw their underlying chemistry and assumed it was real. Slater was very tight-lipped about himself but he'd also let a few things slip around Derrick. Derrick didn't want a relationship right now but he also wasn't opposed to exploring that chemistry down the road—as long as Slater was up for it, too.

"And your parents?" Slater's questions seemed more curious than accusatory, as if testing for all potential future issues.

"My mother will love you for simply having broken through my inability to trust."

Now why had he gone and admitted to that?

Slater squinted at him. "You have trust issues?"

Derrick didn't like talking about his two worst mistakes, but he could give Slater a little bit. "I've been cheated on in the past by people I thought I loved and who I thought loved me. They weren't honest with me about who they were and what they wanted from me. It's why I figured single is better and stick to hook-ups. You?"

"Similar story, I guess. So I get it. The hard-to-trust part. Makes it hard to believe all you want is a fake boyfriend for five weddings, nothing else on the line."

"I mean, there might be a family dinner now and again…"

Slater rolled his eyes. "What the hell do we tell people about how we met?"

Derrick didn't dare hope he'd won Slater over to this plan but so far, so good. "The truth. We hooked up the night of the double wedding, realized we had chemistry, and we've been texting-slash-calling ever since. No one's gonna demand to see phone records proving it."

"If we're dating, how come it took you…a lot of days to come see me?"

He didn't miss the slight slip in Slater's recollection. "My work schedule, and us being a secret, meant I didn't want to be a bother, but then I couldn't stand it another day without making sure you were okay with my own eyes." Which was true enough that it wasn't a lie. He *had* been concerned about Slater. A lot. "I mean, if you really want to sell it, I can kiss you the next time someone walks into the room."

Some of the curious amusement in Slater's eyes dimmed. "I don't kiss."

"At all? Or just the mouth?"

"Mouth." Humor bled back into Slater's expression. "I guess cheek pecks are okay. From my boyfriend."

"Yeah?"

Slater let out a long, slow breath. "Maybe yes but I have questions."

"Okay." Derrick would answer anything if it meant having a permanent date to get him through wedding season. And someone to talk to over a takeout dinner wouldn't hurt, either.

"Do you have in-home laundry?"

Of all the questions Derrick had expected that wasn't it. "Yup. It's a small, stacked set, but it's in the apartment. What else?"

"Who's sleeping on the futon?"

"The bed is plenty big enough for two." Derrick wasn't sure how to interpret Slater's expression, so he treaded with caution. "But seeing as you're the guy with the busted ankle, I guess I can suffer the futon for a few months."

"I don't cook."

"Neither do I. I subsist on takeout, delivery and frozen food. I'm not much of a housekeeper, but the place isn't a mess." A white-and-black terror zipped through his mind. "I should warn you about Lucky, though."

"Who's Lucky? A neighbor?"

"Sort of. Lucky is a stray cat who kind of…bums her way from apartment to apartment. She'll scooch in your door when you don't realize it, meow in your face at three in the morning and sometimes chew on your sneakers. She is, strangely, toilet trained, so you never have to worry about cat shit in your shoes as long as the lid is always up."

Slater stared at him, slack-jawed.

"What?" Derrick asked. "Are you allergic to cats?"

"No, that's just…really weird. And unexpected."

"You just agreed to move in with me, Fake Boyfriend. Start expecting the unexpected. But only in the best ways possible."

"I think I regret this already."

"Regret what?" a new voice chimed in. Derrick twisted around, not too surprised to see Reyes and Hugo in the doorway. Hugo had spoken, and his curious bravado died quickly, shifting right into nervous hesitation. Derrick didn't know the kid well—okay, at all—but he seemed nice enough, if a little skittish.

"Letting him visit for so long," Slater replied, tilting his head at Derrick. "He's exhausting."

"That's not what you said three weeks ago," Derrick deadpanned. Slater choked.

Reyes quirked an eyebrow at them. "Derrick. Good to see you."

"Same, and I should probably go." To Slater, he said, "I'm glad I was finally able to see you. Should I check in after your surgery?"

This close, Derrick could see the subtle flicker of "I'll get you for this" in Slater's expressive eyes. "Sure," Slater replied. "Not sure how doped I'll be, so I'll call you."

"Sounds good." He made a show of gently squeezing Slater's scraped-raw hand before resting it back on the bed. He nearly bent down and kissed Slater's forehead but he didn't want to earn the guy's ire right off the bat. Slater did have to work with these guys again in a few months. "Chin up, you'll be fine."

"Yeah."

"Guys," Derrick said as he passed Reyes and Hugo,

heading for the door. He couldn't hide a smirk as he strode down the busy corridor to the elevators. This visit had ended on a vastly different note than he'd expected when he knocked on Slater's door. They hadn't discussed the particulars of Slater moving in with him, but now that Derrick was committed to the plan, he had arrangements to make.

"Didn't realize you and Derrick Massey were friends," Reyes said.

Slater shrugged one shoulder, unsure exactly how to explain Derrick. And a little annoyed Derrick had bailed without confirming they could start telling people.

What the hell? He's the one who brought it up.

"We hooked up after the double wedding," Slater admitted, keeping his voice as nonchalant as possible. "And we've kept in contact. Texting and stuff."

"Oh? Something there?"

"Maybe. We get along great." True enough. Slater had genuinely enjoyed Derrick's visit, and he had very fond memories of fucking the younger guy. He could see himself being friends with Derrick, as long as Derrick didn't try digging too deep into Slater's past. "He actually stopped by to make an offer I couldn't refuse."

"What kind of offer?" Hugo asked. The kid popped into one of the visitor chairs. He was so earnest during his visits, as if taking his roommate's health and wellness personally, when they were only casual friends. It was...kind.

"Well, getting around the ranch on crutches, or God forbid a wheelchair, while my ankle heals won't be easy, and I don't like the idea of you guys waiting on me, or doing shit for me."

"I won't mind helping out."

"I know, and I appreciate it. But Derrick made a good point about being closer to the city and better physical therapists."

Reyes's eyebrows arched up. "Are you moving in with Derrick Massey?"

"I mean… I guess? Neither of us said it in so many words, but it makes sense."

"You're moving in with a total stranger?" Hugo asked, an amusing sort of shock and horror on his face.

"Dude, you moved in with a stranger when Judson hired you."

"True. So are you guys, like, boyfriends?"

"Dunno. I've never been a huge fan of labels, so I guess right now we're just roommates. Can't really offer him any benefits at the moment."

Reyes scowled. "You sure you're okay with this arrangement? Because we'll work something out if you want to stay at the ranch while you recover."

"Yes, I'm perfectly okay with this arrangement." And the more he thought about it, the more it was true.

The whole "fake boyfriend" thing was kind of brilliant and worked out perfectly for them both. Derrick kept his family off his back about dating during these five upcoming weddings. Slater got a place in the city to recover and get his mobility back.

Win-win.

All they had to do was keep things platonic, stay friends, and things would go back to normal in a few months. They'd go their separate ways.

He just had to get through this damned surgery first.

Chapter Five

The house Derrick shared only had two spots in the driveway and both were empty when he arrived home. They were first come, first served, but there was almost always street parking available in this neighborhood. Derrick had a thirty-minute commute to his job, but it was worth it for the rent and quiet. A lot of the older homes had been converted into affordable apartments for younger, child-free renters who needed a place to crash in between working multiple jobs.

He made a mental note to call his landlord about extra keys for Slater. Each tenant had one to the front door, and each interior apartment had its own unique key for that door. Derrick had liked this place immediately, because the front door opened into what had once been a formal foyer with a wood staircase winding up and then splitting left and right at a landing. A different apartment was at the top of each staircase, while Derrick's was to the right, opposite his neighbors. The foyer had been decorated like a communal living space, with solid outdoor furniture, cushions and pillows, and a coffee table overrun with magazines and books to share.

Derrick didn't hang out here much, because work kept him busy, but it would be a good place for Slater to chill and talk to people. If he wanted to do that. Since Derrick had never really interacted with Slater while the cowboy was around guests, he wasn't sure if Slater was the chatty type like Colt, or the reserved type like Reyes.

He glanced around for Lucky before unlocking his own apartment door. The little bastard zipped out into the foyer and leapt onto one of the armchairs. Turned and meowed innocently at Derrick. "You little shit. What did you destroy?"

Lucky started licking his front paw.

Derrick went inside and paused, taking in the place like a stranger might. The living space was one big room, all restored hardwood, and no clear definition of living room, dining area or kitchen (other than the obvious counters and other appliances off to the left and a small patch of linoleum flooring). His futon was dated and kind of college-dorm-like, but he had an actual entertainment console for his TV and game system. Real end tables bracketed the futon. The walls were blank and boring, though, and the tiny, four-chair dinette set was this fake-bamboo thing straight out of the eighties.

Not much to speak of, but Derrick didn't spend a lot of time here. It was a place to crash, or to occasionally bring a hookup to. Robin had never commented on the décor. But what would Slater think? Then again, the guy shared a small-ish cabin with another dude, so he probably wasn't very picky about his living space.

Using checking for cat damage as an excuse, Derrick moved around the apartment, tidying up areas. Making sure his game cases were lined up and not dusty. Straightening the pillows on the futon. The bathroom could use a fresh scrub, and he made a note to do that in the morning. He also found Lucky's gift floating in the toilet and flushed.

Weirdo cat.

His bedroom was almost too small for the mattress, but he'd wanted a king, and he'd squeezed a small dresser in, too. The closet was big, though, and it held most of his stuff. More boring. But if Slater needed to use a wheelchair to keep pressure off his ankle, or whatever, Derrick could shove the bed against the wall and create maneuvering room. Although the futon was a lot lower and more accessible.

He really needed to stop fussing over this. Once Slater was actually here and the moving in was a done deal, they could figure out the finer details. His stomach rumbled for lunch, and he cursed himself for not hitting a drive-thru on his way home from the hospital. He kept his freezer loaded with high-protein meals, though, so he went into the kitchen.

The faintest scent of pepperoni enticed him toward his door, instead. He peeked out the hole. His two first-floor neighbors, Dez and Morgan, were settling in the foyer with a large pizza box and paper napkins. The couple was super chill and frequently shared their food with neighbors. He didn't spot drinks, so he decided to barter himself a slice of pizza with the six-pack in his fridge.

"Hey, all," Derrick said as he eyeballed the foyer for the cat. "Thirsty?"

"Definitely," Dez replied. She patted the cushion on the love seat next to her. Morgan was sitting at an angle to her in one of the chairs, his bulky body almost too big for it. Dez flipped the box open, revealing some sort of supreme pizza. "Join us for lunch?"

"For sure, thanks." Derrick put the beer down next to the pizza, glad this brand was a twist-off, because he'd forgotten the bottle opener. Then again, Morgan could probably flick the caps off with his pinkie. Dude was some kind of bodybuilder and his muscles had muscles. Meanwhile, Dez was petite at five-two, her entire body the same size as Morgan's thigh. But they were an adorable couple, and Derrick enjoyed spending time with them.

They bullshitted while they ate, and that pizza hit the spot for Derrick. He loved that they ordered from a local place, rather than a chain, because it just plain tasted better. Lucky came snooping around and Morgan fed the cat bits of his crust.

"So," Derrick said after he'd washed his last bite down with a swig of beer. "I may have a friend staying with me for a while."

"Oh, yeah?" Dez waggled her eyebrows. "A friend you fuck, or a friend-friend?"

"Not entirely sure yet, because it's really new. We're only very casually dating." True enough. "He busted up his ankle at work a few days ago, and he needs a place to stay where he can recover, and also have someone around if he needs help."

"So he lives alone?"

"No." Derrick explained a bit more about Clean Slate Ranch and how he met Slater—leaving out the sexy details—and today's conversation about Slater needing a more accessible place to stay.

"That's really chill of you, Derrick," Morgan said. "Helping out someone who's practically a stranger. Trusting him in your place."

Derrick laughed. "He's got a broken ankle. I doubt

he'll be robbing me and making a fast getaway. I trust him." He really did trust Slater, which was odd, because he was very slow to trust nowadays. "Just figured I'd give you guys a heads-up that there will be a new guy in the building soon. But he's open-minded. Nice guy or I wouldn't have invited him to stay."

He added the last bit for Dez, who grinned at him. While Dez preferred she/her pronouns, she also identified as nonbinary and changed her wardrobe depending on her mood. Today she wore a long flowing skirt and peasant blouse, and her short hair was carefully styled. And Derrick was very open about being bi. If nothing else, the first floor had each other's backs.

They polished off the pizza, and Derrick went home with two unopened bottles of beer. Home being literally ten feet away. He loved this setup because it reminded him more of a college dorm than separate apartments. Plus, with the four separate units on one property, the rent was reasonable for their proximity to the San Francisco Bay Area.

He checked his phone. Still an hour or so before Slater's surgery, and calling to check in before it happened felt a little clingy and weird. He would have sent a text if he'd thought to get Slater's number; all he'd done was give Slater his. Putting the ball in Slater's court to actually call tonight or not. If he didn't, Derrick wouldn't take it too personally. This was a casual arrangement after all, not a real relationship.

Still…he hoped Slater called. He enjoyed talking to the guy. Slater had the tanned, slightly lined skin of someone used to working long hours in the sun, but he didn't seem old. Maybe it was the slight air of world-weariness Slater carried with him everywhere Derrick had seen him.

His cell buzzed. Conrad. "Hey, bro, what's up?"

"Dude, I know it's last minute, but are you up for babysitting for a few hours tonight?" Conrad asked, a little out of breath. "There's plenty of pumped milk in the fridge in case Mia gets hungry, but man, I gotta get Sophie out of the house."

"Yeah, you know I'm all in with watching Mia. Sophie getting a little stir-crazy?"

"You have no idea. She hasn't really been out much since the baby was born, and I know her hormones are out of whack, but damn, man. I nearly got taken out by a can of soup for asking what was for dinner, and I wasn't even implying she had to cook, just asking what she wanted."

"Yikes." Derrick couldn't imagine the stress an infant had on a still-new marriage. "Yeah, I can come over and watch Mia for a while. No problem."

"Thank. You. Whenever you can get here. Unless you've got plans with that Slater guy?"

He swallowed a groan. "Let me guess. Wes?"

"Yup. Apparently, Wes overheard Reyes saying something to Miles about you being in Slater's hospital room this morning and weird vibes between you two. Naturally, he blabbed to Sophie, who now wants answers."

"Look, whatever Slater and I are, it's extremely casual. The guy nearly died. Of course I went to see him."

"Because you hooked up at the weddings?"

Derrick let out a frustrated breath. "Yes. We did. He's a nice guy."

"Dude, you really need to stop fucking those cowboys. All they do is break your heart."

"No one broke my heart." Maybe he'd come close with Robin, but Derrick hadn't completely fallen for the handsome cowboy before Robin had declared himself off-limits and in a relationship with Shawn. Close to falling, but not completely. No, most of that hurt had come from Robin not even telling him he was seeing Shawn, casually or not, until that night at Club Base.

Maybe Conrad was right, though. He should keep whatever this thing with Slater was completely platonic so he didn't revert to type and fall for another unavailable cowboy. "Whatever. I'll be there in half an hour."

"I owe you, bro."

Derrick hung up, grateful to have Friday evening plans with a beautiful lady—even if said lady was only three weeks old and would probably sleep most of the night. The distraction would keep him from thinking too hard about the laid-up cowboy with the sexy smirk...

Reyes hated delegating his own ranch duties to others, but he owed Slater. So he was there when Slater was taken into surgery, and he sent text updates to both Judson and Miles as he got them. Miles was busy at the saloon, or he would have been there to keep Reyes from jumping out of his skin.

Miles had been a rock this week, standing strong whenever Reyes thought he might fall apart. He still couldn't get the image of Slater falling out of his head. It haunted him at night, in the dark when he couldn't sleep. Not even Miles's lean body wrapped tightly around his helped him relax. Reyes had, at Miles's urging, made an extra appointment with his therapist for the beginning of the week, so he could talk about the accident before the nightmares got worse. He liked his therapist, who'd been helping Reyes unpack the mistakes of his youth since last fall. Reyes needed to get this latest failure off his chest.

Judson showed up with a thermos of coffee from Patrice. "It's a work-related injury and I'm his supervisor," Judson said. "Some of the other boys wanted to come, but I told them to wait until we see how Slater's feeling. He might not want a bunch of visitors tonight."

"Good call." Reyes poured rich, dark coffee into the thermos's cap. Patrice had an industrial coffee maker for both hands and guests, but she also had a smaller machine for when she wanted to pamper one of her boys. And she made the best coffee.

"Hear anything new?"

"Not yet, but we're getting close to the time they said it would take. Can't imagine it's easy putting steel rods into someone's ankle. Not with all the little bones they say are in there."

"Poor man will probably set off every metal detector in town after this."

Reyes snorted and sipped the coffee. "True story. Could have been so much worse, though."

"I know it, son. I know it." Judson lightly clapped him on the shoulder. They'd all been in a state of panic on Tuesday, until Judson finally got confirmation from the hospital that Slater was alive and in relatively okay condition, considering the length of his slide down the summit.

Still...they'd both needed to see Slater with their own eyes.

"I'm a little sad he isn't coming home to the ranch," Judson said. "But I do understand his reasons for being closer to the city."

"Same." Reyes had shared some of this morning's conversation with Judson over the phone earlier, but he'd left out the part about Slater and Derrick hooking up. That wasn't his gossip to spread to everyone who asked. "Can't fault a guy for not wanting to feel like a burden to the entire ranch."

"It wouldn't be a burden but I do understand the man's point of view. Slater has to do what's best for his recovery."

"Yeah."

Judson chuckled. "Slater better watch out, though. Our hands shacking up with other people has led to quite a few new relationships around the ranch lately. Yourself included, Mr. Arlington."

Reyes smiled at his wedding ring, amused by the last name teasing. He and Miles hadn't made any big plans about taking the other's name or hyphenating. Not yet. Although Reyes did think Arlington-Caldero rolled off the tongue smoothly.

And Judson wasn't wrong about forced proximity leading to romance. It had happened for Reyes and Miles, Colt and Avery, and most recently, Shawn and Robin.

"Big difference," Reyes said, "is all those romances happened at the ranch. There's something special about that land. Not sure Derrick's apartment has the same magic."

"True, true. Guess we'll just have to wait and see."

They did wait and see, and ten minutes later a nurse told them Slater was in Recovery and the surgery had gone well. Judson sent a mass text. Reyes took a chance on Miles being able to speak for two minutes and called him, simply to hear his voice and express Reyes's relief to his boyfr—husband.

He was still working on remembering the husband part. Tomorrow was their three-week anniversary already.

Slater was groggy when they entered his room a while later, but also coherent and glad the surgery was over. "Are you in pain, son?" Judson asked.

"Not much." Slater seemed enamored of his own fingers for some reason, and Reyes silently chalked it up to not being used to anesthesia. "Not from my ankle, anyway."

"We aren't going to stay long, because you need your rest," Reyes said. "But we wanted you to know we were here, and you aren't alone, brother. No matter where you go, you'll always have family at Clean Slate."

Slater blinked hard several times, and it left his eyelashes wet. "Thank you. It means a lot."

"We'll see you tomorrow."

"Sure."

Reyes disliked leaving his friend behind, but the worst was behind them. Now Slater had to do everything the doctor told him to do so he made a full recovery. Any other outcome was unacceptable.

Slater watched his bosses leave, his mind still a bit muddled from being under and not liking the feeling. His brain was already mildly scrambled from his skull fracture, and they'd put off the surgery to decrease the chances of him reacting badly to the anesthetic. He was glad they'd knocked him out instead of doing a local, but now he kind of felt like he had the flu. At least the near-constant ache in his ankle was only a very distant throb.

The surgeon had come by earlier and told Slater exactly what they were going to do, but Slater had only half listened. He didn't care which rod replaced which bone or strengthened what muscle group, or whatever. He'd simply wanted the procedure over so he could start to heal. Afterward, in Recovery, the surgeon said everything went smoothly. With time, patience and ample physical therapy, he would walk again.

Music to Slater's ears.

He dozed for a while, in between the occasional nurse check, and when he woke a while later, it was dark outside his room's small window. Slater reached for his cell. After eight. Damn. He was supposed to call Derrick. It wasn't too late, was it? Nah, not if the stories he'd heard from Colt and Robin about Derrick's fondness for late-night clubbing were true. It was Friday night.

So he found Derrick's contact and called him.

"Hello?" Derrick's slightly suspicious voice replied after four rings.

"It's Slater."

"Oh, hey. I wasn't sure. The name on my phone said Kendall Stamos, so I thought it might be a wrong number."

Slater flinched. He'd had to put his legal name on the paperwork for his cell, and it was why he always texted the other hands. Never called. "Yeah, that's me. I just go by Slater, though."

"So you're like the Pink of the cowboy world?"

"Minus the incredible music talent." Slater liked that Derrick wasn't picking on him for his first name. He'd gotten earfuls of teasing from other boys, and even a few girls, as a kid—until the first time he punched a bully in the nose. His father hadn't even been upset that Slater had gotten three days of detention for it. "Speaking of music, I don't hear any. Aren't you a weekend club hound?"

"Not tonight. Tonight, I am lying in bed next to a beautiful lady."

Irritation rippled across Slater's skin—which made no sense since he had no claim on Derrick's time or attention. "Pre-planned date? She mind you talking to me?"

"No, it was a very last-minute hookup, and I doubt she minds at all since she can't speak yet."

"Huh?"

"I'm watching my niece, Mia." Derrick chuckled, and that deep sound shouldn't have been as attractive as it was. "Conrad called me to babysit because Sophie needed some time away. I can't imagine they get much alone time with a newborn in the house."

"I bet." The mental image of Derrick caring for a newborn baby was...kind of adorable. And since when had Slater started thinking of dudes in terms of being adorable? What the hell had that fall done to his head? "So, uh, I should be discharged Sunday before lunch."

"That's great. I bet you're ready to blow that joint."

"Beyond ready, trust me. I hate being cooped up like this. Used to take walks around the property all the time, and I feel like I'm back—" *Back in a prison cell* dangled off Slater's lips but he swallowed the words. "I hate not being able to just walk out of here." He also hated having to spend another full day cooped up in here without sunshine on his face, but the doctor was still watching his...kidney? Blood pressure. Something.

"I hear you, man. I crashed my bicycle when I was twelve and had to live in a leg cast for most of the summer. Indoors. It sucked ass—I mean donkey ba—crap. It sucked."

"Let me guess. Trying not to cuss in front of the baby?"

"Bingo. I know she doesn't understand a word, but Sophie would read me the riot act if she caught me."

Slater smiled at the thought of big, bad Derrick being scared of someone as small as Sophie Massey, even while his brain took the idea of ass sucking to a whole other level. Did Derrick enjoy rimming? Generally, if Slater was in the mood to have something up his ass, he wanted it to be a nice hard dick, not a tongue. But the few guys he'd rimmed in the past had seemed to enjoy it a hell of a lot. His dick gave an interested twitch at the mental images, but Slater couldn't quite get it up.

It also didn't matter if Derrick liked being rimmed. Slater didn't want or need a sexual relationship with Derrick right now, especially while they were getting this whole living-together situation sorted. "So am I still going home with you on Sunday?"

"If you still want to, then my door is open. We'll have to drive to Clean Slate to pick up your stuff, though. We're close in size, but I can't imagine you want to wear another guy's underwear indefinitely."

Slater snorted and the gesture hurt his nose. "Ow. Yeah, I'll need to pack up my stuff. Reyes and Judson know I'm going to be living with you for a while. Told them a few hours ago."

"Okay. I actually already told my next-door neighbors. They're super chill people. I think you'll like them."

"Great. Uh, what exactly did you tell them about me?"

"Just about hurting your ankle, that we hooked up

once but are super casual, and I offered you a place to make your recovery easy. All the truth."

Tell them just enough of the truth so you aren't caught in the lie.

A lesson Slater had learned quickly and well his first month in prison, so he could navigate life without bringing the ire of the guards down on his head.

"Speaking of your recovery," Derrick continued, "what are you going to be using to get around? I can move some stuff around if you'll have a wheelchair."

"As far as I know, they're sending me home with crutches. My internist doesn't think I'll need a wheelchair, and I don't think the ranch's insurance will pay for any of those fancier devices."

"Fancier devices? Like what?"

Slater shrugged, then remembered Derrick couldn't see him. "Dunno, Wes was saying something about them the other day. Or this morning?" Had Wes visited him today? He couldn't remember. "Doesn't matter, I can figure out crutches."

"Okay. Uh, do you have any favorite junk food or anything? Like I said, I don't cook but my food app game is on point. I keep beer in the fridge and basic snacks like chips and salsa and shit."

"I'm a fan of Cracker Jack. Sweet stuff, I guess, more than salty. Or a mix of the two?" Slater missed his days of thinking clearly so damned much.

"Got it. To drink?"

"I like beer, but I'll be on pain meds for a while. Plain cola is fine. Or root beer, too, I guess."

"Cool. Did I ask if you're allergic to cats? I can't remember."

Derrick can't remember something? Join the club.

"You have a cat?" Something about this sounded vaguely familiar. Had they had this conversation already?

"The building has a cat. The landlord says the cat came with the house when she bought it, and it stuck around during and after renovations, so she named him Lucky and he's just part of the place. Goes from apartment to apartment using our toilets and being a general nuisance."

Okay, Slater's head wound was fucking with his hearing. "Did you just say the cat uses your toilet?"

"Yup. You'll be living with a toilet-trained cat."

"How the fuck do you toilet train a cat?"

"I asked the same question when I first moved in, so I searched online. Apparently, there are methods that work. Someone took the time once to train Lucky, so it kind of surprises me he's a stray."

"Yeah. And to answer your question, no, I'm not allergic."

"Good thing, or I'd be stocking up on antihistamines and tissues, because now that you've agreed to move in and be my fake boyfriend, you're locked into the deal."

Fake boyfriend. Right. Slater studied the boring artwork on the wall across from his bed, trying to remember why—oh, yeah. Wedding season. That's why he was moving in with Derrick temporarily.

Stupid bruised brain.

"Then I guess you're stuck with me," Slater said. "You've locked me into five weddings, if I recall correctly, but I do have one stipulation of my own."

"Fire away."

"I have to be somewhere in June, and it's non-negotiable that I attend. I'll likely need a ride, but you aren't obligated to stay, or to go as my date."

"I'm intrigued. Do I get to know ahead of time what this obligation is?"

Slater contemplated his answer a beat. "Not yet. Look, I'll text you when I have a firmer release time."

"All right. And I agree to your stipulation. I'm intrigued. Good night, Kendall."

Slater groaned. "You tell anyone about that and I'll make sure Lucky learns how to shit in your bed. There's a reason the only people I call on my cell are Reyes, Judson and Arthur."

"Don't worry, I can keep a secret. Night."

"Yeah, good night." Slater ended the call and hooked it up to the power cord Hugo had brought for him from the cabin a few days ago. He'd kind of miss living with the kid, who was earnest, eager to please and exceptionally good at problem-solving. He'd definitely miss the ranch and his fellow horsemen. But he wasn't saying goodbye on Sunday, just "I'll see you later."

On Sunday, a brand-new adventure began.

And Slater would never admit out loud that he was kind of terrified.

Chapter Six

Slater purposely gave Derrick a pickup time fifteen minutes later than what he actually expected, so he'd have a few moments to himself. Well, sort of to himself. The orderly who'd wheeled him down to the lobby and pickup area stood casually nearby, apparently unable to leave his charge until someone else showed up.

He fingered the crutches perched across the arms of the wheelchair, unsure how he felt about them. They'd been adjusted to his height and reach, and he'd practiced walking with them yesterday and this morning a bit but still felt unsteady. They made his bruised ribs ache like crazy, but he'd deal. His headaches were almost completely gone, and he hadn't had a dizzy spell yet today. Part of him wanted to see if his doc would write a prescription for a wheelchair, in case the dizzy spells came back. The last thing he needed was to pitch over and bang his brain around more.

Just gotta get used to the new normal.

A new normal in which he lived away from the ranch he loved, with a guy he was attracted to, and then pretended to be his boyfriend for a couple of months. A new normal where his ankle was tender and sore, his ribs still hurt and would for a long time, especially with using crutches. And he had a lot of scabbed cuts that needed ointment frequently so they didn't leave scars.

Not that Slater gave too many shits about scars on his body, but he'd like to at least help his face heal back to normal. Didn't want to scare future ranch guests, after all.

A blue, four-door sedan trundled up to the curb, and Derrick sprang out of the driver's side. He didn't notice Slater was already in the lobby until he walked in the automatic doors. "Hey, am I late?"

"Right on time," Slater replied. Derrick's jeans hugged his hips and package, and the half-tucked-in band tee was almost too tight. "Wouldn't have taken you for an Aerosmith fan."

"I went through a phase when *Armageddon* came out. I might have been a little bit in love with half the male cast of that movie."

"Dude, wouldn't you have been about ten when that movie came out?"

"When I first rented it, whatever. Actually, it might have been one of the movies I watched on repeat the summer I broke my leg." Derrick looked down at his T-shirt. "Huh. Funny coincidence."

"Yeah. Funny."

"Ready to go?"

"Definitely."

Derrick took the crutches and the paper bag with Slater's prescriptions. Slater's handler came over and dutifully wheeled him out to Derrick's waiting car. He would have preferred riding up front but his ankle was throbbing again, and he really needed to elevate it. So he hobbled into the back seat and stretched out. Derrick got a blanket from his trunk and used it to prop Slater's foot up. Because it was his right foot, Slater had to sit behind the driver's seat so he didn't risk his foot sliding off the seat, and it put him in the unfortunate position to smell Derrick's cologne really well.

And he liked it.

"Do you need to stop anywhere on the way home?" Derrick asked. "Pharmacy?"

"Nope, got everything filled at the hospital. To be honest, all I really want right now is to stretch out on something soft and watch anything besides basic cable."

"I can manage that. Before or after we drive to the ranch?"

Shit, Slater had somehow forgotten that particular chore. And once he parked his ass, he didn't want to move the rest of the day. Might as well get this over with. The guests would all be busy in the big corral, watching Reyes and whoever else do mounting and riding demos, so they wouldn't interrupt anything. He was glad Reyes would be busy, because the poor guy acted like he owed Slater a blood debt or something, and he didn't. Slater would have let go of anyone before pulling them down that mountain with him.

"I guess after," Slater said. "Unless you've got plans?"

"Nope. Not a thing except getting you settled."

"Okay."

Derrick blasted an R & B station on the drive out to Garrett. Slater wasn't used to this route in a car; he always took it on his motorcycle, and today he enjoyed the ability to listen (and occasionally sing along) to the music. Derrick had a surprisingly good voice and could mimic quite a few artists.

As the car trundled closer to Garrett town limits and Derrick turned the volume down, Slater asked, "How come you aren't a professional singer? You're really good."

"Too shy, honestly. I did choir in school and in church, but never bothered auditioning for solos. Conrad used to needle me about auditioning for one of those reality singing shows, but I never had the stones. Singing is for fun, not a career."

"Makes sense."

"So what about you? What did you do before Clean Slate?"

Slater considered his possible responses and in the end, went with the simplest truth. "I worked for a shipping company that specialized in large freight and animals. It was good work, a lot of time on the road, but I liked it. Did that for a few years until one job had me bringing an abused pony up to Arthur's horse rescue. I fell in love with the work they do, and after some calls, Arthur gave me a job at the rescue. Eventually, I ended up at the ranch working with the guests and horses there."

"Cool." Derrick navigated the country road that eventually revealed the two large boulders marking the entrance to Clean Slate Ranch. He drove slowly, avoiding the worst of the dirt road's potholes and ruts, and Slater's ankle thanked him for that.

Their arrival only garnered a few curious looks from guests, who were at the corral as expected. Derrick helped Slater slide out and get situated on his crutches. Derrick had offered to drive right up to the cabin, but Slater needed to practice more on the crutches, and he'd been on his ass for almost a week.

Before they'd gotten five feet from the car, Patrice swooped in and cupped her hands over Slater's cheeks.

"It is so good to see you again, hon," Patrice said. "Your poor face."

Slater smiled. "My face will heal, but it feels incredible to be out of that hospital." The warm sun against his skin was pure heaven, and he really hoped Derrick's place had some kind of patio, or at least direct sunlight part of the day.

"I won't keep you. You don't need to be on that ankle any longer than necessary."

"Thanks, Patrice. I'll see you, okay?"

"Bless you, hon." She kissed his cheek before heading back to the guesthouse, and Slater's heart panged. She was the ranch's den mother and, in some ways, a mother figure to many of the men who worked here, Slater included. His own mother had vanished when he was a kid, and he'd gotten along with his stepmother just fine, but something about Patrice exuded warmth and hominess. Unconditional support.

Love.

Things he'd never returned in kind, always deflecting her gentle questions about his past, or even his current likes and dislikes. Refusing to get to know yet another person who'd only ever tried to include him.

He and Derrick went down the worn path to cabin row, Slater taking his time so he didn't stumble or trip over a divot of grass. His underarms ached by the time they reached his cabin, and he was grateful to slide into one of the sitting chairs.

"What can I do?" Derrick asked.

"Got a suitcase under my bed. The one on the left there. Dresser on the left is mine. Just toss shit into it."

Derrick did exactly that, emptying the dresser drawers and stuffing things into the large suitcase. Slater didn't own a lot, because he mostly wore the same four pairs of jeans and his Clean Slate polos—which he directed Derrick to leave behind—and he told Derrick which of the toiletries were his. Slater wasn't sure if he'd come back to this cabin when he returned to work, or if Hugo would get a new temporary roommate so he made sure Derrick packed everything personal.

Including the box under his bed with his most private items, which Derrick thankfully didn't nose into. He simply tucked it into the suitcase with everything else. As he zipped it up, it hit Slater how sad it was that his entire life fit into that single piece of luggage. A big piece of luggage, but still. Someone could easily toss that into a ditch on the side of the road, and Slater would be forgotten. Only a memory to the people he'd once worked with.

Except his stuff wasn't being tossed into a ditch. Slater was heading into a suburb of San Francisco to live with a guy he barely knew, but who he trusted on a deep-down, instinctive level. Derrick was a good guy who babysat newborns and took in broken cowboys, and he wouldn't screw Slater over.

The cabin door swung open and Hugo let out an excited squawk. "Oh, good, you're still here. Ernie said he saw you guys headed this way." He squatted in front of Slater. "I wanted to say goodbye before you headed out. And to say you're a really sneaky roommate. I had no idea you and Derrick were close enough to be dating, much less moving in together."

Slater nearly choked on air. "We aren't living together because we're that serious, Jesus. It's just…more convenient than me living all the way out here. And it's temporary. Don't get too comfy living alone, kid."

Hugo grinned. "Good. For an old guy, you're actually pretty cool."

"Brat." Slater gently swiped at the kid with his crutch, but Hugo dodged out of the way. "Take care of the horses while I'm gone."

"I will. Get well soon, yeah?"

"I'll do my best."

Slater swallowed against a thick lump in his throat as he followed Derrick out into the afternoon sunshine. May was just around the corner, and the weather was gorgeous. Warm but not too hot. The rainy season was behind them, and thank God for small favors. He'd kind of miss the upcoming summer tourist traffic, but this wasn't forever. With any luck, he'd be back before the end of the summer, his ankle back to normal, and no more weird memory glitches.

A few of the hands stopped by the car while Slater was getting situated, and he rolled the rear window down to shake their hands and say goodbye-for-now to his friends. Reyes was busy, thank God, and after a couple minutes of idle chatter, Derrick drove away. Slater stared at his hands, unwilling to watch the ranch fade into the background, swallowed up by the dusty horizon. This ranch was home, and he was leaving his home, but he'd be back.

Living with Derrick was temporary. A bump in the road.

"You hungry for lunch?" Derrick asked once he was back on the interstate. "I know all the best places in town if you've got a craving for anything in particular."

Slater was kind of hungry after his "meh" breakfast of pancakes and applesauce. "You know what I could really go for right now? A fully loaded Italian sub."

"I've got an app for that. Here, take my phone."

He did and opened the app Derrick named.

"Type in your order, and then go to saved favorites, and I'll tell you what I want," Derrick said. "Should be ready and waiting by the time I get us there."

"Awesome, thanks." Slater had never looked into these sorts of phone apps, because he lived in the sticks. Garrett had exactly one restaurant and they didn't deliver. He found their classic Italian sub and loaded it up with mayo, oil, banana peppers, hot peppers, oregano, onions, pickles and tomatoes. No lettuce because yuck. He didn't like grass on his food.

Derrick's saved favorites were a hot meatball sub and a hot chicken carbonara sub that sounded really good. Maybe Slater would get that for himself next time. Derrick asked for the meatball sub and said to add a bag of spicy corn chips. Nice. They both liked hot food. On a whim—and because he'd almost fucking died last week—Slater added two homemade fudge brownies. If Derrick didn't want one, he'd eat them both.

They didn't chat much after that, and Derrick cranked up the radio again. Slater closed his eyes and listened to Derrick sing, and before he knew it, Derrick pulled into a pickup spot outside a deli. He dashed inside for their food and came out a few minutes later with a loaded plastic bag. The new scents in the car made Slater's mouth water.

Derrick pulled into a residential neighborhood that was a mix of old and newer homes, and he cursed as he parked on the street in front of one of the houses. "Damn it, I'd hoped there would be a driveway spot open so you didn't have to walk as far."

"I'll be fine."

Slater wasn't sure which house was their destination, so once he was situated on his crutches, he waited for Derrick to grab the bag of food and Slater's prescriptions. Then he followed Derrick up the sidewalk to a driveway. The two-story home had some age and was painted blue and white. It took a minute for Slater to get up the three steps to the small front porch, but he managed without toppling onto his ass.

Derrick unlocked the front door. The foyer surprised Slater with its living room look, and he eyeballed the interior staircase. Thankfully, Derrick led him to a locked door on the right. "Home sweet home," Derrick said.

The apartment was tidy, had a pleasant lemon-polish scent to it, and had sunlight streaming in through the living room windows. The windows overlooked a modest backyard that had a simple cement patio surrounded by a narrow swath of grass. "How do you get out to that?" Slater asked.

"You have to go out the front door and around. It's not the most convenient thing, but when the owner remodeled there wasn't an easy way to keep a rear exit for everyone to use."

"Got it. Cool. Food now?"

Derrick laughed. "Make yourself comfortable."

Slater did, stretching out on the futon with one throw pillow behind his back and another propping up his right foot. He'd barely done anything today but it still hurt, and he could probably take a pain pill soon.

Derrick took their food into the kitchen area and opened the wax-paper-wrapped sandwiches. "You want some of my corn chips?"

"Yeah, sure."

"Cola or root beer?"

"You got both?"

Derrick shot him a sheepish grin over one shoulder. "Maybe."

"Surprise me."

"Cool."

A few minutes later, Derrick put a chilled can of cola on the end table closest to Slater's body and handed him a porcelain plate with his sub and a handful of red-dusted chips. Derrick had a similar plate, plus a bottle of beer, and he settled on the floor with his food. Slater felt like a douche for taking up the only piece of sitting furniture in the living room, but Derrick didn't seem to mind. He tore into his meatball sub with gusto, leaving a smear of tomato sauce on his chin.

Slater kind of wanted to lick that sauce off, so he picked up his own sub, which dripped oil onto his plate. Perfect. The first bite was food nirvana as so many flavors mixed together in the very best way. Heat and spice and fat and meat and crunch and oh, hell yes! This was a deli he was absolutely ordering from again. The spicy corn chips were a shockingly good combo with his sub, and the great food helped him forget about his aching foot.

They didn't talk while they scarfed down their lunch, and that was fine by Slater. He wasn't huge on conversation, preferring solitary walks through the land to boisterous beer and poker nights with the other hands. Besides, why fill the air with small talk when the food was so good?

The six-inch sub plus chips more than filled Slater up, so the brownies would keep until later, and he sipped at his cola while Derrick licked sauce off his own fingers. Slater wasn't used to being waited on. In Patrice's kitchen, the hands served themselves and put their own dishes in the dishwasher basket. But Derrick offered to take his empty plate with a gentle smile, so Slater handed it over. Unsure how Derrick's TV system worked, he waited for the guy to clean up and return to the living room. Derrick sitting on the floor of his own home kind of sucked, but Slater was pretty tall and took up the whole futon.

"I can prop my ankle up differently if you want to sit up here," Slater said. "On a stool or something."

"It's fine. I don't really have anything for you to use, but Dez and Morgan might have something we can borrow. Their apartment is nuts."

"Who?"

"Our neighbors. Really nice couple. Morgan is a bodybuilder and Dez is a clothing designer-slash-up-cycle blogger. She's actually got a pretty good following on social media."

Slater blinked. "What does upcycle mean?"

Derrick stared at him as if Slater had asked the world's dumbest question. "She reinvents old or broken things into something new. Like broken pottery into a mosaic tabletop, or she's really good at taking worn-out clothes with holes and recreating them into new pieces. She takes photos and blogs about the process, and sometimes she sells at swap meets. She wears a lot of the stuff she makes, too, and is really into reusing and recycling."

"Oh. That's cool. Really creative." He was impressed by creative types, especially artists, poets and authors. People who created new things out of nothing but the thoughts or images in their heads. Slater had never possessed much creativity.

Rachel was creative. She enjoyed drawing, painting and acting. Her mother wasn't like that, though, so Slater wasn't sure where she'd gotten her talent from. Latent genes from a grandparent, maybe?

"How's their apartment nuts?" Slater asked, putting his mind back into their current conversation.

"They just have a lot of stuff. Dez loves tag sales and thrifting, and she's always picking up a new project, so they have boxes and bags of things all over the place. Random furniture parts, cheap clothes, bits and bobs of all sorts. It's not messy, exactly, just very full. But I bet they have a padded stool we can borrow. If not, I'm sure I can find something at Goodwill."

"Okay, good. I just… I know my ankle needs to be elevated, but I don't want you to sit on the floor in your own place."

Derrick grinned up at him in a way that made Slater feel as if they'd been friends for years, rather than weeks. "No trouble, man. I should have thought ahead and didn't. Want me to check in with Dez next door about a stool? Once we get settled, we can stream a movie or play a game. Do you game?"

"Not really. I play a few on my phone, but the last time I played a video game was on a Super NES system back in the day."

"Damn, man, you're old."

Slater pretended to swipe at Derrick's head and the motion made his ribs ache. "I'm only thirty-five, you ass. Not that much older than you."

Except I have a seventeen-year-old daughter no one knows about.

No one in his current life knew the whole truth about Rachel, and Slater planned to keep it that way for now.

"You said you're turning thirty soon, didn't you?" Slater asked.

Derrick rolled his eyes. "Yeah, and I'm dreading whatever Conrad and Wes are cooking up for me. Although, I guess whatever Conrad dishes out, I get to serve right back to him in two years when he turns thirty."

"Well, the easiest way to head them off at the pass is simply to say you're too busy taking care of your broken boyfriend, and you don't have time to go out and play." Slater meant it as a slight joke, because the apartment seemed easy enough to maneuver around on crutches, but Derrick seemed absolutely delighted by the excuse.

"You're a lifesaver." Derrick lurched up from the floor and planted a hard kiss to Slater's surprised forehead. "And the perfect excuse to stay in for the foreseeable future. I mean, I do love to go out dancing to let off steam and occasionally find a hookup, but the last thing I want is some kind of ambush at a nightclub."

"Have you tried telling your brother that? You guys talk, right?"

"Yeah, we talk."

"So tell him you don't want a surprise party. Tell him you'd rather stay in, or go out on a simple dinner date or something. It's your birthday, pal."

Derrick blinked at him several times from his kneeling position before a strange kind of wonder softened his face. "Damn, you're right. I really would just rather go out to dinner as a family. Or hell, even us all getting together at Mom and Dad's for one of Mom's big spaghetti dinners. She makes awesome from-scratch meatballs."

"Sounds perfect to me."

"And it'll give you a chance to meet my folks before the first wedding next month. Third weekend in May."

"And your birthday is…?"

"May fourth."

Slater's lips twitched with humor. "How often do you get greeted with 'happy birthday and may the fourth be with you'?"

Derrick snorted. "A lot more in recent years, especially on social media. You a *Star Wars* fan?"

"Yup. Between me and some friends on the same block, we wore out our video rental place's VHS copies of the original trilogy. Dad took me to see the theatrical re-release back in '97 and then finally bought me my own VHS set. It was pretty awesome, but I wasn't a fan of all the changes Lucas made."

"Sounds like you and your dad are close."

Slater didn't like talking about his family, but Derrick's comment seemed genuine, rather than leading, so he didn't change the subject right away. "We were when I was growing up. My mom left us when I was young, so it was just us two for a while, until Dad met my stepmom, Kim. Then I did the usual rebellious teenage shit, and Dad and I kind of grew apart. We don't talk much but we're still in contact."

He's the only way I know what's going on with my own kid.

"I'm sorry you guys aren't close anymore," Derrick said softly. "My parents have always been great and supportive, even when I came out as bi. I mean, they weren't thrilled about that, but they didn't do the whole 'it's a phase' crap some of my other relatives pulled. I also think it helps that Conrad is married with a kid, and probably a few more in the future."

"Less pressure on you to settle down?"

"From my parents, anyway. Between them, they have

a collection of seven siblings, who also have spouses and kids, so I have a lot of cousins. That's why you're my buffer against all the women in my family who will want to partner me up or marry me off to some friend of a friend."

"Buffer. Gotcha."

"Buffer and friend." Derrick's eyes flickered to Slater's lips, then back up. But he seemed to recall Slater's declaration that he didn't kiss. Not hookups, anyway.

Slater did kind of want to kiss Derrick, which confused the hell out of him. He also wanted to keep this as platonic as possible, so Slater cleared his throat. "So about that stool from your neighbor?"

"Yeah, right. I'll pop across the foyer and be back in five."

"I'm not going anywhere."

With a wink, Derrick stood and headed for the apartment door. Some of the lingering sexual tension faded the moment Derrick was out of proximity, but damn. This entire afternoon had been way too easy. Too... nice. But he could not get attached to Derrick as anything other than a friend.

Period.

Derrick closed the apartment door and then leaned against it for a few moments, desperate to catch his breath and keep his half-chub from getting any bigger. Kneeling next to Slater, whose long, muscled body was stretched out on his futon like a feast, had given Derrick all kinds of dirty thoughts. Thoughts he'd kept completely to himself, not wanting to jinx this before it truly began.

Besides, Slater had just had surgery and was probably on pain meds, and Derrick didn't want to accidentally take advantage of the guy. Ever. But the attraction was still there, damn it, and Derrick needed to keep better control over his dick.

"You lock yourself out or something?" Orry Thompson was perched on one of the sitting chairs, phone in hand, but his attention was on Derrick. Orry lived upstairs with twin brother George, and they didn't hang downstairs as much as some of the other residents.

"Nah, I'm good." Derrick wasn't about to share his guy problems with Orry, and Orry seemed content to shrug it off and go back to his phone. Business as usual.

Derrick strode across the foyer and knocked on Dez's door. Morgan answered with a wide grin. "Hey, dude, what's up?" Morgan asked. "Your roommate here yet?"

"Yeah, he's settling in. You remember I said he busted his ankle? I was hoping you guys had a padded footstool or something he can use to keep his ankle elevated."

"Sure, we've got something. Come in."

The sheer clutter of the place made Derrick's skin prickle with unease the instant Morgan shut the door. Their apartment had a similar open floor plan but also included the home's original kitchen, so the bedroom was right by the front door. Organized chaos was the best Derrick could do as a description, but he did see a couch and TV in the mess.

Something whirred briefly behind a mound of clothing, and then Dez's head popped up. She was doing something on the sewing machine. "Hey, Derrick."

Derrick returned the greeting, and Morgan explained his visit.

"Oh, yeah, what about that green stool in the bedroom?" Dez said. "If you put a pillow on it, it should be high enough for his ankle. Especially if he's on the futon."

Morgan disappeared into their bedroom.

"Working on something new?" Derrick asked politely.

"Yep. An online friend asked me to turn a bunch of her old college and sorority tees into a quilt for her bed, so I'm working on that."

"That's a thing?"

"Yup. It turns shirts you'll probably never wear again into something useable, instead of them taking up space in a dresser or closet."

"Huh. Cool." He learned something new every day.

Morgan returned with a hideous wooden stool with a lime-green, cracked leather cushion. Two out of six upholstery buttons were missing. But it had sturdy legs and would do the job. "Here you go, dude. I hope your friend's leg heals fast."

"Thanks. He's pretty exhausted from all the moving around today, but maybe you guys can stop over tomorrow night and meet him."

"We'll do that."

"Cool. Thanks again for the stool."

"Not a problem. Let us know if we can help."

Derrick nodded and left, grateful for his generous neighbors. Orry was still on the chair, on his phone, and he didn't look up when Derrick passed him again. Opened his own apartment door.

Slater was snoring softly, flat out now and head on a pillow. Derrick smiled at his friend, then quietly put the stool down by one end table. It was strange having another person asleep in his living room like that, but he'd have to get used to someone else being in his space. Derrick had some work to catch up on, anyway, so he pulled out his laptop and let his "boyfriend" sleep.

Chapter Seven

Slater woke in a dim room to the sound of someone... typing? The nurses didn't type shit in his room, so what the—oh, yeah. Derrick's place. He tried to sit up but his stiff body and sore ribs protested, and he let out a pained groan, annoyed at himself for falling asleep in a strange place—and for being unable to move.

"Slater?" Derrick appeared quickly, his face creased with concern. "You okay? Do you need a pill or something?"

"Yeah. Forgot to take one before I dozed off. Ow." The throb in his ankle reminded him why taking his pills on time was a very good idea. He'd have to program reminders into his phone or something.

"Which one?"

"I'm not sure."

"Okay." Derrick disappeared and then reappeared with both pill bottles. He read the names and compared them to his discharge paperwork. "So looks like you get the ibuprofen on the regular, but the oxy is only for the first few days for intense pain."

That sounded right. "Pain's pretty intense."

Derrick handed him the oxy tablet and the warm cola to wash it down. Slater managed it while still mostly flat on his back. "You just wanna lay there for a while?" Derrick asked. "Until the pill kicks in?"

"Yeah, I think so. This was a lot easier in an elevated hospital bed."

"I bet."

Slater's bladder gave a pang and he groaned again. "Shit, I have to piss."

"Then let me help you sit up."

Helplessness was not something Slater enjoyed, but Derrick helping him sit up was far less embarrassing than waking up in the hospital with a catheter up his dick. He'd demanded that thing be removed, preferring to piss in a damned bottle until he proved he could get to the bathroom without a dizzy spell.

No dizziness today, thank fuck, but his body protested every single action, especially his ribs. Nothing could be done for bruised ribs, though, besides time and patience, and he did not look forward to weeks of this.

Better than being dead. Or worse.

His injuries could have been far more devastating. Anything from permanent paralysis to multiple broken limbs. So Slater could suck it up and deal with his aches and pains. Nothing was keeping him from seeing Rachel graduate in June.

He hadn't really explored the apartment beyond the futon, but there also wasn't a lot to see besides dated furniture and a tiny kitchen. The appliances were clean, if a little old, and he got curious. "How long ago was this place renovated into apartments?"

"About eight years, I think," Derrick replied. He had one arm around Slater's waist, and the warmth seeped through Slater's shirt as Derrick reached for the crutches. Got them under Slater's pits. "I've only lived here for about two years. Moved the summer after my ranch vacation, actually, to be closer to work. The landlord offered to replace the appliances but they work just fine, so I didn't see the point in spending the money."

"Got it."

Slater hobbled his way toward the door Derrick indicated, Derrick following along behind as if he expected Slater to topple over. The bathroom was small and decorated in white subway tile and laminate flooring. A white pedestal sink and medicine cabinet. The only bits of color in the room was the vinyl palm-tree-covered shower curtain hiding the tub, and two green floor mats. Behind the door, he spotted a metal rack full of towels and toilet paper rolls.

"Nice," Slater said. Definitely bigger than his bathroom back at the ranch. When Derrick didn't move from the open doorway, Slater quirked an eyebrow at him. "You gonna hold it for me or just watch?"

Derrick laughed out loud. "Sorry, man," he said and pulled the door shut.

Chuckling, Slater did manage to relieve himself while standing and without banging his ankle around. Washing his hands was more of a challenge. Task complete, he couldn't help peeking behind the shower curtain to inspect the tub. Clean with a single bottle of all-in-one shampoo and body wash. Didn't surprise him with how basic the rest of Derrick's apartment was, but he was surprised by the shower seat inside the tub.

"Dude."

Derrick was leaning on the wall across from the bathroom door when Slater crutched his way out. "You bought a shower seat for me?"

"Sure. They aren't that expensive. Plus, my showerhead is detachable so it'll be the easiest way for you to shower without splashing a lot of water on the floor." Derrick's eyebrows wiggled. "Unless you'd rather I give you sponge baths."

"No, thank you. Plenty of those in the hospital. And I'll pay you back for the chair."

"No sweat."

"How long did I sleep, anyway?" As Slater hobbled back to the futon, he realized the apartment wasn't dim because Derrick had drawn the curtains shut. It was dark outside.

"It's after seven."

"Really?"

"Yeah. I let you nap, because I figured you didn't get a lot of good sleep in the hospital, what with nurses in and out of your room looking at things."

"You're right. Thank you." Slater felt wide-awake for the first time in days. "I don't sleep well in general, which I'm sure you figured out by now."

"Most people who do aren't in home gyms working out at three in the morning. Are you hungry? I snacked on some leftover Chinese earlier, but I can heat something up."

Slater's stomach wasn't grumbling, but it did feel somewhat queasy after taking that pill on an empty stomach. "I should eat something. Nothing too greasy or heavy."

"I've got leftover steamed rice and one egg roll left. If you just mix the cabbage with the rice and don't eat the egg roll wrapper, it shouldn't be too heavy."

"Cool, that sounds good." Instead of the futon, Slater aimed for the hideous dinette set and sank into one of the cushioned chairs.

Derrick brought over an equally hideous green stool and helped him prop up his foot on an extra pillow that hid some of the horrid lime color.

"Who's your decorator?" Slater deadpanned.

"Table and chairs came with the place, and the stool is from my neighbors. Water or soda?"

He really hated being waited on like this, but no way could he manage getting himself a drink while on crutches. It was also kind of…nice for a change. "Water, thanks."

Derrick fetched him a glass of water from a filtered pitcher, then went about heating up leftovers. "Fork or chopsticks?"

"Fork."

Soon, a steaming pile of white rice and egg roll innards landed in front of him, and it smelled good. Really good.

"Want any sort of sauce? I have a whole packet drawer."

"Packet drawer?"

"Yeah, you know how every bag of takeout comes with some kind of packet sauce, like duck sauce, ketchup, even little packs of Parmesan? I keep it all."

"Got it." Slater was tempted to add red pepper flake but didn't want to risk his stomach rebelling after such a heavy, spicy lunch. Puking all over Derrick's kitchen floor on the first day was not a good look for a new roommate. "Soy sauce?"

Derrick opened a drawer near the sink and tossed two packets of soy onto the table. He even brought Slater a goddamn paper napkin from some delivery place or another. "I feel like I should tip you for your service," Slater said.

"I don't mind being a bit more hands-on your first few days here. Once you get better on the crutches, you'll be able to do more for yourself."

"Right." It made perfect sense but Slater didn't have to like it.

"So are you a morning bather or a nighttime bather?"

Slater tore a packet of soy sauce open and squeezed it over his rice bowl. "Usually at night, so I don't go to bed smelling like horse and shit, especially if it was my turn to muck the stalls. I can't wait to shower the hospital smell off me." He didn't smell all that medicinal but the way Derrick's eyebrows jumped amused him.

"We can put that on the agenda after you eat."

"You can fix me dinner, Derrick, but I don't need you to scrub my back, too."

Derrick's dark eyes pinned him in place. "I promise not to look while I help you onto the shower seat."

Slater was too damned sore and tired to figure out if Derrick was teasing or flirting, and he really didn't need either tonight. "I can manage on my own, thanks. Wait, is my suitcase still in the trunk?"

"Nah, I brought it in while you were sleeping. I left it on top of the bedroom dresser, unzipped, for easier access."

"Bedroom, huh?"

Derrick shrugged. "No matter where we end up sleeping or not, I didn't figure you'd want your clothes strewn around the living room."

"Thanks. Did you, uh, look in the box?" Slater hated asking but that was his private stuff.

"Nope. You're taking a risk moving in with me, too, Slater, and I won't pry into your personal belongings. As long as there's not a gun or anything in there."

"Nah, nothing like that. Just mementos from my old life before the ranch."

"Got it. So I do have a question for you that I've been dying to ask."

Slater paused with a fork of rice and cabbage by his mouth. "Okay."

"Where did you get the nickname Slater?"

Prison, and I am so not going into that with you.

"About ten years ago," Slater said, picking his words carefully, "a guy I knew said I looked like that Lopez guy from *Saved by the Bell*. My dimples, I guess, because I didn't see the resemblance. So he started calling me Slater and it stuck."

Derrick tilted his head. "Yeah, I can kind of see the dimples and the dark hair, but other than that, like you said there isn't really a resemblance. I like it. You look more like a Slater than a Kendall, or even a Ken."

"Yeah, I don't know what the fuck my mother was thinking with that first name."

"Your mom named you? What is it with women and strange names? We have upstairs neighbors. Twins named Orry and George Thompson, and their mom was a huge fan of this TV miniseries called *North and South*. The American one, not the British one, and the twins are named after the male heroes of that show."

Slater had vague memories of the miniseries. His stepmom, Kim, had watched it on some cable channel or another when he was younger, and he'd watched the war scenes. The romance stuff had bored the crap out of him, but Patrick Swayze had looked damned fine on a horse. So had the guy who played George. "Do you like them?" Slater asked. "The twins, I mean?"

"They're okay. Pretty much keep to themselves, so I

don't know much about them or their story, and I only got the *North and South* connection because Dez said something to them when they first moved in."

"How did Sophie and Conrad come up with the name Mia? Is it strange to you?"

Derrick grinned. "Nah, I love that name. No big story that I know of, they both liked it and agreed on it for a girl."

"So they didn't know the sex ahead of time?"

"Nope, they wanted the surprise, so they did the nursery gender-neutral and asked people to buy shower stuff in all the colors. I think Conrad said they'd agreed on Michael for a boy, so if their next kid is a boy, he'll probably be a Michael."

"I'm surprised Uncle Wes hasn't demanded a name-sake."

"Yeah, well, I wouldn't be surprised if the boy ends up being Michael Westin Massey. Which actually has a nice ring to it. They both want at least three kids, as long as their careers can support them."

Slater searched his memory as he ate more rice, hoping to keep their conversation on Derrick's family so Slater didn't have to navigate any more land mines in his own past. "I know Sophie works with you, but what does Conrad do again?"

"Believe it or not, he designs and installs custom closets."

"Come again?"

"It's a thing, believe me. I had no idea it was a thing, but he's got an eye for design and space, and with some of the salaries folks make in Silicon Valley, they can afford to drop a few grand on a custom closet."

"Huh." Slater speared a bite of both rice, cabbage and bits of carrot. "So he kind of makes his own hours?"

"For the most part. It helps him be home with Sophie and Mia more right now, between client bookings."

"Do you want kids?" The question burbled up and out of Slater without warning, helped along by Derrick's bright smile whenever he mentioned his niece.

"I don't know, to be honest." Derrick fiddled with his glass of water. "I like other people's kids, but I never saw myself as the guy with a minivan, wife and a pack of kids inside. I adore Mia to bits, and I love the kids my cousins have. I'm just not sure I'm cut out to be a dad." He shot Slater a crooked grin. "You?"

"I'm not really cut out to be a dad, either." And that was the God's honest truth. He'd tried his damnedest with Rachel, but all he ever seemed to do was screw up.

"So any siblings?"

"Only child."

"Bummer." Derrick winked. "No one I can needle blackmail material out of."

"Oh, you're on now, Massey. I am so getting Conrad's number and getting dirt on you."

"My life is an open book, man. Ask whatever you want to know."

Slater considered the statement as he continued eating. He enjoyed chatting with Derrick and did want to get to know the man better. But Slater's life was *not* an open book, and he didn't need Derrick demanding some sort of quid pro quo on information. "Meh, I doubt you're all that interesting."

Derrick flipped him off.

After he finished eating, Slater resigned himself to being waited on again by Derrick, who cleared the table.

Whatever. It would only be for a few days, until Slater got used to the crutches. He investigated his suitcase, as well as the very small, boring bedroom. Nothing about the place seemed to reflect anything about Derrick as a person. Not that Slater had done much in the way of decorating his cabin, but Hugo had hung a colorful poster over his bed and filled their shared bookshelf with knickknacks and personal things.

None of his jeans would be useful until the stupid cast finally came off, and Slater only had the one pair of sweatpants he was wearing. He'd have to order some online. But he had several pairs of gym shorts he could use for now, so he grabbed those, a clean undershirt and his own all-in-one wash. Time to attempt a shower.

Derrick watched him from near the bathroom door. "You need a hand?"

"Dunno yet. I'm going to try this myself, but I won't lock the door in case you hear a crash."

"I'll keep an ear open." He handed Slater a plastic garbage bag. "For your cast."

"Thanks."

Once inside, Slater nearly locked the bathroom door out of habit. He'd be naked and vulnerable to anyone who came inside once he was on that shower seat—but deep down, he knew Derrick wouldn't come in unless Slater called for him.

It took some doing and Slater was a little out of breath by the time he was finally undressed and seated on the bath chair, with his plastic-wrapped foot situated on the edge of the tub. Not terribly comfortable but he managed to wash himself. After six days in the hospital, no shower had ever felt so good. He avoided the mirror, aware he needed to shave soon but not really caring tonight. He was thoroughly exhausted by the time he dried and dressed, and he didn't even ask his host. Slater collapsed onto the big king bed and groaned.

"What do you need, pal?" Derrick asked.

"Pill for me, pillow for my foot."

"On it."

After Derrick gave him the pill and a glass of water to sip, he helped Slater get under the actual covers and prop up his foot. Derrick's touch as he situated the cast for Slater was gentle and warm, and the kindness chased away the remnants of Slater's first-day jitters. All of today's activity crashed down on him, and Slater fell asleep before he could say thank you.

Derrick watched his new roommate sleep for a few minutes, impressed with how stubbornly Slater had managed the last hour. The guy had an independent streak that was going to be a pain in the ass, especially if Slater wore himself out trying to do everything on his own. One of the top things in his discharge papers—Derrick had read them over twice during Slater's nap earlier—was rest. Lots of rest.

At least the stubborn cowboy had allowed Derrick to fix his dinner.

They hadn't managed the "where are we sleeping?" conversation before Slater passed out, either. Slater was situated on one side of the bed, and it was big enough for them to share without touching. Derrick wasn't into groping people while they were asleep, so Slater was perfectly safe if they shared. But Derrick hadn't shared with another guy in a long time. He also didn't know if Slater would react badly if he woke with someone else in bed with him when he wasn't expecting it, and Slater had enough to deal with right now.

Derrick grabbed his pillow and an extra blanket from the closet, then shut the light off. Closed the door most of the way but not all, in case Slater needed help in the middle of the night. It was still early-ish, only a little after nine, so Derrick settled on the futon with his phone and earbuds to watch Netflix for a while.

He woke with the sun barely rising and Slater shouting his name.

Derrick nearly fell getting off the futon, not used to sleeping on its lumpy cushions, and he scrambled to the bedroom. "What's wrong?"

Slater glared in his general direction. The covers were thrown back, and his cast dangled off the side of the bed in a way that looked painful and awkward. "I need help," Slater said, tone clearly indicating his displeasure with the statement. "My ribs are killing me and I can't manage sitting up, and I've gotta piss."

"Oh. Okay." So not an emergency, then. Good. Now Derrick needed to get his racing heart to calm down. He'd never been woken up by someone screaming his name before and he'd panicked. "How urgent is the need to pee, because I can get a bottle—?"

"You fucking well will not. I can hold my bladder until I get to the toilet. I'm just…going to have to sit. My foot hurts like hell, and I don't have the energy to stand and balance."

"No problem. Um, do you want to grab my hands and pull, or should I support you from behind and push?"

"Push."

Slater let out a long, unhappy groan when they finally got him sitting upright. He pressed one hand to his left side. "How is it possible I feel worse today than I did yesterday?"

"Yesterday you did a whole lot of moving around you haven't done since before your fall. You gotta rest and take it easy, or you aren't going to heal." Derrick brought the crutches over, and he helped steady Slater as the man rose. The fact that they were similar in height made the whole production easier.

Once they were in the bathroom, Derrick asked, "You need me to pull your shorts down, man? I promise not to cop a feel."

"I'm only saying yes because I really need a pain pill right now."

"Cool." Derrick politely averted his eyes as he tugged the gym shorts down and then helped Slater sit on the can. "I'll get the pill."

He gave Slater a few minutes as he gathered up his meds, water and two crackers to take with the pills, because Slater was due for an ibuprofen, too. Slater stuffed the crackers into his mouth after he took the pills. Derrick helped him stand and pull his shorts back up. Waited by his side while he washed, not liking the stiff way Slater moved.

They got him settled on the futon, and Derrick fetched the stool for his ankle. Got an ice pack and a towel, too. "You're a lifesaver," Slater said.

"This lifesaver needs to take a shower and get ready for work."

Slater stared a beat. "Oh, yeah. I guess it is Monday."

"Do you need me to take the day off? I can if you think you'll need help." As much as Derrick adored his job, he'd take time off in a heartbeat if Slater asked him to. Slater was still figuring out his crutches and getting used to the apartment, so—

"Nah, I can manage. Do your thing, you don't have to babysit me."

Derrick held Slater's gaze but the guy had a great poker face, and if Derrick insisted he should stay, Slater would just insist Derrick leave. Slater was stubborn as hell, and while he accepted the help Derrick offered, he clearly didn't like it. "Okay." He showed Slater how to use his TV and gaming system before hitting the shower.

After he dressed, Derrick made them both a quick breakfast of frozen waffles. Wrote a list of phone numbers for Slater including his office number, Dez's cell (since she worked from home), the landlord's number, and just to be an ass, added, "911—in case of emergency."

Slater rolled his eyes at that.

"Seriously, though," Derrick said. "If you fall or get too tired to do something, call me or Dez. She's super chill and lives right across the foyer."

"I will. Thank you. Now go to work."

"Yes, dear."

Derrick grabbed his laptop bag, double-checked his phone was in it, and headed for the apartment door. "Don't burn the place down while I'm gone."

"It'll all be cinders by lunchtime."

With a snort of laughter and a tiny ounce of worry for his friend, Derrick went to work.

Chapter Eight

Two hours into his morning, Slater ran headfirst into a problem he hadn't truly considered with this living arrangement: boredom.

He'd never been much of a TV-show watcher, preferring contained stories in movies, and even then he was picky in what he watched. He was a fan of horror and SF and some comedies, but he preferred smart humor to fart jokes. Nothing caught his eye as he scrolled the hundreds of choices on Derrick's streaming apps. His own tablet got a free signal but he'd forgotten to get Derrick's WiFi info before he left. He could read, but ever since the fall, reading for too long gave him headaches.

Hell, reading the lengthy discharge paperwork had given him one yesterday.

Slater was supposed to sit and rest, but by the time lunch rolled around and he'd managed to cobble together a ham sandwich and chips from Derrick's food—he definitely needed to give the guy money for groceries, or do an online order, or something—Slater was going out of his mind. And he had weeks of this left ahead of him!

Derrick called him at twelve thirty, and Slater simply said all was well. He'd figure out the boredom issue on his own. He managed to waste all of five minutes ordering more sweatpants on his phone. Played a few of his games. Nope. He just wasn't used to sitting on his ass all day long. He needed to be *doing* something.

Curious about this person named Dez, Slater hauled himself up onto his crutches and headed for the door. Derrick had showed him where he kept his spare apartment key, but did Slater really need to lock the door if he was going twenty feet away? Probably not, because Derrick mentioned the house having a separate front door key he needed to get a copy of for Slater.

Should be fine for a five-minute neighborly chat.

The foyer was empty and quiet, and Slater crutched his way across the hardwood floors. He took a moment to really look around. The house had probably been charming back in its heyday, and the owner had done a good job restoring the original molding and banisters. With more and more younger people remaining single and/or child-free, creating apartments out of former homes made a lot of sense.

He ran a hand through his messy hair before knocking.

A moment passed before the door swung open. A very petite person smiled up at him from a good ten inches down. They wore paint-stained overalls and a black tee, and had short hair. "Hey, uh, Morgan?" Slater asked.

"Dez O'Connor, and you must be Derrick's boyfriend, Slater," they said with a grin.

Crap, he was so unused to socialization he couldn't even get a new introduction right. "Yeah, I am. It's nice to meet you, Dez."

"Same. Derrick asked me and Morgan to stop by later tonight to meet you, but this is great. I was taking a stretch break, anyway."

"Stretch break?"

"Yeah." She ushered him into the most cluttered apartment he'd ever seen. "I'm going back and forth between a quilt project and some clothing redesigns, and when I get caught up, I get really stiff. Taking regular stretch breaks is good for my back, muscles and digestion."

"Oh. Cool."

"So how do you like Derrick's place?"

"It's nice. I'm grateful he's letting me recover here, instead of the ranch."

"I bet. He told us a little bit about that. Being in a smaller space and closer to people is probably better in the long run. I mean, I'm almost always home."

"So he said." Slater gazed around the piles of shopping bags, plastic totes stacked on each other, bits of furniture peeking out. "Um, you mind if I sit?"

"Sure." She led him to a couch, and he sank into it, grateful to get those crutches away from his armpits. Dez plunked down beside him. "So what brings you by? Bored already?"

"Very. I'm used to structured days and chore lists, not sitting on my ass watching TV."

"I can empathize, I think. I was bullied so much when I was a kid that my mom ended up homeschooling me until high school, and there were some days I craved human interaction so badly I wanted to scream at the top of my lungs."

"Yeah, that's kind of how I feel. I mean, I'm not the most sociable guy on the ranch by far, but I was always around other people. Tourists, horsemen, even the horses. Being completely alone is…stifling."

"Then I'm glad you stopped over." Dez lightly poked him in the shoulder. "Hey, you should take up some kind of art or hobby project. Then we can hang out together and do our stuff, so you won't be lonely."

"I'm not very artistic or creative."

"I bet you have some sort of hidden talent. And I have tons of craft kits and materials hiding around this place."

No kidding.

"I have a blog," Dez continued, "where I show off the things I make and show the project from start to finish, and sometimes I post videos online, too. So once in a while, a fan will send me something to try for fun, but I always insist it's either a kit they got super-clearance or from a thrift store. My whole thing is making the old or worn stuff new and fun again."

Slater understood why Derrick liked Dez so much. She was interesting and had so much positive energy, he just wanted to sit there and absorb it. He also appreciated her worldview on reusing things instead of trashing them—even if the cluttered apartment made his skin itch.

"The blog thing is kind of cool," Slater said.

"It's a lot of fun, and it's helped me really accept my true self, and I saw the confusion when I answered the door. I'm nonbinary, but I prefer she/her pronouns."

"Oh. Okay." Slater actually knew what that meant, thanks to Hugo and his frequent evening rants about the LGBT+ community accepting all parts of the rainbow. "And Morgan?"

"Straight cis male. But he is amazing and loves me for who I am, not how I present one day to another."

"Good. I'm glad you have that kind of acceptance."

Dez tilted her head. "You don't?"

"At the ranch, I do. Did. Do? It's a totally accepting place, but my past is…murky."

"Got it, and if this is way too personal for a first conversation, please change the subject. I'm just glad to see Derrick dating one person for a change. He's such a great guy, and he deserves a great person." Her eyes narrowed. "So if you're taking advantage of him for a place to stay…"

"Totally not doing that." Especially since living together had been all Derrick's idea. "I like Derrick a lot, and the only reason we're living together this soon is because of my stupid fucking ankle." He also liked knowing Derrick's friends were protective of him. Derrick wouldn't be alone when Slater eventually left.

"Good," Dez said. "So is there anything you have a special interest in? Besides horses, I guess? Like I said, I have all kinds of craft things and starter kits. Or I can just randomly pick something and you can try it out."

"I can honestly say I've never walked into a craft store in my life, so I wouldn't know one thing from another. As long as it's something I can do with my hands and concentrate on for long periods of time, I'm game for whatever." His hand-to-eye coordination had improved immensely in the last few days, but it never hurt to keep exercising it.

"Cool, okay. Sit tight."

"All right." A little nervous, but also intrigued, Slater watched Dez jump up and disappear behind a stack of plastic storage tubs. Things shifted and moved, and she muttered to herself quite a lot, and Slater found the entire thing kind of hilarious. It was a great distraction from his throbbing ankle. He twisted so he could rest it on the arm of the sofa. Keeping it elevated was key, and he should probably get an ice pack on it soon.

"This one was on top," Dez said triumphantly, "so let's try this kit." She came around the tote tower with a box in her hands. "Ever done a latch hook rug?"

"Nope." He had no idea what that even meant.

Dez perched her butt on something across from the couch that he hoped was a coffee table, and she held the kit out. "It's basically small pieces of yarn you hook through this mesh canvas, and you produce a pattern. You can finish the edges and use it as a small rug. It was really big in, like, the seventies and eighties, but it never went away."

Slater studied the box, which showed a picture of a fuzzy green frog rug. "This is somehow enjoyable?"

She laughed. "For some people, yes. I did a few when I was a kid. They're fun and easy, but you also end up with something useable at the end of the project."

He tried to imagine that frog rug in front of Derrick's apartment door, and Slater grinned. "Yeah, okay. I'll give this a shot. Sounds like more fun than staring at the walls."

"Awesome." Dez clapped. "I'll show you how to get started."

Thus began Slater's very first tutorial on how to make a latch hook rug. It took him a few tries to get the basic moves down, but then he was hooking piece after piece of pre-cut yarn onto his pre-painted canvas. He didn't mind the slight cheat in having the image already on the canvas, because it helped him not fuck it all up completely.

Once he had the idea, Dez went back to her sewing machine, and they worked together with thirties swing music playing over her sound system. When Slater's phone alarm went off, Dez offered to dash next door for his pill, and he was grateful. He really liked Dez, and Slater was nearly halfway done the latch hook kit when the apartment door opened.

A huge, muscle-bound guy stepped inside and froze. "Who are you?" he asked.

"Uh, Slater?"

Dez's sewing machine stopped whirring and she popped into view. "Hey, babe, this is Derrick's boyfriend. He got really bored, so I gave him something to do."

"Oh, cool." The man who had to be Morgan took three long strides so he could bend and shake Slater's hand. "Morgan Flaherty."

"Hi." Slater shook the guy's meaty palm. "Dez is right. I had no real idea how cooped up I'd be healing this fucking ankle, and I'm not a huge TV guy."

"No problem. Dez has enough projects stored up to keep six people busy for the next five years."

Dez flipped him off before jumping up to kiss his mouth. "What do you want for dinner? I can do a tofu scramble. Slater, are you staying?"

"For tofu?" Slater replied. "Not a chance."

"Trust me, I had the same reaction the first time," Morgan said. "Two years with Dez and I'm a firm believer in tofu. Even if I do love my pepperoni and sausage pizza once in a while."

"Relationships are about balance and compromise," Dez added. "He gets his porky pepperoni and I get my tofu."

"Are you a vegan?" Slater asked.

"Mostly vegetarian with occasional meaty treats,

but we do try to eat more plants than meat whenever possible. And it's not an animal rights thing, it's just healthier for our bodies and minds. I try to invite Derrick over on healthy food nights but he's determined to over-salt his body with frozen dinners and takeout."

Dez made a lot of good points, and after three years of eating Patrice's home cooking in the guesthouse, Slater had a feeling he was going to start disliking frozen food and takeout pretty quickly. Maybe once he was better on the crutches, he could learn to cook simple meals.

"If it's getting close to your dinnertime," Slater said, "I can make myself scarce."

"You don't have to leave," Morgan replied. "But if you want to, I can carry the latch hook stuff over for you."

"I appreciate it. Maybe I should get a little wagon I can tie to one crutch to carry stuff for me."

"Or a backpack."

"Good point and much easier." How had Slater not thought of something so obvious? He could take anything anywhere with a simple pack. More online shopping was in his future tonight.

Frantic knocking made all three of them jump, and Slater nearly fell off the couch. Morgan strode over and flung the door open. Derrick stood there, eyes wide, mouth agape, and started to ask, "Have you seen—?" Then he spotted Slater and instant relief made his rigid posture sag a bit. "There you are. Why aren't you answering your phone?"

"I didn't hear it ring." Slater picked it off the couch cushion, but the screen wouldn't light up. "Shit, the battery must have died. I didn't put it on the charger last night. Why? Is something wrong?"

"Not anymore." Derrick stepped inside so Morgan could shut the door. "I called to ask if you wanted anything special for dinner, and after the third time to voice mail, I panicked. Thought maybe you'd fallen or something."

"You were worried about me?"

"Yeah." Derrick shoved his hands into his slacks pockets and looked at his feet. The posture was…kind of adorable, and Slater liked knowing Derrick worried about him. And thought enough about him to ask what he'd like for dinner.

"That is so cute," Dez said. "This is the first time I'm seeing you together, and you make a charming couple."

"So what are you doing here?" Derrick asked him.

"Trying not to lose my mind from boredom," Slater replied. He held up the half-finished frog rug. "Dez gave me a project."

"Really?" Derrick sat beside him and looked at the rug, and no, his cologne did not make Slater's skin prickle with awareness. And nearness. "My mom used to do these when I was little. You were really that bored?"

Slater shrugged. "I can only watch so much TV before my brain wanders. I like doing things with my hands." He wiggled one eyebrow at Derrick. "This is pretty hands-on."

Dez giggled. "And Slater is welcome over anytime. You're both welcome. Especially if you want to stay for dinner."

"Do you have enough for four?" Slater asked before Derrick could say no, because he really, really wanted to watch Derrick eat tofu.

"Definitely enough." Dez's eyes sparkled with *I see*

what you did there mischief. "I'll start cooking. Derrick, you want anything to drink?"

"I'm okay for now, thank you." Derrick picked up the latch hook kit box. "This really takes me back. If you enjoy it I can swing by a craft store and pick up a few more."

"I'm not sure." Slater rubbed his finger over the latch hook tool itself. "I mean, I enjoy working with my hands and it's fun to watch the image appear in yarn, but it's simplistic."

"Can't you buy the canvas plain?" Morgan asked. "Then you can cut your own yarn colors and make your own design. Instead of a frog or unicorn or whatever those kits come with. Wait a sec." He threaded his way to a big bookcase on one wall and scanned the spines until he found two. Pulled them out and brought them over to Slater. "These are for cross-stitching but they're just patterns. You can probably use them for latch hooking, too."

Slater accepted the two heavy books. One was customizable cross-stitch patterns that ran the gamut of phrases and Bible quotes to animals and winter scenes. Super simple and extremely complicated. Growing up, he'd had an elderly neighbor, Mrs. Phillips, who'd park herself and her sewing basket in a rocking chair on her trailer's tiny front porch, and she'd cross-stitch all day long on these big wood hoops. He had no idea where those finished projects ended up, because her family moved her into a nursing home when Slater was eight, and he never saw her again.

"What's this one?" Derrick slid the second book out from under the first. Then started laughing.

Slater glanced at the cover. "*Subversive Cross-Stitch*. The hell?"

"Oh, I love these. They're all cussing and *fuck this*, *fuck that*. I can just see Conrad's place with an entry rug that says, 'Bless This Mother-Effing House.' Oh, my God, these are priceless."

"See?" Morgan said. "All you have to do is use markers to draw the words or patterns on the latch hook canvas, pick your own colors, and then hook away. Or I guess you could learn to cross-stitch, too, and do wall samplers or something." Off Derrick's funny look, he added, "What? I've lived with Dez for two years. I've picked up on some of her language."

"These are great," Slater said. He kind of liked the idea of using these books for inspiration and designing his own patterns. "Now I just need raw materials."

"I know Dez has a few totes full of yarn, but I dunno if she's got any canvas."

"I don't want to keep taking Dez's supplies. I can buy my own stuff."

"You aren't supposed to be out and about for at least two weeks," Derrick said. "You need—"

"To rest, yes, I know. Thank you, Nurse Massey."

Morgan chuckled. "Are you two sure you haven't been dating longer than a few weeks?"

Slater quirked an eyebrow at Derrick, who looked bemused by the comment. Technically, they weren't really dating. Fucking on the gym mats had not been a date. Even dinner last night, as nice as it had been, wasn't technically a date. But they were telling everyone that they were boyfriends, so... "If you can't have fun with and tease your partner, who can you have fun with?" Slater asked.

"True story." Morgan cast a longing look in the direction of the kitchen. This apartment didn't have the same open floor plan as Derrick's. "Dez was still figuring herself out when we met, and watching her embrace being nonbinary and being able to just…exist? I fell in love so hard."

"How about after dinner," Derrick said to Slater, "I'll run out to the closest craft store and get stuff for you. I can even video-chat the call so you can see what I'm buying and choose what you want."

Slater stared at Derrick, whose earnest smile woke up the deep-down part of Slater that was lonely. So fucking lonely, and here was a fun, funny, friendly guy eager to do Slater all kinds of favors. Even going to a craft store at six thirty in the evening after a surprise dinner of tofu scramble, or whatever Dez was concocting in the kitchen. "Really?"

"Sure. I didn't think about you being bored and cooped up here day after day. Especially when you're used to an independent life. If you want to spend tomorrow latch hooking cuss words onto canvas, I'm all for getting you supplies."

"Thank you." Slater briefly resisted the urge to lean over and press a gentle kiss to Derrick's cheek. But why resist? Couples, even fake ones, kissed each other as thanks for a favor. So he lightly pressed his lips to Derrick's warm cheekbone. "I mean it. Thank you."

"No problem." Derrick's dark eyes flittered toward Slater's lips, and Slater drew back. Not only because they weren't alone—not that he imagined Morgan would judge them—but because Slater didn't kiss on the mouth. Not with hookups and not with random guys he lived with but barely knew.

"I'll give you my debit card," Slater said.

"Okay."

With a plan firmly in place, Slater, Derrick and Morgan spent the next twenty minutes or so poring over both cross-stitch books, looking at patterns, phrasing, color combinations, and laughing a lot over some of the bawdier ones. Slater started making a mental list that included permanent markers in different colors, so he could "sketch" his designs on the canvas before he added the rows and rows of yarn. The entire project had him kind of excited, because he'd never been the creative type who produced art for others.

But this was something he could do with his free time and not feel like he was sitting around being lazy while his ankle healed. He'd have physical proof of time and energy spent. Maybe he could even sock away some future birthday and Christmas gifts. No way he'd be good enough at this to make anything for Rachel for her graduation gift, though…

Apparently, in the combined O'Connor and Flaherty apartment, there was no dining table or official meal spot. A few minutes after some lovely, warm aromas began circulating the apartment, Dez emerged with a tray loaded with what looked like soft tacos at first. Slater definitely smelled chili and cumin and something sort of eggy but not quite.

"It's Faux-Huevos Rancheros Tacos," Dez said. A dozen tortillas loaded with faux-egg, beans, red peppers and onions were accompanied by side dishes of sliced avocado, shredded lettuce, shredded cheese, what he assumed was sour cream and chopped cilantro. Also a jar of salsa with a spoon in it. "Dig in!"

Derrick shot Slater a dirty look for the tofu trickery. Slater winked and then grabbed a taco. Loaded it with cheese and salsa, and then took a big bite. The tofu had a shockingly good texture against the beans, somehow mimicking the texture and flavor of actual eggs. "Damn, this is excellent," he said.

Dez beamed at him. "Thank you. I actually came up with this a few months ago when Morgan was craving Taco Tuesday but we didn't have any actual meat in the house. You can use the same mixture and roll it up into a kind of breakfast burrito."

"Very cool." Slater had no desire to go full vegetarian—Patrice's sausage gravy was too fucking amazing to ever give up—but he could see adding a few new things to his regular diet. Especially if they were as good as this.

Derrick ate his taco more slowly—and loaded with every possible topping—but he seemed to enjoy the meal. "I hate to say it," Derrick drawled as he loaded up a second taco, "but there might be something to this tofu thing."

Dez pretended to faint. "All it took was a boyfriend to get you to eat tofu? Can Slater tempt you into trying tempeh next?"

"What is tempeh?" Slater asked.

"Don't ask," Morgan replied with a pained face. "I can do it certain ways but just don't ask."

Slater wasn't sure if he wanted to try this mysterious tempeh or not, but he'd also spent five years eating whatever was dumped on his prison lunch tray without questioning it. He didn't have to do that anymore, though. Not now and not ever again. He'd just look up tempeh on his phone later. Once he charged the damned thing.

Dinner was delicious and the company was beyond charming. Morgan and Dez took turns feeding each other bites of their tacos, and the obvious love the pair shared shined in their smiles and simple gestures. Two years of love and acceptance. Slater's own heart ached with jealousy and loneliness, and while he wasn't a forever kind of guy, Slater was glad to have Derrick as a friend.

Dez was completely cool with Slater borrowing her books. After complimenting the meal up and down, Derrick carried the books and rest of the latch hook kit across the foyer to their place. Derrick didn't seem annoyed at Slater for leaving his apartment unlocked all day long. Slater hooked his phone up to its charger and got his ankle back up on the ugly green stool, while Derrick quickly searched for any online coupons for the craft store he planned to hit.

"Hey, Derrick?" Slater said before his roommate left. Derrick paused by the apartment door, a silent question in his dark eyes. "Are you okay with lying to your friends about us being a couple? I mean, knowing you have to do it and actually doing it are two different things."

Derrick bit his bottom lip for several long seconds. "I'm not okay with it, exactly, but it was part of the deal we made, right? Fake it for the summer until we break up?"

"Right. I just…" *Don't want you to start resenting me screwing up your life after only one day.* "Cool, I just wanted to check in. Now go shopping for me."

With a wink, Derrick left.

Video-chatting with Derrick while he scoured the aisles at the craft store was…kind of hilarious. He mostly showed video of the shelves, but his commentary was priceless. Slater didn't want to invest a lot of money into this until he was sure it was a hobby he'd continue long-term, so Derrick rustled up half-a-dozen skeins of cheap yarn in the clearance aisle—the colors were odd, but whatever—and even an as-is latch hook kit marked down because it was missing half the pre-cut yarn.

Derrick found a big package of plain canvas, a roll of rug binding, plus markers and a few more on-sale skeins of yarn in different colors before promising to be home soon and signing off. When he did arrive home with his purchases, he also had a pair of craft scissors and a storage tote for all of Slater's supplies. Slater was tired and achy by the time they sorted and stored everything for the night, and even more exhausted after he managed a quick shower.

Derrick helped wrestle him into bed, and Slater kind of hated that his fatigue always seemed to dominate Derrick's evening. His arrival had completely upended Derrick's routines, but Derrick didn't seem to mind. Maybe because he knew Slater wouldn't always be this helpless? Slater mumbled something to Derrick about not being afraid to share if he wanted, before drifting off to sleep. His first day cohabitating with Derrick Massey was down. Only roughly eleven weeks and six days left to go.

Derrick spent a long time standing in the doorway of his own bedroom, a pillow in his hand, uncertain where to go. Slater had been half-asleep when he said Derrick could share the bed, so what if he didn't mean it? What if it had been the oxy talking? Why hadn't

Derrick brought it up before Slater exhausted himself showering?

Yes, Derrick wanted to sleep in his own bed. Yes, Derrick wanted to sleep next to Slater. Slater had given him sleepy permission before passing out. But if Derrick slept there tonight, he'd want to do it again tomorrow. And every night after, for as long as Slater was here. Derrick enjoyed sharing his bed with another warm body beside him. But the last time he'd shared his bed with someone who wasn't open about who he was, Derrick had gotten hurt.

But he had time to learn more about who Slater was, deep down behind the flirty swagger and broody stares. They'd only been actual friends for a few days. It wasn't a marriage proposal, it was sharing a giant king bed as platonic fake boyfriends, for fuck's sake.

So Derrick slid into his side of the bed and closed his eyes. Listened to the steady cadence of Slater's breathing. Enjoyed the scent of his body wash until Derrick fell asleep. And when he woke the next morning, it was to Slater poking him awake instead of shouting his name. Derrick was in a much better position to help him sit up, and Slater flashed him a grateful smile as he crutched out of the bedroom for the bathroom, taut ass encased in tight workout shorts.

A guy could get used to that sort of wake-up call.

When Slater returned to the bedroom, Derrick asked, "Are you okay that I slept in here?"

"Sure, why? I said you could, right?"

"Yeah, but you were pretty loopy when you did. I needed to be sure."

Slater nodded slowly. "Cool. Go shower. I want to

see if I can manage my own pills this morning. Maybe even two toaster waffles."

"Don't burn my apartment down."

"Cinders," Slater said in a faux-villain voice as he turned to leave the bedroom. "Cinders by noon."

Derrick laughed, grateful his choice had been the right one, and got ready for work.

Chapter Nine

By Saturday, Derrick and Slater had established an easy routine between them. As Slater got used to life on crutches and managed his meds, he became more independent. Even used a backpack to take his supplies across the hall to Dez's place in the afternoons where they worked together on their individual projects. Derrick had come home last night to find the pair in the foyer, Slater hooking away while Dez hand-stitched a pair of jeans.

The finished frog rug sat outside Derrick's front door, and he kind of loved the cartoonishness of it. Slater had also finished the as-is kit with his own yarn, and the small cat rug adorned Dez and Morgan's doorstep.

Other small things began to change around the apartment, too. A set of free weights appeared in one corner of the living room. Slater's clothes began creeping out of the suitcase and into two dresser drawers Derrick had purposely emptied and left open for him. Food appeared in the fridge and cupboards. Slater wasn't going out shopping, so he must have been making great use of his phone.

Saturday morning, Derrick spent an hour on his laptop doing some work-related stuff he hadn't finished yesterday. Then he and Slater met Dez and Morgan in the foyer for a Monopoly tournament. Dez had put together a platter of sliced veggies for snacking, plus a bowl of vegan "ranch" dressing that…tasted kind of good with the red peppers and carrot sticks.

Conrad would be busting his balls so hard right now if he knew Derrick was actually eating and enjoying vegan shit.

They played and ate and joked like they'd been doing it for years, rather than for the first time, and for a while, Derrick forgot he and Slater weren't actually a couple. They did everything couples did, except have sex— shared meals, shared a bed, shared friends, talked and teased and watched TV. It was so damned domestic and easy Derrick didn't want it to be fake. But Slater hadn't made any moves on him or made any attempts to open up about his past, and Derrick would respect that.

Then again, it had only been a week since his ankle surgery, and he was still in moderate amounts of pain.

Orry Thompson passed through the foyer once, ear-buds in and phone in hand, and he barely spared their group a nod.

"Does he ever talk to anyone?" Slater asked after Orry disappeared out the front door.

"Not really," Morgan replied. "And you almost never see George. Don't know why."

"Yeah." Dez picked up the dice and rolled. "When they first moved in, me and Morgan took them a fruit basket, and neither one of them wanted to talk for more than two minutes. They're pretty secretive, but I guess as long as they aren't doing anything illegal up there, it's none of our business."

At noon, they ordered an extra-large veggie pizza, wings and a two-liter of cola to share. The game went far into the afternoon, until Slater had declared bankruptcy after landing on Boardwalk with two hotels owned by Morgan. Morgan and Derrick owned most of the board between them, and Dez went out a few rolls later. Derrick had never actually finished a game of Monopoly, and he wasn't sure how it was supposed to end. Especially when all he and Morgan did was hand their wads of cash back and forth, one never quite able to bankrupt the other.

Slater and Dez had their heads together, mostly ignoring the game in favor of working out a new pattern on grid paper—Dez's suggestion so he could figure out his design before putting it down on the blank canvas. Made sense to Derrick, and he liked the way the tip of Slater's tongue stuck out of his mouth when he was really concentrating.

"Dude, your roll," Morgan said. "Unless you're ready to call it a draw? I feel like we could go all night like this."

Derrick checked the time on his cell. A little after five. He'd stuffed himself with lunch but would have to start thinking about dinner soon. "How about two more rolls each, and if nothing dramatic happens, it's a draw."

"Works for me."

Nothing dramatic happened. Derrick sorted all the fake money into the banker's tray while Morgan put the rest of the board away. Since they were right there in the foyer, neither he nor Morgan had completely shut their apartment doors, and the box just inside Derrick's place buzzed. Each apartment had a call box and attached buzzer outside to let in guests.

Who was trying to see Derrick on a Saturday night?

Curious, he strode to the front door and swung it open. A very unexpected sight grinned at him from the porch, and Derrick stepped aside to allow his guests inside.

"Dudes, what the fuck?" Slater squawked.

Mack, Reyes, Colt, Ernie, Hugo and Robin surrounded their friend and leaned down to hug him. Mostly quick bro-pats but the attention left Slater obviously overwhelmed. He took a moment to introduce everyone to Dez and Morgan, then asked, "What are you all doing here?"

"Came to see you, duh," Colt replied. "Derrick been keeping you out of trouble?"

"He has, actually."

"What is that you're working on?" Hugo asked, pointing to the grid paper pad on his lap. "That kind of looks like what my mom would draw up before she began a knitting project."

"You're taking up knitting?" Robin asked.

"No, not knitting." Slater didn't seem embarrassed at all as he explained his new hobby. "It helps keep me focused and it's actually pretty fun. So everyone can expect at least one profanity-laden throw rug for your cabin by the end of the summer."

"Sweet."

"I can't believe you guys drove all the way out here to see me on your only night off. Well, except for you two." Slater pointed at Mack and Robin, who no longer worked at the main ranch but still lived on the land. "How's the house hunting going?"

Wait, the what now?

"Slowly," Robin replied. "We've got a decent budget, but right now everything is either newly renovated or in such piss-poor condition we're better off demolishing it and rebuilding it from the foundation."

"You and Shawn are house hunting?" Derrick asked.

"A little bit, yeah. Shawn and I have talked about it a lot. Getting our own place with a real kitchen so he can keep teaching me how to cook. But options are limited in the Garrett area. And neither one of us wants a long commute to the ghost town. So we're taking our time."

"Not like Arthur's going to kick you out of cabin row," Mack said with a grin.

Listening to Robin talk about his future with Shawn hurt a little bit, but it also helped squash the last of Derrick's lingering feelings for Robin. Sure, they'd burned hot and heavy for a while, but Robin was clearly in love with the ghost town cook, and they were buying a house. Definitely serious stuff.

Meanwhile, Derrick had a fake boyfriend for the summer and not much else. Maybe he should get a pet. The lease didn't allow anything with fur, because of Lucky, but maybe a lizard?

"So how's married life?" Slater asked. Reyes simply smirked at him, while Colt launched into a story about his own husband, Avery.

Derrick hung back, a bit out of place among the group of cowboys, but happy to see Slater around his friends again. He was isolated here in the house, but as his ankle healed, his mobility would increase. They bullshitted for a while, until Dez and Morgan excused themselves to their place.

"So have you guys had dinner yet?" Mack asked.

"Not yet, why?" Slater waved a hand at his elevated foot. "You can't exactly kidnap me into the city for a meal."

"No, but we can have a picnic. Patrice packed up a cooler with food for us, and I've got beer in the car."

"Seriously?" For a split second, Derrick thought

Slater was going to burst into tears. He recovered quickly, though. "I cannot tell you how much I've missed Patrice's home cooking. I mean, Derrick can nuke a mean frozen meal, but nothing compares."

"I've had her food, and I agree," Derrick said with a grin. "You guys are welcome to take the party into my place. There are about as many places to sit as out here but the floor's probably cleaner."

"Sounds good," Mack replied.

Derrick collected Slater's stuff while Slater levered himself up and onto his crutches. Hugo grabbed the ugly green stool while the other guys went outside to collect the food and beer. They got Slater settled on one end of the futon with his foot up, and Derrick grabbed a fresh ice pack, because they hadn't iced it in a while. Then he grabbed a flat sheet from his closet and spread it out on the living room floor like a picnic blanket.

The delicious scents of food filled the apartment the moment Mack opened the cooler and Derrick's mouth watered. With a little help from the guys, they got plates out and the food arranged. Hugo seemed delighted to prepare a plate for Slater, who turned down a beer in favor of a cola. Derrick waited until his guests had served themselves before piling his own plate high with meatloaf, mashed potatoes, steamed vegetables and her famous corn bread.

"So this latch hook thing is keeping you busy, huh?" Ernie pointed his fork at the tote of supplies by Slater's end of the futon.

"It's definitely keeping me sane," Slater replied. "You get used to one routine, and then *bam!* need to find a new one."

"Change isn't always easy," Mack said. "But sometimes a new direction is absolutely worth it."

"Something tells me my new direction isn't as exciting as renovating a ghost town."

"Maybe not the same, but it can still be exciting." Mack slid a curious gaze in Derrick's direction. "Sometimes life isn't subtle about pointing us to where we're supposed to be."

Slater met Derrick's eyes briefly before glancing away. "Maybe."

The conversation shifted to less intense topics, and Derrick enjoyed the camaraderie between the other men. Mack, Colt and Reyes especially had an easy rapport, but they folded Ernie, Hugo, Robin and Slater into things. Reyes spoke the least of anyone, but from what Derrick knew of the guy, that wasn't unusual.

They started talking about hobbies again, and Robin brought up his wood carving and how it was adding up to extra cash. Said he wanted to take Shawn on a trip this summer, and Derrick grinned at how completely smitten the guy sounded when he talked about Shawn.

Colt reached into one of the reusable shopping bags they'd brought the beer in, and he tossed a Rubik's cube at Slater. "Here's something to keep your brain occupied. Avery gave it to me a few months ago, but I can't figure the damned thing out."

"Are those things actually solvable?" Ernie asked. "Never seen it done."

"What is it?" Hugo said. Everyone in the room stared at the kid. "What?"

Slater fiddled with the cube in between eating his dinner. Derrick helped himself to two beers, using the alcohol to stay nice and mellow. Today had been...

a great day. Full of friendship and time with Slater. Maybe not the hot, naked sexy-times his body craved with the man, but this was good, too. An emotional connection and strong friendship would only help sell their relationship when the first wedding rolled around.

He made a mental note to take his suit to the cleaners next week. Hadn't worn it in a while because the double wedding at the ghost town had been business casual, rather than formal.

Does Slater have a suit?

Did it matter right away? He'd never get dress slacks on over that cast, so until it came off, black sweatpants and a nice shirt would have to do. Unless Dez could finagle something for Slater. He'd have to ask.

After they cleaned up dinner, Colt broke out a deck of cards and a box of wooden matches, and everyone except Slater and Reyes settled in to play Five Card Draw. Derrick wasn't very good at poker, and he went out first in a big bluff against Hugo. Then he spent the rest of the game watching, listening to the conversation, and keeping an eye on Slater, who was more interested in the Rubik's cube than the game.

At nine thirty, Slater tossed the solved Rubik's cube back at Colt, who gaped at him with open admiration. "Holy shit, you did not just do that."

Slater shrugged, then tried to stifle a wide yawn. "You just have to figure out the patterns."

"That's nuts. Damn."

"We should probably start packing up," Mack said. "But before we leave, we have one more little surprise for you, Slater."

"Another one?" Slater eyeballed Mack. "You're not gonna kiss me, are you?"

Mack chuckled. "Hell no, you ain't my type. Reyes?"

"Reyes is gonna kiss me?"

"Smart-ass," Reyes said. He opened the apartment door and reached for something out of sight. He brought in an angled object Derrick didn't recognize at first. Not until Slater let out a startled gasp. It was a top-of-the-line hands-free crutch, with a padded spot for Slater's right shin to rest on so the cast hung over the back edge, and a vertical brace for his upper thigh. With some practice, it would allow Slater to walk without the use of two crutches and with free use of both hands.

"I don't... Fuck." Slater gaped at the gift, his eyes glistening. "You guys didn't have to buy that for me."

"Yeah, we did," Reyes replied. He knelt beside Slater. "You've asked me to stop thanking you for saving Sam and not taking me over that cliff. This is my final thanks, Slater. You deserve this freedom of movement."

Derrick's heart squeezed tight with emotion as unspoken things passed between the pair. Slater offered his hand, and Reyes shook it. Held tight for a long moment before releasing him.

As Slater said goodbye to his friends that night, Derrick noticed a new lightness in his voice. A true acceptance that he did have family back in Garrett, and a job waiting if he chose to return. And as much as Derrick was happy for Slater over that, he was also sad for himself.

But a fake boyfriend didn't get to feel sad over Slater's happiness. Right?

Slater hated seeing his fellow hands leave, but he was also exhausted after a very long day of social interaction—almost more than he typically saw working a day at the ranch. He was also overwhelmed by so many things: that they'd come here at all, the food Patrice had sent, the fun times and jokes, and most of all, the new crutch. He was a little scared to try it, but also excited for the possibilities it offered.

"That was unexpected," Derrick said once he'd returned from walking their guests to the house's main door.

"Yeah, it was." Unexpected and kind of awesome.

Derrick picked up the solved Rubik's cube Colt had left behind. "I'm really impressed you solved this, by the way. I've never met anyone who could."

"It just...made sense." Slater couldn't describe it any better. He'd seen the puzzle box before but never attempted one until tonight. "Maybe if I'd applied myself in high school, instead of being a stereotype, I'd have managed college and some genius-level career."

"What kind of stereotype?"

Slater grunted. "The trailer park trash who gets his girlfriend pregnant when they're only seventeen, so he drops out to work to support them." Oh, shit, he hadn't meant to say all that, and Derrick's shocked expression only made Slater feel like a bigger fool for his past choices.

Derrick sank down on the opposite end of the futon. "You have a kid?"

This would be the optimal time to lie and say no, but hadn't he already enlisted Derrick as his ride to Rachel's graduation next month? Might as well fess up now. "Yeah, I do. A little girl named Rachel."

"How old is she?"

"Seventeen."

"Holy shit."

"Yeah. The date I insisted on in June? It's her high school graduation."

"Wow, man. That's wild."

"That I'm so much older than you?"

"Nah." Derrick shook his head. "I mean, I always knew you were older but to have a kid who's seventeen? You were a young dad, huh?"

"A really young dad." One of the proudest moments of Slater's life had been holding Rachel moments after she was born. The first person after the doctor and nurse to hold his baby girl. But he had made so many bad choices after that day. So many horrible decisions that had led him to some pretty awful places.

"Does she live with her mom?"

"No. Her mother is…unreliable. In and out of her life whenever it's convenient. No, my father and step-mom have full custody. She's lived with them for the last eleven years."

"Damn." Derrick's expression softened. "Do you see her often? Rachel, I mean, not the mom."

"Not a lot." Derrick's curiosity and lack of outward judgement helped Slater keep talking when he would normally clam up. "When I get my week of vacation at the ranch, I try to go home and see everyone. She knows me, but we aren't close." *Not like I wish we were.*

"Do any of the guys know about Rachel?"

"Arthur knows. I told him about her, briefly, when I interviewed for my first job at the horse rescue." Weariness settled deeply in his bones, and not just from today's activity. "I've made a lot of mistakes, Derrick, but I've spent a lifetime trying to make up for them. And then for all my hard work, the universe decides to bust up my fucking ankle."

"Maybe there's something to what Mack said earlier about life putting us where we're meant to be." Derrick's dark eyes flickered down to Slater's lips. "Thank you for telling me about Rachel. I won't tell anyone, I promise."

"I trust you." Slater didn't trust easily but he did trust Derrick Massey. Maybe more than he should after knowing the guy for a month.

"Same," Derrick said, "or I wouldn't leave you alone in my house every single day. Or have invited you to live here in the first place. I don't...trust easily."

Slater didn't have to phrase it like a question, but he did. "Because someone broke your trust?"

"Two someones, and pretty badly. I thought I'd learned after the first time, but apparently not. Fortunately, I never had to watch Conrad go through the same pain. Maybe he saw what I went through and figured out what not to do."

"Everyone fucks up. There's no shame in that as long as we learn from our mistakes and try to do better."

"You should hook 'Everyone Fucks Up' onto a rug."

Slater grinned. "Maybe I will. Or I'll save it for my first wall sampler."

"You're going to try needlepoint?"

"Dunno. Dez made me watch a few beginner videos yesterday, and I might try it if I get bored with latch hook. It's not like I don't have the time to try new things."

"True." Derrick yawned, which made Slater yawn in turn. "So, we survived our first week together. Wasn't so bad, was it?"

"It wasn't bad at all. You ever call Conrad about your birthday next week?"

Derrick sat up straighter and grinned. "I did. We're having a small family dinner at our parents' house on Thursday, and you are, as my boyfriend, invited to join us."

Slater chewed on his bottom lip. He knew this moment would come, and he'd already been introduced as Derrick's boyfriend to the neighbors. No one had to find out they weren't fucking. Hell, even if they'd been actual boyfriends, who would expect them to be fucking a week after Slater had ankle surgery?

"Okay," Slater said. "I, uh, guess it's too late to ask, and also kind of a dumb question considering Sophie, but will your parents mind that I'm white? And, you know, a guy?"

"Nah. I mean, they were a little surprised by Sophie at first, because Conrad had never dated white girls before. But they saw how happy she makes Conrad. Mom might fuss a little about me not giving her grandbabies, but Sophie wants at least three kids, so she's covered."

Slater tried to imagine a future with Derrick where he introduced Rachel to Derrick's parents. He could almost see it…but Slater also saw himself back at work on the ranch, surrounded by guys he'd known for years, living on the most beautiful land he'd ever seen. This thing with Derrick was temporary, anyway, and trying to imagine something different was pointless. Slater would enjoy the friendship while he had it and focus on the present. No more distant futures and pipe dreams.

Except as Slater fell asleep that night to the newly familiar rumble of Derrick's soft snores, he couldn't help dreaming for a little while longer.

Chapter Ten

Slater needed to keep his ankle elevated and iced for at least another week, so he could only practice a bit with the hands-free crutch, because of the way he had to position his leg. He still used the regular crutches for most things, but the hands-free made fixing his own sandwich for lunch so much easier.

He had a doctor's appointment Friday to have his soft cast switched to a hard one, and Dez had volunteered to drive him so Slater didn't have to pay for a Lyft. No way was he letting Derrick take off work for it. But before that, he had to get through dinner with the Masseys. Not that he expected a disaster or anything. Slater had seen the couple from a distance the few times they'd been up to the ranch, and they seemed incredibly kind.

Still, other than the first time he'd taken Nina on a date when they were sixteen, he'd never done the whole "meet the parents" thing. Derrick was relaxed on the drive over, so Slater tried to relax, too. Nothing to stress over. This wasn't even a real "meet the parents" dinner. It would be fine.

As Derrick pulled into the driveway of a nicely tended, mid-century rancher, Slater blurted out, "Don't bring up Rachel tonight."

"I won't." Derrick shifted into park and angled to face him. "I promised I'd keep your secret and I will."

"Thank you. It's not that I thought you would mention her, but…"

"I get it, pal." He quirked an eyebrow. "Do I get to call you 'babe' in mixed company now?"

Slater flipped Derrick off and reached for his door handle, grateful for the familiar way they teased each other. Today was the first big hurdle in their fake relationship, and Slater didn't want to say or do anything to screw up Derrick's plan.

He eased his cast out of the foot well and swiveled his body. He still had to wait for Derrick to bring the crutches around from the back seat, but he no longer needed help getting up, even from such a low sitting position. Still made his ribs ache, though. Conrad pulled in behind them before Slater was completely situated, and Derrick instantly migrated to the baby in that car's back seat. Slater hadn't met the newest addition to the family yet, so he waited while proud Uncle Derrick carried the tiny bundle over to him.

"This is my girl, Mia," Derrick said. "Isn't she gorgeous."

"She's beautiful," Slater replied, mostly to a beaming—if tired—Sophie. "She's got your eyes, I think."

"That's what people tell me," Sophie said. "I think she looks more like Conrad, but she's still so young. She'll probably grow up and look like neither of us."

"Or the perfect blend of you both," Derrick added. "At least we know she won't look like Wes."

Sophie giggled.

"Why not?" Slater asked.

"Because Wes is adopted," Sophie replied. "Derrick never told you that?"

"I guess it never came up." Slater had had no idea Wes and Sophie weren't biological siblings. Huh.

"Well, now you know, and can we move this inside? I have to pee."

Their group moved up the cement path to the front door with Slater bringing up the rear. Robert and Sharon Massey greeted them at the front door with smiles and hugs for everyone, Slater included, and a chorus of "happy birthdays" for Derrick. Sophie dashed into the house. Sharon gave Slater an extra-firm hug, then pulled back to look him over. "You are a handsome young fellow, aren't you?" she said. "No wonder Derrick's kept you all to himself."

Slater blushed, because his face was still a bit of a healing mess he applied ointment to twice a day. "Thank you, ma'am. You're lovely yourself. I can see where Derrick gets his looks."

"And a charmer to boot."

"Damned shame about your ankle, son," Robert said. "But I hear you saved a little boy that day."

"Yes, sir." Slater tried to shrug it off because he was tired of being called a hero for doing something so instinctive as yanking a kid back from the edge. "I did my job that day, nothing more."

"Charming and modest," Sharon said. She wrapped her hand around Slater's forearm and squeezed. "Come into the living room and sit. You probably need to get off that ankle."

"Thank you, I appreciate it."

She led him into a warm, cozy living room full of dark furniture and framed family photos. Slater spotted a few of the brothers when they were kids, and he kind of wanted to see more. But Sharon helped him settle on the couch and leaned the crutches on a side table within easy reach. "Can I get you a drink? We have diet cola, iced tea, apple juice or beer."

"A cola would be great." Slater didn't usually drink this much soda, but he also hadn't kept it on hand at the ranch, and Patrice didn't buy it for the guesthouse. Might as well take advantage of its availability.

Apparently, the other kids could fend for their own drinks, because Conrad followed Sharon into the kitchen and returned with beers for him and Derrick, who'd seated himself and Mia right next to Slater. The baby was awake and staring wide-eyed at her uncle. When Sharon returned with a diet cola for Slater and a cup of coffee for Robert, she asked Slater, "Do you need to elevate your foot?"

"I'm okay for now—"

"No, you need it up," Derrick interrupted. "Conrad, go get him a chair from the dining table. And an ice pack."

Conrad rolled his eyes then did as asked. Derrick's insistence on the ice pack and the way he ordered his brother around were amusing as hell. Sophie returned and shared the love seat with Sharon. Once Slater's foot was elevated on a chair and covered with a towel-wrapped ice pack, Derrick asked, "Do you want to hold Mia?"

"Maybe in a little while." Slater hadn't held a baby that tiny since Rachel was a newborn, and he wasn't sure he remembered how.

"Okay." Derrick gazed around the living room. "People, I know I said I wanted a low-key birthday but this is dead silent. Not even a card?"

"Your gift is our company," Conrad snarked.

Derrick blew a raspberry at him. "Fine. This little one's company is all I need, anyway."

Slater couldn't help admiring the easy way Derrick held his niece. The way he smiled and his eyes gleamed simply by looking at her. He'd felt that way about Rachel. Even when he'd come home late at night, exhausted from a double shift at the gas station, just looking at her slumbering face had made Slater feel alive. Aware that everything he did, he did for Rachel.

"So, Slater," Robert said. "Living this close to the city must be a big change from being out on that ranch."

"It is different but it's not unfamiliar," Slater replied, careful to keep his tone light and conversational. Time to try and sell this fake relationship. "I grew up north of here, so I've been in and around the area my whole life."

"How long have you been at Clean Slate?"

"A bit over three years." Slater told them about the shipping company he'd worked for previously, and how he'd ended up working for Arthur Garrett, while Sophie and Sharon put the finishing touches on dinner in the next room. Conrad told a story about an exhausting client who kept changing her mind about his closet designs, until the women said dinner was on the table. Sophie settled Mia in a carrier to chill while the adults gathered in the dining room. Derrick helped him get situated at the far end so he could keep his foot propped up, and Slater's mouth watered at the spread.

"Birthday boy gets to pick his favorites for dinner," Sharon said.

"Your favorite is corned beef and cabbage?" Slater asked Derrick.

Shit, should I have already known that? Don't boyfriends know those things?

"One of my favorites," he replied. "Never had it growing up, but a college roommate turned me onto it. Why?"

"It's just something we ate a lot growing up, that's all. My dad could get the cut cheap from a butcher friend, and cabbage was even cheaper." This pot smelled way better than the thin soup Dad used to batch up before he married Kim. His stepmother couldn't stand the smell of cooked cabbage, so they only ate it on the rare occasions Kim went out of town to visit her folks.

"It took me a while to find a recipe we all liked," Sharon said. "But it's hearty stuff. I've gotten compliments on it at potlucks over the years."

"Well, it smells amazing, ma'am."

"Thank you, dear."

The side dishes included potatoes gratin with Brussels sprouts, crescent rolls and a gelatin mold with canned fruit inside. All favorites of the birthday boy. For someone who existed on takeout and frozen meals, Derrick had an eclectic palate. Slater hoped that once he could use the hands-free crutch more, he could put his free time to good use and cook them both healthier (and cheaper) meals.

Dinner went more smoothly than Slater expected, with casual conversation all around the table. Mia squalled once to be fed, so Sophie disappeared into the living room for a while. But with the layout of the house, she was close enough to the table to still contribute until Mia was satisfied. And since Slater had stuffed himself full of good food at that point, Sophie decided it was time for him to hold the baby.

She eased the precious bundle into his arms, and Slater's heart melted instantly. Mia had been small at birth and she hadn't grown much, but she was gorgeous. Tiny pink lips smacked together, and her dark eyes drooped shut as he gently rocked her. No goo-goo noises or silly words, he simply held her close and inhaled her baby smell.

"You're a natural, dear," Sharon said.

Slater couldn't bring himself to admit he was a father of his own kid, so he swallowed back a thick lump in his throat and said, "Thank you, ma'am." He glanced to his left at Derrick, whose sad eyes made that lump grow.

"What do you charge to babysit?" Sophie asked, and she didn't seem to be entirely joking.

"I have no idea what the going rate is. Besides, I can't manage a baby on crutches."

"Derrick told us about that hands-free crutch your friends gave you. I have another six weeks of maternity leave, and even when I go back to work, it'll only be part-time because Conrad makes enough at his job." Sophie flashed a dazzling smile at Sharon. "Momma S has already agreed to help out but I don't want to rely solely on her and Papa Rob."

Slater couldn't make himself turn down the offer to watch this little angel. "How about we wait and see how I do on that new crutch? I need to get myself from one end of our apartment to the other without pitching over, never mind while holding a baby."

"Fair enough," Conrad said. "And no pressure. We'll get the childcare thing figured out before Sophie goes back to work. Right, Soph?"

"You're right, no pressure, Slater." Sophie's gaze

flitted back and forth from him to Derrick. "You guys would make adorable parents, you know."

Derrick nearly inhaled his beer. "Jesus, Sophie."

"Sorry. I mean, you guys are dating and are already living together."

"For convenience," Slater said. "We are nowhere near serious enough to discuss adopting kids. Right now, I can't think further than my next doctor's appointment, much less a year from now."

"Which is completely understandable," Sharon added. "You've already had one huge life upheaval recently. Baby steps until your ankle is better."

"Exactly. Thank you." He truly did like Sharon Massey and her quiet strength. She reminded him a bit of his own dad, fighting like hell for his kid no matter what. Believing in Slater despite every bad choice he made. Visiting him every goddamn week during the five years Slater was in prison.

And he took the compliment Sophie had quietly paid him by trusting him with her baby, when she didn't really know him. Maybe she trusted him via his association with Derrick, and that was cool. He genuinely liked the Massey family, and regretted the way he'd fooled them all today, selling them on his fake relationship with Derrick. He truly hoped they never found out the truth—for Derrick's sake.

Derrick had never had a better birthday. Low-key and still fun. Full of good, home-cooked food. Easy conversations with the people he loved most. Sure, he'd have liked to see Wes and Mack in the group, because he loved ganging up against Conrad with Wes, but they had their own jobs at the ghost town and couldn't always duck out early. This was enough.

And watching Slater fall in love with Princess Mia? Priceless. After dinner, they had coffee and chatted more, until Sophie brought out a chocolate ice cream cake with big 3-0 candles on it, surrounded by a bunch of smaller, sparkling candles. Unsure if they were trick candles or not, Derrick had Slater hand Mia over to Gramma so Slater could help him blow them all out.

They were trick candles.

Eventually, Mom took the cake away with a laugh and dunked the candles in a bowl of water to get them to stop sparking back to life. Derrick didn't expect gifts, but Mom and Dad gave him a gift card to a fancy restaurant nearby—"for when Slater is feeling better and able to go out," she'd said—and Conrad said he was welcome to take back all the extra beer overcrowding his fridge. Sophie rolled her eyes, then handed him a card with a gift card to the nearest movie theater.

Last year, he'd gotten basic Visa gift cards.

Turn thirty with a boyfriend and suddenly you're flush to romance him right.

The idea of romancing Slater intrigued him, because Derrick got the sense no one ever had. He'd never been cared for and spoiled, and Slater deserved that. They'd only lived together for a little over a week, but Derrick was hooked, and he couldn't wait to spoil Slater with a fancy dinner and IMAX movie. A real date.

If Slater wanted that. The chemistry was real, and his parents seemed to like Slater, but this was still an arrangement. No matter what they told other people, he and Slater weren't really a couple.

After cake, Dad pulled out their battered box of The

Game of LIFE, and they gathered around the board to play. Well, Mom, Dad, Conrad, Sophie and Derrick gathered around, while Slater sat with Mia sleeping in his arms. They had a crib for her in one of the spare bedrooms, but Slater seemed content to hold the baby. LIFE had been a favorite growing up, and while everyone else played with the same enthusiasm as always, Derrick found less enjoyment in the task of traveling from college to retirement, marrying and packing up kids along the way.

Who said life had to include marriage and kids?

Derrick watched Slater and Mia when it wasn't his turn to spin the wheel. It still surprised him sometimes when he remembered Slater had a nearly-grown daughter of his own, but he was so natural with Mia. And from what little he knew about Slater, arguably a confirmed bachelor. Probably wouldn't want to adopt and start a family.

Not that Derrick wanted to adopt kids, or that Slater was his future. Birthday musings, that was all. But the entire evening was so perfect and comfortable, with Slater fitting right in and Derrick's parents accepting him.

Sophie won the game. Slater was drooping around the edges and still on his final two weeks of rest, so Derrick made their excuses. With some leftovers for tomorrow's lunch, he helped Slater say goodbye and got him into the car. Derrick dropped kisses on little Mia before hugging his family and leaving with his "boyfriend." Slater dozed on the way home, and he was so lethargic when Derrick parked that he got Slater undressed and into bed before he fetched the leftovers from the car.

It had been a perfect birthday. The exact right way to ring in the big 3-0. And as Derrick slowly fell asleep later that night, he couldn't help wondering if someone special would be there with him next year to celebrate thirty-one.

The strangest thing happened the Saturday after Slater's follow-up appointment: his friends from Clean Slate showed up again with food and to play poker. This time it was Mack, Reyes, Colt and Robin, so fewer people, but it meant the absolute world to Slater. They ate, joked and had a great time, and when they left that night, Slater told them to bring their significant others next time.

If they came again.

All that following week, Slater used his hands-free crutch more often and three nights he had simple dinners ready for himself and Derrick when Derrick came home, thanks to Dez and her kitchen wizardry. He and Dez spent their afternoons together crafting, either at her place or in the foyer, depending on Dez's project, and whether or not she needed the sewing machine. Slater was learning to cross-stitch and kind of enjoyed it. He got headaches, sometimes, because of how small the stitches were, so he mixed it up with latch hooking, which was less a strain on his eyes.

So far, his first three weeks as Derrick's fake boyfriend were off to a great start, and they got along like peas and carrots. Bacon and eggs. The perfect platonic couple, and on the third Saturday in May, Slater woke up with morning wood for the first time in weeks.

The alarm hadn't gone off yet—usually they slept in but today was wedding number one—and Slater slept flat on his back, because of his ankle. So the coverlet was impressively tented by his erection, and he stared at the hump in front of him. Unsure what to do about it, he stared at the ceiling and tried to focus on anything except the softly snoring man in bed beside him. The king mattress was big enough that they rarely touched at night, but all Slater had to do was reach out an arm. Brush warm skin.

No. Platonic relationship, that was it. No matter how much fun dinner at the Massey house had been, they weren't a romantic couple.

Slater also hadn't gotten it up in weeks, and the urge to slip his hand beneath the covers and fist his erection was overwhelming. But he couldn't beat off in Derrick's bed, especially not while the guy was two feet away. He could do it in the bathroom. The problem was, even though Slater now managed to sit up in bed without help, he often let out a morning groan of stiffness and pain that always woke Derrick. So he tried to ignore his bladder until Derrick's alarm went off and he wasn't disturbing the other guy.

He poked at his sore ribs until the problem boner started to fade. Sore ribs that weren't as awful as before but still an issue with general movement. He was getting better with the hands-free crutch, though, mostly using it around the first floor between theirs and Dez's place. He'd been briefly introduced to Orry Thompson but not the reclusive brother George yet. And the single father and daughter pairing who shared the other second-floor apartment were sweet if standoffish.

Slater didn't take any of it personally.

Derrick's alarm went off at eight, giving them both plenty of time to wake up and get Slater settled on the futon before Derrick showered. The preprogrammed coffee maker spat out its nectar and Slater managed to serve his own cup, without sloshing on himself or the floor, thanks to the hands-free crutch. He even had waffles in the toaster by the time Derrick emerged, dressed for the day in black slacks, a white button-up shirt and a green tie.

Dude liked green.

And he looked really, really good in it.

Slater let out a soft wolf whistle that made Derrick grin. Someone knocked, ruining the moment before either of them could actually flirt—which they'd been doing a lot of. Subtle flirting that teased and poked without turning into an outright pass at the other guy. Slater crutched to the door, not surprised to see Dez on their stoop with a shirt box in her hands.

"Morning guys," she chirped. "I meant to drop this off last night but Morgan had me way distracted." Her shining eyes suggested they'd been distracted in the bedroom.

"What is it?" Slater asked.

"Your pants."

"My what?"

"Come see." Dez strode to the dinette set and put the box down. Slater and Derrick crowded around as she whipped the box top off to reveal a pair of black slacks. "Derrick told me your size, so I made you custom slacks that are flared on the right side so the material will close around your cast. You won't have to hit a wedding in sweatpants."

Slater lifted the slacks and inspected the right leg. Dez had sewn extra fabric into both seams, which made the calf area wider. "Yeah, but how do I get my cast into the slacks?"

Dez beamed and shocked the crap out of him by ripping the right side open from waist to ankle. "Velcro. I patterned it after those sweatpants that runners wear and can just rip off without stopping, but I only did it on the right side. So you put your left leg in like normal and then Velcro it up around your right leg. Easy peasy."

"Wow." Slater stared at the slacks, completely humbled by the unexpected gift. "You have to let me pay you something for these."

"It's taken care of. Besides, you keep me company while I'm working, and I was more than happy to do it."

"These are fantastic, Dez," Derrick said. "Thank you."

"Yes, thank you." Slater didn't usually hug, but he wrapped one arm around Dez in a loose, sideways embrace, anyway.

She hugged him back, then leaned up on her tiptoes to kiss his cheek. "You are more than welcome. Now, go get dressed. I want to see how they fit."

"Yes, ma'am."

Slater went into the bedroom, detached the crutch, and shucked the sweats he'd put on. He'd always been a right-leg-first guy when it came to putting on his pants, but he sat on the bed and slid his left leg into the regular side. After a bit of fussing with the seams, Slater got the Velcro smooth and even on all sides of his right leg and around the cast. The crotch was a tad tight, but once he put the crutch back on and stood, everything evened out.

Dez beamed at him when Slater returned to the living area. "They look like they fit okay. Turn around and show that ass off to your man."

Slater hid his initial surprise behind a cough. "They feel great, thanks. And Derrick will have plenty of time to ogle my ass later."

"They look great," Derrick added. "You're a crafting wizard, Dez."

"Friends help each other out, right?" Dez punched Derrick lightly in the shoulder. "You two have tons of fun today, okay? Eat all the free food you can."

"Trust me, I will. My cousin had this one catered by the ladies at her church, and they make fantastic food. It's the same church I attended when I was a kid, so I know their food."

"Do you still go to church?" Slater asked, unsure why that had popped out of his mouth. He'd never seen Derrick leave on Sunday mornings. Derrick usually slept in until ten or so on Sunday.

Dez said goodbye and ducked out before Derrick replied, "Our parents took us when we were young, but they also said when we were fourteen we were old enough to choose if we wanted to continue. I did for a few more years because I enjoyed singing in the choir. But as I started figuring out I was attracted to women and men, I started seeing the latent homophobia, and after I graduated high school, I stopped going. I still attend Easter and Christmas Eve services with my parents at their new church, but that's about it."

"Oh."

"How about you?"

"Nah." Slater brushed a bit of lint off his new slacks. "Dad wasn't into that kind of thing, and some weeks we barely had enough to survive on cabbage soup, nevermind tithing anything to a church. It's like they tax their members to sit there for two hours a week and be told how to think. No thanks."

Derrick chuckled. "You aren't wrong about that. I also prefer the term *spiritual* to *religious*, anyway."

"Same." Slater liked knowing they looked at religion and spirituality in a similar way. The one and only time he'd been inside of a church was when Dad married Kim, and he'd found the place dark and creepy and somber. Definitely not for him. "What time are we leaving? If you told me, I forgot." The memory slips irritated him less and less, because they were simply part of his new normal. TBIs sucked.

"In about an hour. The ceremony starts at noon, and then the reception is directly after in the church's auditorium. But it'll take us about forty-five minutes to get there, depending on traffic."

"Got it." Slater eased onto the futon and unstrapped the crutch so he could elevate his ankle for a while. He probably wouldn't get many chances to today. "Can you make sure we don't forget my pills?"

"On it already." Derrick was at the counter and he held up a tiny pill carrier.

"When did you buy that?"

"I already had it. In my early twenties, I went on a huge health-nut kick and took all kinds of vitamins and supplements. I used this to take pills to work with me."

"Oh." The health-nut kick had paid off, if that's how Derrick got such a fine body. And this knowledge made Derrick's steady diet of frozen meals and takeout even more amusing.

Derrick fussed in the kitchen for a few minutes before joining Slater on the futon. They watched part of a movie they'd both seen before, so it didn't matter they didn't see the ending before it was time to leave. Slater used his regular crutches to get outside to the car, because strapping in and out of the hands-free was sometimes a pain. He probably wouldn't use the hands-free until the reception, so he could play his boyfriend role and mingle with Derrick's family.

Slater wasn't familiar with this side of the Bay Area, so he trusted Derrick to navigate them. They hit a small traffic snarl that seemed to make Derrick nervous about being on time, but they pulled into the church parking lot with ten minutes to spare. Other people were still streaming in through the church's front entrance, and Slater followed Derrick's lead as they left the parking lot and went to join the throng.

Showtime.

Chapter Eleven

Derrick had discreetly taken an antacid before leaving the house, and he had a few more in his pocket, wrapped in a tissue next to Slater's pills. Bringing his "boyfriend" to meet his parents had been minimally stressful compared to this moment, walking up familiar stone pavers toward the front of the church he'd grown up in. Familiar faces and family and friends all around him.

The program attendants were second cousins Derrick didn't know well, so he thanked them for his and Slater's programs. He spotted Sophie and Conrad in the large vestibule, which was still somewhat crowded, and Derrick helped Slater navigate his way through on crutches. Several of his already-married cousins were cooing over Mia, who looked adorable in a yellow dress and bow headband.

"There's my princess," Derrick said as he dropped a kiss on Mia's forehead.

"This is her first big outing," Sophie said, her fatigue overshined by her proud mama bear smile. "So far, she's been a hit."

"Of course she has, she's amazing."

"Hey, Derrick, good to see you," his cousin Trevor

said. They shook hands. Trevor was two years younger than Derrick and had gotten married four years ago. His wife, Trish, was already expecting their second, and their eldest clung to Trevor's pant leg.

Trish gave Derrick a hug around her big belly. "So did you actually bring a date to a function for a change?" she asked.

"I did." Derrick angled so Slater was more prominent in their group. He kind of wanted to hold Slater's hand to sell it more, but the crutches made it difficult. So he gently squeezed Slater's forearm instead. Trevor knew he was bi so this should be easy enough for a first introduction. "This is my boyfriend, Slater. Slater, my cousin Trevor, his wife, Trish, and their boy, Gus."

"It's a pleasure," Slater said. "I'd shake your hands, but I'm just trying to keep my balance here."

"It's all good," Trevor replied. "How'd you bust your leg?"

"Work accident."

Ushers began urging everyone into the sanctuary, so their conversation ended. Since they were family on the bride's side, their group sat together in a pew with Mom and Dad, who'd been waiting. He and Slater ended up on the far right side of the sanctuary, so Slater could lean his crutches against the wall and stretch out his leg without worrying about tripping the bridal party.

Slater leaned over and whispered, "So far, so good."

Derrick winked.

The ceremony was a bit long for his tastes, with a lot of music and even a number by the church's choir, which left Derrick a bit nostalgic for his choir days. But he couldn't see himself joining a church just to sing when he could do it at home. The entire production took close to an hour before the minister finally pronounced them man and wife, and the happily married duo walked down the aisle together.

Derrick applauded along with everyone else, but he wasn't able to picture himself as the groom. Hell, if Derrick ever did settle down and get married, he'd probably just want to drive out to City Hall and have it done there. No big ceremony or public displays of mutual adoration. A wedding certificate was just paper, after all. Nothing to fuss about.

Since the reception was attached to the church, they didn't have far to go. Round tables covered in white cloths and blue lantern centerpieces dotted the room, with a long table at one end for the bridal party. Church ladies were setting up a hot and cold buffet, which wasn't open yet, but a drinks station was already seeing brisk business. Their entire group settled at one table, then Derrick and Trevor volunteered to get everyone drinks.

"So how long have you and Slater been dating?" Trevor asked as they joined the line.

"About two months, give or take a week. He works out at Clean Slate Ranch."

"The place near the ghost town where Sophie and Conrad got married?"

"That's the one. We met the same day Sophie had Mia and we hit it off. Kept in contact. When he busted his ankle, things got a bit more serious between us." They poured the requested drinks for their table. Not everyone wanted something yet, or they'd have needed an extra set of hands. Derrick gave Slater his cola, and their fingers brushed lightly. They shared casual touches all the time but something new buzzed across Derrick's skin.

Slater's bright blue eyes met his, wide with surprise, before he looked away.

Since Mia was the newest member of the extended Massey clan, their table got busy very quickly with family members eager to meet the tiny angel. Slater surprised Derrick by holding his hand on top of the table, claiming ownership of his "boyfriend" to anyone who stopped by. It also pleased Derrick all over the place, because it clearly showed his family that him being bi was not a phase. He also loved that Slater had reached for him first, which he hadn't expected.

He introduced Slater to anyone who asked, until the hired DJ asked everyone to please be seated for the arrival of the bridal party. The DJ introduced the pairs of bridesmaids and groomsmen one at a time, until it was time to welcome the newly married couple. Derrick only released Slater's hand long enough to clap. Then the DJ said everyone could get their plates before the speeches.

"Do you want me to go get your hands-free from the car?" Derrick asked. "Or I can make you a plate."

"The crutch would be great, thank you." Slater didn't look excited to be left alone but at least he knew the friendly faces at their table. And it didn't look like Mom and Dad were getting up for food just yet. He'd be fine for three minutes.

"Be right back." Derrick stood and, on a whim he couldn't explain, leaned down to kiss Slater's temple.

Slater flashed a wry grin that seemed to say, *You're a big dork.*

"I know you are but what am I?" Derrick darted away from the table before Slater could properly retort.

He got caught in two brief conversations on his way to and from the car, so it took nearly ten minutes for him to get back. And his heart melted at the sight of Slater holding a sleeping Mia. Sophie and Conrad were in line for food, but Trevor and Trish were back with loaded plates. The scents made Derrick's mouth water.

"What's that contraption do?" Trevor asked.

"Helps Slater walk without using regular crutches," Derrick replied. "It's called a hands-free crutch."

"I love it for getting around our apartment," Slater added. "Makes cooking a lot easier when I've got two free hands."

The "our apartment" had probably slipped out without thought, but Trevor focused in on it fast. "Wait, you two are living together?"

Slater glanced at Derrick. Derrick said, "It's not that we're super serious, but it was the best solution for Slater's recovery, so I offered."

In exchange for five weddings and his daughter's high school graduation.

Derrick would never live it down if Trevor found out he'd had to negotiate for dates this summer.

Conrad and Sophie returned with plates of food, and Slater eased Mia into her carrier so he could strap on the crutch. They joined the line, which moved at a steady pace as the ladies who prepared the food served portions of whatever folks asked for. Derrick followed behind Slater, in case he tripped or had trouble with the crutch, but they got through the line and back to their table without incident.

The food was incredible, and it was probably close to an hour before everyone, including the bridal party, had their food and was seated. Derrick half listened to the Best Man and Maid of Honor speeches, the other half of his attention on Slater. Their proximity at the table, the way their elbows sometimes brushed. The faint scent of Slater's skin and sweat. Derrick felt eyes on him and looked up, right into Conrad's smirking face.

Derrick kept eating.

As the meal slowly came to an end, folks rose and mingled, and the DJ played dance music in the far corner of the auditorium. A few of his aunts stopped by the table to investigate Slater, probably hearing through the grapevine that Derrick was no longer available to them for pairing up with a "nice girl from church." Which was the entire point of bringing Slater along.

The trouble was, every time Derrick introduced Slater as his boyfriend, the entire thing felt more real. Less like the illusion it was supposed to be.

After all the official dances were over, the DJ invited everyone out to dance floor. "I'd ask if you dance," Derrick said to Slater, "but you've got a bum foot."

Slater snickered. "I'm a decent dancer, I guess, but nothing quite beats my wrestling moves."

"I remember." He'd loved how Slater had tossed him around on those blue mats—nope. Sexy thoughts would lead to a boner his thin slacks wouldn't be able to hide. "But yeah, dancing would be a bad idea. You'll need to get that ankle elevated as soon as we get home."

"It's already throbbing a little."

"You need a pill?"

Slater considered it. "In a little bit. I want to be able to tolerate some pain and don't want to risk getting hooked."

"Good man."

"You men are adorable," Mom said from across the table. "Never thought I'd see the day when Derrick genuinely fussed over a romantic partner."

Derrick hid a grin and sipped his soda, both pleased by the compliment and slightly embarrassed by the lie behind it. Slater wasn't his partner, and he likely wouldn't ever be. Despite Slater's confession about Rachel, he hadn't opened up about anything else in his past since, and he did his best to avoid Derrick's subtle attempts to engage him in personal conversation.

Sophie returned from feeding Mia. She promptly handed the baby off to Derrick, grabbed her husband's hand, and led him to the dance floor. Mom and Dad headed out during a slower number. Derrick enjoyed watching everyone dance to "The Time Warp."

"If you want to go dance, you can," Slater said. "You're wiggling in your chair like you want to."

"Are you sure?" He kind of did want to dance, especially if "The Electric Slide" came on, because he could bust that out.

"Absolutely. Go. Have fun for both of us."

Derrick didn't want to leave Slater's side, but it had been ages since he'd gone out dancing, and his body missed it. Missed writhing around in close quarters to other gyrating bodies. Not that anyone was gyrating at a wedding reception full of kids, but Derrick could make do with what he had. He joined a diverse group of cousins and danced.

The DJ was good, mixing up the dance songs with party songs, and then a slow one once in a while. Derrick ended up dancing with his Mom to "Wonderful Tonight" because Dad's bad knee needed a break.

"I think you've broken a lot of hearts today," she said as they swayed to the music. "The family's prize bachelor is off the market."

Derrick grinned down at her. "Took me long enough,

huh?" And in that moment it didn't feel like a lie at all. He truly enjoyed his life with Slater, and he wanted it to be more than an arrangement, but so much of that hinged on Slater opening up. Sharing himself with Derrick the way Derrick was sharing his entire family with Slater.

"You and Slater look like you make each other happy."

"We do." Truth. At least on Derrick's end. But Slater wasn't the same broody guy Derrick remembered from the ranch. This Slater smiled frequently, did needlepoint and latch hooking, and he'd even made friends with Lucky the cat, who joined him and Dez in the foyer some afternoons.

"Then you hold on and you fight, if this is what you want." Mom's eyes were serious a beat, before she smiled. "All I've ever wanted for my boys was for you both to be safe and happy."

"I am, I promise."

They finished out the dance in a warm hug, and then Mom went to sit with Dad. Slater was holding Mia and chatting with one of Mom's sisters. Slater seemed completely at ease, so Derrick kept dancing.

Slater had had no real expectations for how today might go when he got up this morning, and the entire production had gone smoothly. He got a few hostile looks from some of the older folk, and he didn't read too much into it. Derrick had mentioned some of his relatives were not very accepting of him being bi, and the looks rolled off Slater's back.

And he totally understood why Derrick was charmed by Mia. She was a very quiet baby compared to Rachel, who'd fussed about everything for the first six months or so of her life. Mia calmly took the world in, and he could tell Sophie was glad for the break. Holding the infant also reminded him of all the years he'd missed with Rachel.

He'd missed out on a lot of her childhood, but she turned eighteen this summer, and Slater truly hoped they could have a relationship as adults. He wanted that more than anything else in the world.

"You okay, honey?" the woman beside him asked. She was one of Derrick's aunts and had been nattering on about something when Slater's mind had wandered. He'd been terrible with names before his fall, but after? He likened his new memory to a colander: the big stuff stayed in but the little things slipped out and disappeared.

"Yes, sorry," he said. "You were saying?"

She continued the story of how the law office she worked for had ordered Dream Boxes from Derrick's nonprofit and how much fun it had been to decorate small totes and fill them with travel toiletries for distribution at a local women's shelter. The story endeared Slater to Derrick even more as he learned more about what the man's job was and who they helped. He'd had no real concept of nonprofits before now. But in a way, Arthur Garrett's horse rescue was a similar animal. They took in horses that needed help, made a modest salary and did good work bringing abused creatures back to life.

His heart panged for that ranch in a way it hadn't in weeks. Despite being somewhat limited to the house, Slater spent some mornings simply sitting on the front stoop, enjoying the sunshine. Not the same as his long walks around the ranch property, but he wouldn't be going on any long walks for a few more weeks, at the earliest.

Maybe it was the fact that Derrick's living room alone was larger than the entire ranch cabin, and that he had the foyer, too, but Slater didn't feel as cramped or claustrophobic in that house. He didn't need those long walks as much as he used to.

But is it really the house, or is Derrick part of the equation, too?

What if Clean Slate Ranch wasn't his final destination after all?

Eventually, his bladder panged and Slater reluctantly gave Mia over to Sharon Massey, who was delighted to hold her grandbaby. She also pointed him in the direction of the bathrooms, which were back near the auditorium's entrance. Without Derrick as wingman, navigating the room on the hands-free crutch was more daunting, but he managed without stumbling or falling. The throb in his ankle was getting worse, though, so he'd have to get an oxy from Derrick soon. Take the edge off.

On his way back from the bathroom, a young woman he didn't recall meeting inserted herself directly in his path. "Are you really dating Derrick?" she asked.

Slater gaped at her. "I…yes. Who are you?"

"I'm his cousin Jada. Are you guys really dating?"

"Yes." Despite the dating thing being a ruse, it still felt real to Slater. Not that he'd ever say as much out loud to Derrick or anyone else. Really dating meant really talking, and he wasn't ready to do that. Maybe ever. Not about certain things. "Why wouldn't you think we are."

"Well, he's dancing alone."

Slater waved a hand at his crutch. "I can't exactly

bust any moves right now. And Derrick is a great guy. I'm lucky he wants me around." So much truth in those words. "I'm not going to tether him to our table if he wants to dance."

Jada eyeballed him for a few more seconds before smiling. "Okay. I love Derrick, and he's never brought a boyfriend or girlfriend around, so we're kind of protective."

"I get it." Sort of. Slater didn't have a big, extended family to rely on, but Derrick did and he was glad for that. Glad that when this arrangement inevitably ended, Derrick would have his brother, parents and cousins around to help soften the blow of their "breakup." Derrick wouldn't be alone.

Slater would receive sympathy from his coworkers at the ranch, but he couldn't imagine confiding in any of them. Or wallowing in his own feelings over the matter. Not that he expected to wallow. It wasn't as if real feelings were involved here. He and Derrick were friends, and after they "broke up" they'd remain friends. No drama. No mess.

They'd each go back to their own, separate lives.

"So rumor is," Jada said, "you broke your ankle on a dude ranch?"

"I did." Slater really needed to sit, and Jada wasn't going away, so he told her a bit more as she followed him back to the table. Then she managed to get Mia from Sharon and cooed over the baby, her focus finally off Slater. He hated talking about himself, but that's what people did at these gatherings. Hopefully, by the end of the summer, he'd become a lot less interesting.

Derrick returned a while later, his skin glistening with perspiration, and he gulped from a cold bottle of water. "Damn, I haven't done that in forever. Miss dancing but my body is telling me why I don't go out like I used to."

"He just turned thirty, and he's already ancient," Sharon teased her son. "Wait until you're my age."

Slater fiddled with his own cup of soda while Derrick's words floated around in his head. The last couple of Saturdays, Derrick was home when Slater's ranch friends came over to eat and play cards. Instead of going out and doing whatever he wanted, he'd chosen to get to know the ranch guys.

I can't read too much into that. He has to be there or we won't sell the couple thing.

Instead of commenting on the dancing, Slater quietly asked Derrick for one of his pills, then washed it down with warm soda.

"Ankle bothering you a lot?" Derrick asked.

"More than usual, but this is the most moving around I've done on it since I got the cast."

"If you're ready to head out, we don't have to stay for the garter belt and bouquet toss."

"Are you sure?" Slater was getting tired and really wanted to put his ankle up with an ice pack.

"Definitely. I already congratulated the bride and groom. Let me find Sophie and Conrad to say goodbye, and then we can go."

Slater squeezed his wrist. "Thanks."

"No sweat."

Derrick kissed his temple again as he stood, and Slater…didn't mind. The gesture was oddly sweet and slightly possessive, and it didn't seem forced at all. A casual thing between boyfriends. He tracked Derrick around the auditorium this time, admiring the way Derrick's fine ass moved beneath those dark slacks. The memory of fucking that fine ass over the workout bench flashed through his brain, and Slater bit the inside of his cheek hard.

When Derrick returned, they both said goodbye to the Masseys and little Mia. At the car, Slater said, "I hate to be a wimp about this, but do you mind if I stretch out on the back seat?"

"Of course not." Derrick helped him with the crutch and got that blanket out of the trunk so Slater could elevate his ankle. His woodsy cologne tickled Slater's senses and it was not helping his unwanted sexy thoughts.

They'd been on the road for about five minutes when Derrick asked, "So did you have fun?"

"Sure. I've never been to such a big wedding before. Six bridesmaids?"

Derrick chuckled. "Yeah, the groom has a lot of sisters, which paired well because the bride has a lot of brothers."

That made Slater laugh. "One of your aunts said you were breaking hearts by being off the market now."

"I'm sure those broken hearts will find solace somewhere else." The statement was forceful and also…possessive? Of Slater?

He poked a little more. "You aren't afraid of potentially losing dates after we break up?"

Derrick didn't respond right away, and Slater swore the steering wheel creaked. From this position, Slater could only see a sliver of Derrick's profile, so he couldn't read the guy's expression.

"I didn't date before we met," Derrick finally said, "so I don't see that changing too much after."

"Back to club hookups, then?"

"Dunno. Guess I'll find out when it happens."

Slater dropped the subject and watched the scenery go by. They were both subdued when they got home. No one was in the foyer, so they took their somber moods into the apartment. Slater hobbled to the refrigerator to get an ice pack, then found himself standing by the counter staring at it. Fingers going numb but unable to move. He disliked the idea of Derrick going back to club hookups, because Derrick deserved someone stable and emotionally open. Someone who could love him the way he should be loved. Not someone who fucked up every relationship in his life, including the one with his own daughter.

Not an ex-con like Slater.

Footsteps shuffled up behind him, followed by a light waft of cologne. His body prickled with awareness but Slater didn't tense up. Hands rested lightly on his hips, and the simple touch sent blood rushing to Slater's dick. For weeks, he'd slept next to a man he was incredibly attracted to. A man he enjoyed spending time with. Eating with. Doing nothing more taxing than watching a baseball game on a Sunday afternoon.

"I don't want to think about the future right now," Derrick said, his voice soft, earnest. "Not when the present feels so good." Warm lips brushed the back of Slater's neck, and he gasped. Put the ice pack on the counter but wasn't sure what to do with his hands. Slater was upside down and turned around, and maybe they could blame this on wedding fever.

Slater grabbed the hand on his right hip and slid it down and around, leaving it over his hard cock. Derrick groped him, kissed his neck again, and Slater said, "Bedroom."

"Fuck yes."

Derrick must have momentarily forgotten the attached crutch, because his attempt to turn Slater around ended with Slater's extended calf slamming into Derrick's knee. Slater fell into him so he didn't hit the counter, and they both started laughing. Once they righted themselves, they managed to get into the bedroom and unstrap Slater's leg from the crutch. The cast was still a heavy problem, but hey, tear-away trousers!

Slater tugged at the buttons of Derrick's dress shirt, wanting to see the guy's bare torso again but he didn't want to ruin his clothes. Then again, Dez could probably sew on any missing buttons. All rational thoughts fled when Derrick leaned down to suck on Slater's collarbone. He wasn't sure how they'd both ended up naked, but Derrick was slotted between Slater's spread legs, hard dicks rubbing, and he was making a snack out of Slater's chest. His pecs, nipples, shoulders and neck. Even up to his cheeks and chin.

Everywhere except Slater's mouth, because Slater didn't kiss.

I don't kiss hookups. This is more than a hookup.

But a mouth kiss felt too much like a declaration he wasn't ready to make yet, so Slater surrendered to whatever Derrick wanted—for now. Derrick seemed content to taste every exposed patch of Slater's skin, exploring him in a brand-new-to-them way. Far more intimate than wrestling in a shed. Because they knew each other this time.

Really knew each other.

Their first time together, Derrick hadn't done much

more than kiss the tip of Slater's cock. This time, Derrick sucked him steadily into his mouth, using his hand and tongue to drive Slater crazy with pleasure and desire. He grabbed at Derrick's short hair, unable to get purchase, and then resigned himself to whatever Derrick had in mind. Slater had a handicap with his hurt foot and giving Derrick control this time intrigued him. And it felt fucking amazing.

Derrick sucked him, rolled his balls, rubbed his taint, but didn't go any closer to his hole. Slater was down with being fucked if that's what Derrick wanted; he trusted Derrick to get them both off.

"Fuck, that feels good," Slater gasped. "Damn."

Derrick sucked on his nuts a beat before lifting his head. "What are you up for?"

"What have you got?"

"Hmm." Derrick shifted until he knelt between Slater's spread legs, and he clasped both their dicks in his hands. Jacked them lightly. Seemed to debate something in his own head. The intensity in Derrick's dark eyes made Slater's belly squirm.

Finally, Derrick lunged for the bedside table and produced a bottle of lube. Rubbed some on both of their cocks before lowering himself, pressing their groins together. Slater groaned at the intense pressure, then hitched his left leg up to wrap around Derrick's ass. They thrust together, Derrick doing most of the work, driving them toward release. Maintaining eye contact almost the entire time. Slater wasn't sure what his eyes showed, but Derrick's showed desire, intent and pure arousal.

And maybe a little bit of affection?

Slater didn't think about it too hard. He'd woken up

horny, he had a hot guy rubbing off with him, and they were both going to come very soon. "Come on, Tiger," Slater demanded. "Get us there."

"Working on it." Derrick latched onto Slater's pulse point, and Slater groaned at the intensity of that pressure on his throat. Almost more intoxicating than a kiss. He slid one hand around to dip his fingers into Derrick's crease and rub his hole. Derrick grunted and thrust harder. Sucked harder. Slater's release winked just beyond his reach. It had been too fucking long, and he needed to come, damn it!

"Fuck!" Derrick rutted hard as warmth splashed between them, slicking his way more, until he stilled atop Slater. Breathing hard, his big body a comforting weight against Slater's.

Not so much against Slater's rock-hard cock.

"Damn." Derrick licked his pulse point again before sliding down the length of Slater's body. He licked Slater's dick clean before sucking him down. It only took a few seconds before Slater shouted a warning and came down Derrick's throat. Derrick sucked him through it, not missing a single drop, and that was insanely hot. Not all the guys Slater had been with over the years liked to swallow, but Derrick definitely seemed to enjoy it. And he was good at it. The entire experience had been…way too perfect. Too right.

And kind of a little scary.

He tugged at Derrick's shoulders until Derrick crept back up Slater's body. Derrick pressed his forehead to Slater's but didn't try to kiss him. Didn't take something Slater wasn't yet willing to give. Derrick's come-scented breath gusted across Slater's lips, and Slater imagined sharing the taste. But wasn't that for couples? Not for fake boyfriends?

Nothing about what they'd just shared was fake, though.

Derrick slid to the left so he was half draped over Slater and rested his head on Slater's shoulder. "Any regrets?"

"None. That was hot. Felt great."

"Same." Derrick sat up, a bit of wariness in his eyes. "It's just when we made our agreement, I said I wouldn't expect sex in return for you living here."

"I remember." Slater was too boneless to sit up, so he squeezed Derrick's knee. "The sex we just had was about us. Two guys with chemistry getting off. Doesn't have to be more than that." Slater kind of wanted it to be more, because both times he'd gotten off with Derrick had been incredibly intense—a kind of passion he'd never experienced with anyone before. A kind of passion that also terrified him to his bones.

"Right. Just sex." Derrick grinned. "Really great sex I hope we can have again?"

"Definitely." Slater faked a yawn so he had a moment to tamp down his hurt. No reason to feel hurt at all, since this *had* just been sex. Nothing else. No room for the tender feelings that had first tickled behind his breastbone at the wedding, watching Derrick interact with family. The ways Derrick doted over him and treated Slater like a proper boyfriend.

Well, duh, he has to sell it. Stop seeing more into this mess than is there.

"I think we could both use a shower," Derrick said. "How about I pop in and rinse off, and then I'll help you bag your cast?"

"Yeah, okay."

"Cool."

Derrick dashed out of the bedroom. Slater stared up at the plain ivory ceiling, annoyed at himself for allowing the magic of today's wedding to get inside his head. To make him want and dream when the entire day had been a fantasy. Nothing more, nothing less.

No more dreaming. Only four more fantasies to deal with and then Slater could go back to his single life at Clean Slate Ranch.

Chapter Twelve

The day after the wedding, Derrick noticed a slight change in Slater that he couldn't put his finger on. Slater wasn't giving him the cold shoulder, or suddenly being touchy-feely now that they'd had sex again. Nothing in their established routines had changed. But he was... cooler.

Derrick chalked it up to a post-wedding hangover and let it go. Wedding number two was two weeks later and the days in between passed as normally as they had before the first wedding. They shared a bed every night and no longer hid their morning wood from each other, but that was all. Slater was the one healing, so Derrick would let him initiate sex.

They also shared breakfast and dinner every day, occasionally eating over at Morgan and Dez's place. Slater kept improving his needlepoint game. Derrick went to work and did his job. Conrad sent him photos of Mia constantly as she grew and did more interesting things than eat, sleep and poop.

He couldn't believe she was already almost eight weeks old.

The wedding was a three-hour drive south. Mom and Dad sent a card but couldn't attend because Dad's knee was acting up again, and his doctor had said to rest. Since Conrad drove an SUV, they decided to road trip as a group. The back seat was more spacious for Slater to sit in the middle and stretch his leg out. It separated Mia from Derrick, but whatever. He'd get his cuddles during the inevitable pit stop.

Slater was cheerful during the trip, and he cooed at Mia when she wasn't sleeping. She was, of course, the star of the show at this wedding's reception. The entire production was outdoor at the family's house and spacious backyard, and the weather was perfect for an afternoon wedding. Slater eased right back into Boyfriend Mode, even going so far as to hold Derrick's hand a few times when they walked somewhere. They ate and chatted and went through the motions, and Derrick had a ball.

He really, really liked Boyfriend Slater more than Roommate Slater.

I need to take him out on a real date. Romance the guy with my birthday gift cards.

Derrick watched Slater balance a small plate of appetizers as he crutched his way over to Derrick, who was lurking at the edge of the yard. Fewer people he knew well here, and he quickly got bored of the whole, "So what's new in the last four years since I've seen you?" conversation. He had managed a quick chat with the groom, who was a cousin Derrick and Conrad had been tight with as kids before the uncle had relocated them for a new job. It had been good to reconnect in person, instead of just online.

Slater joined him and offered the plate. Derrick snagged some sort of shrimp skewer and ate it. This wedding was finger foods only, no big meal. Their return plan was to grab a bite someplace local before hitting the road home.

"Is it weird," Slater said, "that I'm a little disappointed no one is freaking out about things like Steve Martin did in *Father of the Bride*?"

Derrick chuckled. "I love that movie, but Conrad said if I showed it to Sophie while she was still planning their wedding, he'd beat me over the head with the DVD case."

Slater nearly choked on a bite of food. "Probably a good call. But they got through the wedding jitters eventually." Something in Slater's expressive blue eyes shuttered briefly. Then he shoved the plate at Derrick. "I have to take a leak, and there's probably a line. See you in a few."

The abrupt departure worried Derrick, because what on earth had either of them said? He got it when Slater was melancholy around Mia but what about Sophie's wedding had shifted his mood? Maybe it was wedding talk in general. He still didn't know as much about Slater as he wanted to know at this point, but they were also still playing the roles of fake boyfriends. They didn't confide in each other, so it was hard to guess what this was all about.

Slater didn't have to piss, but it was the perfect excuse to find a quiet part of the home's downstairs and get his thoughts together. The kitchen and den had guests but the formal living room was empty. Slater sat on a chair by a dark fireplace, closed his eyes, and breathed.

It had been a joke between brothers. Conrad beating Derrick over the head with a DVD case. A joke. But that hadn't stopped Slater's thoughts from flashing back to eleven years ago. The brawl that eventually sent Slater up the river for five years. The final blow to the head with a heavy piece of lumber that landed his victim in a coma for a week.

The prosecutor repeating Slater's life mistakes over and over, that Slater had been perfectly sober and in control of his actions. The initial charge had been attempted murder, but it was eventually dropped to assault. Assault charges still carried a lot of time, though...

"Slater?" Sophie's soft voice shocked him into looking up. She had Mia and a blanket, and her gentle smile held a tinge of concern. "You okay?"

"Yeah, I just needed a minute to myself." Slater pulled on enough truth that he wasn't lying to her. He genuinely liked Sophie and Conrad, and somehow the pair completely believed he and Derrick were a happy couple. "I'm not used to big crowds like this. Life on the ranch is a lot more solitary even when guests are around."

"Makes sense. I came in to feed Mia but I can find another spot."

"You struck me as the kind of person who would be on board with public breastfeeding."

Sophie laughed. "I am all over it as a basic right, yes. Women should be able to feed their kids wherever they are and without covering up. I'm just not there myself yet. Maybe when she's a little older I'll be able to whip out a boob and let her latch."

That made Slater chuckle. "Nina was like that with Rachel." A chill spread through his chest as he realized what he'd let slip.

She sat on the sofa near his chair and rocked a fussing Mia. "Rachel?"

"Yeah." He studied Mia's scrunched, unhappy, hungry face. "My daughter."

"Oh. Wow." Her eyes widened. "I guess that's why you're so natural with Mia. I didn't know you have a daughter."

"Derrick knows but no one else. It's really complicated, and I don't get to see her much because of custody agreements."

"How old?"

"Eighteen in July."

"Holy shit." Sophie glanced around because that had been sort of loud. "You don't look old enough to have an eighteen-year-old."

"Because I had her when I was that age. Too young and too immature. I don't tell people about her because it just reminds me of how badly I did by her growing up. Mia is a precious gift, Sophie. Make sure you guys give her and her future siblings all the love you can."

"We will."

Sophie seemed close to tears, and Slater didn't want to make the young mom cry. "You go on and feed Mia," he said. "I've got to go bother my boyfriend."

"Okay. And I'll keep your secret, Slater. I promise."

"Thank you." An unfamiliar sense of loyalty and kinship washed over him, and it was the only reason Slater reached over to squeeze her shoulder. "I mean it. Thank you."

"No problem. You make Derrick smile. I hope you and I can become better friends."

"Same." And he meant it, too. Sophie had a genuinely kind spirit, and in some ways, her quiet strength reminded him of Rachel. "How long is this shindig supposed to last?"

"Another hour, I think, but we can head out whenever our guys are ready."

"Okay. See you in a bit, then."

Slater found Derrick exactly where he'd left the man, and as he hobbled forward, he took in the delicious sight of Derrick's form packed into those dark slacks and a white, short-sleeve top. It showed off his toned arms and waist, and Slater wondered why he'd avoided sexual contact for the last two weeks.

Don't. Get. Attached.

Yeah, that was it. As much as Slater craved another amazing orgasm, he didn't want to get too used to them. They wouldn't always be available to him, and Derrick had been very clear about that after wedding number one. And part of Slater resented their arrangement down to his bones. He wasn't a hearts-and-flowers guy but even he recognized real chemistry when he felt it. He also wasn't the guy who went begging for attention or tail.

The magic of the wedding wove a different spell as their group excused themselves around five o'clock. Derrick volunteered to drive this time, and after finding a casual dining place for dinner, their quartet—plus precious Mia—settled into a booth with nachos and a round of drinks. The chatter was easy, if dominated by the Massey brothers, who told stories of their childhood with today's groom that made everyone laugh. The camaraderie was so easy and real, and Slater wanted to believe in it. But by August, it would be gone. Slater would be home on the ranch with his friends.

Friends who showed up every Saturday night—except for the ones on wedding days—in various combinations, and he adored the men for their loyalty and support. It helped knowing he had a soft place to land when he inevitably left Derrick's apartment.

And Dez. He treasured his friendship with Dez, who was probably his second-best friend after Derrick. She was loyal, fun, eclectic, funny, supportive and so many things he'd miss when he was gone. They'd stay in touch, he was sure, but it wouldn't be the same as crafting together in the foyer. And he was getting pretty damned good at cross-stitch, even if he did toot his own horn. Latch hook, too, and he had three rugs stashed away as Christmas gifts already for his fellow horsemen. Dez had even urged him to open an online storefront and sell his bawdy wares.

Slater wasn't so sure about anyone wanting to buy his shit, but it was a nice compliment.

He picked at the stuffed pork chop he'd ordered, not terribly hungry tonight and unsure why, while everyone else ate their fill. The only reason he asked to pack up the leftovers was because Derrick could take it for lunch on Monday. Might as well not waste the food, especially when Conrad insisted on paying.

That night, he and Derrick had sex again, much like they had two weeks ago. A lot of rubbing and nipping and frotting, until they both blew like volcanos. Slater couldn't seem to bridge the gap into full-on fucking again, and Derrick didn't push. Derrick seemed perfectly content with what physical affection Slater gave him, and in some ways, it made Slater feel like shit. In other ways, it put control back in Slater's court, and he needed that to help cushion the inevitable hit when they broke up.

The first week of June sped by, and too soon, it was time for their trip north for Rachel's graduation. His dad had room at the house, but the custody agreement meant a hotel for the night, and Slater booked a nice room for himself and Derrick in town. The ceremony was on a Tuesday evening, with a small party at the house directly after, and Derrick didn't mind taking a few vacation days to drive Slater out that Tuesday morning.

Slater was a ball of nervous energy, and Rachel's graduation gift was carefully tucked into their shared suitcase—why bother with two when it was a one-night stay? Being the passenger in Derrick's car felt strange after so many years of driving north on his bike, alone, but it was also a nice feeling. He'd never really come out to his dad, stepmom or daughter, because Slater still hadn't embraced any particular label for himself or his sexuality. He just...liked who he liked.

And right now? He really liked Derrick Massey.

Derrick didn't push. Not for information, backstory or sex, and that lack of conflict helped Slater find a kind of inner peace he wasn't used to feeling. This was the best, most solid, short-term relationship of his life, and he'd enjoy it while he had it. And the fact that Derrick didn't push for more only drove home the short-term part of their relationship.

The drive took about two hours and they made it with the windows down, enjoying the summer air, even if it was a tad hot. The wide-open spaces of the interstate were nowhere near the same as the ranch lands, but it made Slater feel less confined in the blue sedan. Then again, small spaces didn't feel as confining as they used to as he put more and more time between himself and prison.

As he learned from and healed from his mistakes.

And as he tried very, very hard not to fall for Derrick Massey and all his charm.

About ten miles from their exit, Derrick said, "So it's probably way too late to ask, but are we still playing up the whole fake relationship while we're here?"

Slater blinked at him, surprised by the left-field question. "Why wouldn't we?"

"Well, when you first asked me to come it was just to give you a ride, not actually go to the ceremony and party. I wasn't sure how you wanted me to play this."

It hadn't occurred to Slater to drop the fake relationship thing around his family, because it had become... real-ish. He'd feel strange about referring to Derrick as just a friend or roommate when to the rest of the world they were "boyfriends." He also liked the idea of showing up with someone as incredible as Derrick on his arm. "Play it as boyfriends," Slater finally replied. "Is that okay?"

Derrick winked, then reached across the seat to squeeze his knee. "Definitely okay."

Slater covered that hand with his own and held on, enjoying the physical contact. He gave Derrick directions once they exited the interstate, and a familiar town rolled by. Not much had changed in the few months since his last visit, other than the weather. He pointed out a few local landmarks but it was really just another sprawling suburb of Sacramento and not all that interesting.

The house was a squat, single-story box with three bedrooms, one bathroom and a big front porch. Dad had given it a new coat of paint recently, so it didn't look as drab as other homes on the street that had all popped up during the cheap housing community phase of the fifties. Dad's truck and Kim's car were in the driveway, and a few other cars were parked on the street nearby. Slater had called yesterday and told Dad they'd be there around noon for lunch, but he hadn't thought to ask if anyone else was planning to stop by before tonight's ceremony.

They were going to check in to the hotel post-lunch and pre-graduation, so they didn't bother with the suitcase. Slater did crutch around to the trunk to fetch his gift, because he wanted to give it to Rachel quietly this afternoon, before the hubbub of a party. The front door swung open before he could knock. Kim flashed him a warm smile then wrapped him up in a familiar hug.

"You look pretty great for someone who tumbled over a mountain two months ago," she said as she released him. "Not a scar on your face."

"Good ointment," Slater replied, then kissed her cheek. "You look fantastic."

"You flatter." Her gaze went to his right. "Philip didn't mention you were bringing a friend."

He felt more than saw Derrick tense. "Surprise." His turn to do the introducing. "Kim, this is my boyfriend Derrick Massey. Derrick, my stepmom Kim Stamos."

"You're kidding." Kim slid right past him to embrace Derrick. "You must be someone special, because in all my years, this boy hasn't brought anyone home to meet us since first taking up with Nina."

"Haven't found anyone worth the trouble until now." Slater smiled at Derrick's bemused expression as he hugged the woman back. "This one's pretty good."

"Jerk." Derrick took a half-hearted swipe at him once Kim released her hold.

"Come on inside," Kim said. "We don't have to stand

out here like strangers. Rachel and your father are in the kitchen finishing lunch."

"What are they making?" Slater asked as he stepped inside a house that hadn't changed since he was a kid. Same faded rug, same brown couch and love seat, same worn wooden end tables. The flat-screen TV was new, though, as were some of the accessories, thanks to Rachel's good taste and keen eye for bargains.

He followed the slightly spicy scent of seafood through the living room and into the kitchen. The island was littered with bowls containing all sorts of steaming ingredients that seemed vaguely Mexican. Dad and Rachel were both standing over the ancient gas range and staring into a skillet Rachel kept stirring.

"Happy Graduation Day," Slater said.

Rachel looked up and smiled, and Slater's heart panged with love for his little girl. Blonde like her mom, Rachel looked like both her parents—although Dad liked to tease she looked like Nina when she smiled and Slater when she was grumpy. "Hey, Dad." She handed a pair of silver tongs to Slater's father and walked over. Gave him a loose hug. "You look really good for someone who fell off a mountain."

Slater chuckled. "Kim already used that line, but thanks. I feel really good, considering. You look amazing."

"Thanks." Blunt as always, she asked, "Who's that?"

"My boyfriend." He introduced Derrick to both Dad and Rachel, and they each shook his hand. Dad was a little stiff but Rachel seemed completely charmed by the idea of Slater having a real boyfriend.

"How long have you guys been dating?" Rachel asked as she returned to moving shrimp around in a hot skillet.

"Two months, give or take. We met at the ranch where I work."

"Oh?"

Slater and Derrick tag-teamed their origin story while Rachel scooped cooked shrimp into a serving bowl. Apparently, lunch was shrimp burrito bowls so they took turns loading their bowls with rice, beans, salsa, shrimp, corn, avocado and other fixings. Their quintet sat at the eat-in kitchen table with an additional folding chair to accommodate everyone.

A few minutes into the meal and small talk, Dad said, "I'm really sorry we couldn't get down to visit you in the hospital."

"It's okay," Slater said automatically. Dad was on disability from a hip injury and Kim only got part-time hours at a local grocery store while she applied for better full-time jobs. Slater sent money every month, but their small family had a fixed income and not a lot to spare for traveling. Today's shrimp lunch was a luxury. "I had my ranch friends around me. And Derrick."

"Still. You're my only child, and I wanted to be there."

He studied his father, whose broad frame had withered a bit in recent years, leaving him thinner and paler. "You were here for Rachel, Dad, exactly where I needed you. Please don't second-guess that."

"So, what do you do, Derrick?" Rachel asked.

Derrick grinned and launched into his standard speech about Open Hearts, Open Hands while everyone continued eating. He had a strong, deep voice that commanded you to listen, and even though Slater knew all this, he listened along while shoveling food into his mouth. Rachel engaged Derrick, asking questions about the company and Dream Boxes specifically. When Derrick mentioned setting up his coworker Sophie with his own brother and whipped out pictures of Mia, both women at the table melted.

Slater adored Mia, but said, "Promise me you won't have one of those until you're at least thirty," to Rachel.

He'd only meant to tease but she cast him a withering, teenage glare. "I've had an IUD since I was fourteen, Dad, chill."

That bordered on the edge of good-to-know and TMI. At least they'd made sure Rachel wouldn't be repeating the mistakes of her parents. He caught Kim's sympathetic smile. Rachel was strong-willed and stubborn like Slater, but she was also a brilliant kid. A full ride to CSUS to study government in the fall. Almost eighteen and the world at her feet.

To be that young and full of possibilities again.

Rachel continued thumbing through photos of Mia, then paused. "Where was this taken?" She flashed the photo at both him and Derrick. It was a selfie Derrick had taken of himself and Slater at wedding number two when Slater was holding a sleeping Mia. Slater loved the picture and had demanded Derrick text it to him.

"My cousin's wedding two weeks ago," Derrick replied. "Your dad was a very gracious plus-one for me. And he's great with Mia."

Rachel met Slater's gaze and smiled. "You look happy."

"It was a great day," he said. It had been a wholly terrific day, his minor panic attack aside. "I've enjoyed getting to know Derrick's family better."

"So are you two pretty serious?" Dad asked.

"It's complicated, so we're taking things slow. I mean, I'll be back on my feet and at work by the end of the summer, and long distance isn't for everyone.

Baby steps work for us. These shrimp are delicious by the way."

"Thank you. Rachel has been teaching me new things and staying within our grocery budget. All those food shows she watches are paying off in big ways."

"There's the internet, too," Rachel added. "Those two ministrokes you had back in April won't happen again, Pop, you hear me?"

"Ministrokes?" Slater went rigid. "You didn't tell me you had a stroke, Dad."

Dad tossed Rachel an annoyed glare before looking at Slater. "I didn't want to tell you, because you had your own medical crisis going on. But that's the biggest reason we didn't get down to see you after your accident. My doctor was doing all kinds of tests and warned me against the stress of seeing you like that."

"Shit, you could have told me sooner."

"Like he said," Rachel interrupted, rising to her grandfather's defense, "you had other things going on. He's eating better, we're watching his blood pressure, and he quit drinking. We've got this."

The blunt way Rachel said all that made Slater feel like a scolded child. And a little unwelcome in this house at all.

"I'm glad you're doing better, sir," Derrick said.

"Thank you, son," Dad replied. "It was a wake-up call for sure. I'm only fifty-six and got a lot of years left to live with my girls."

Slater hid a flinch. Kim, ever the peacekeeper, reached over to squeeze Slater's wrist. "We're taking good care of him, I promise," she said. "Just like it looks Derrick is taking good care of you."

"He is," Slater replied. "We make a pretty good team."

"How do you keep yourself busy all day while you aren't working?"

"Well, that's actually a great segue into something." He glanced at Derrick, who excused himself to fetch the box Slater had left in the living room. Derrick handed it to Slater, who offered it to Rachel. "I've learned a few new tricks thanks to one of Derrick's neighbors who's a blogger and upcycler."

Rachel unwrapped the flat box and took off the lid. Both eyebrows went up as she lifted the framed sampler from its nest of tissue paper. "You made this?" she asked.

"Yup. I cribbed some of the pattern from a book and designed the edge myself." Slater had cross-stitched the phrase "She Believed She Could, So She Did" in the center and surrounded it with colorful swirls and shooting stars. "I never thought I'd take up arts and crafts, but it's good for dexterity and brain cognition, which was super helpful after my head injury. Plus, it keeps me busy."

"Thank you, Dad, I love it." She came around the table to give him another rare, precious hug. "You're really good at this."

"It is amazing," Kim agreed. "I never had the patience to learn needlepoint of any kind. Have you done any others?"

"Definitely." Slater had taken pictures of every finished product, from the first frog rug to this particular piece, and he proudly showed them off on his phone.

Some of the cussing on the designs made Rachel laugh. "These are really cool," she said. "A neighbor taught you this? Can you text me a link to her blog?"

"Definitely." He couldn't remember the last time his

daughter asked him to text her anything, not even a "Happy Birthday." Maybe, just maybe, they could fix their relationship and find a way to peacefully coexist.

Derrick loved every moment he witnessed between Slater and his daughter, because even when she was being snarky, Slater's love for her glowed in his eyes and face. In the way he watched her and smiled at her, and Derrick adored that she'd accepted Slater's gift and loved it.

He was also silently sad, because he didn't know if he'd ever witness it again. Slater's earlier comments about them going slow and trying long distance only reminded Derrick how temporary this was and how much he was going to miss Slater when he returned to Clean Slate. Derrick never realized he had a hole in his life until Slater fit neatly inside and filled it with his charm and humor. He didn't want to lose Slater, but Derrick was terrified of long-distance relationships.

His freshman year of college, he'd fallen in love with a woman named Eugenie and he'd been smitten. When she transferred out of state the following year, they promised to remain exclusive. Derrick had wanted to surprise her with a visit a few days before her birthday that December, and she'd opened her dorm door in her robe and had a guy in her bed. His senior year, he met and fell for Antoine, and they burned hot and heavy for about six months, until Antoine admitted he was also fucking other guys.

Derrick had been done with relationships after that, and now he'd fallen for Slater almost against his will. Maybe Slater would agree to date long-distance once his ankle was healed, but what if Derrick wasn't enough for him? His heart would never heal again if Slater cheated on him.

He doesn't seem the type, though. He's too loyal to cheat.

Then again, he'd thought Eugenie was loyal, too.

Not appropriate thoughts for lunch with his fake boyfriend's family, so Derrick tried to pay attention to the conversation. Everyone had finished eating. Rachel was looking at something on her phone, while Slater helped Kim clean up the kitchen. Philip remained at the table and sipped his glass of water. "You seem a very decent fellow," Philip said to him. "You looking to settle down with my boy?"

Derrick wasn't sure how to answer that. "Like Slater said earlier, we're taking things slow. Finding our way. He's a terrific guy, and I'm lucky to have him in my life."

Rachel muttered something he didn't catch.

"Time changes people," Derrick continued now that he knew she was listening. He'd enjoyed engaging with the teenager, and he wanted her to give her dad a chance. "From what I've heard from my friends, Clean Slate Ranch is a place that gives extra chances to folks who've maybe messed up their first or second chance at life. Plus, it's a really fun vacation spot. I spent a week there two years ago and loved it."

Philip laughed. "Don't bother selling me a vacation package, I can't afford it." But he smiled as he spoke, and Philip glanced over his shoulder to where Slater was helping Kim with the dishes. "I take it he told you about his stint in prison?"

Derrick's chest went cold and tight.

"Dad!" Slater whirled around, both hands dripping

with soapy water, his face red and pinched. "Jesus Christ, really?"

Philip frowned. "You're living with the man and didn't tell him? He has a right to know." Next to Philip, Rachel went stiff all over.

"Can we not do this in front of Rachel, please?" Slater asked, his pleading eyes fixed firmly on Derrick. Derrick wasn't sure what to say, do or think, so he just nodded his consent. They were definitely talking about this when they got to the hotel.

Someone banged on the front door, and then a chirpy female voice said, "Yoohoo! Anyone home?"

Slater groaned, and Rachel didn't look any happier about the new visitor. Before Derrick could ask, Slater mouthed, "My ex."

Uh oh.

Chapter Thirteen

Slater resisted the very real urge to raid his dad's cupboards for the bottle of whiskey that was always on hand for "medicinal" purposes. Rachel said he'd stopped drinking but Dad kept the whiskey well hidden. Well, except from his bullheaded, rebellious teenage son, because Slater had gotten good at taking nips and refilling it with water.

The last thing he needed to navigate after Dad accidentally dropped the prison bomb on Derrick was his ex-wife, Nina. As much as it pissed Slater off that Derrick found out about prison this way, Dad thought their relationship was real, and he'd probably assumed Slater wouldn't move in with someone without revealing he was a felon. Now that was a conversation he needed to have with Derrick.

Later. Right now, he had Nina to deal with. He'd loved her once, a long time ago, but time, resentment and her own string of bad choices had left her limited to one weekend a month with their daughter. She was also the harpy who'd gotten Slater's time with Rachel reduced to supervised visits.

His only saving grace was that his father or Kim could act as the supervising person, rather than a social worker. And they kindly gave him access whenever he got vacation time to come up here and hang out.

"This is going to be fun," Rachel said softly as she rose to answer the door.

Slater grabbed a towel and wiped off his dripping hands. He couldn't stoop to mop up the floor because of the crutch, so Kim did it for him. In the other room, Nina let out excited squeals that hurt Slater's ears. He couldn't bring himself to look at Derrick as their entire quartet braced for the new arrival.

Nina was still slender and pretty, her blond hair cut short in a way that suited her round face, and she had one arm looped around Rachel's waist. She stopped short when she spotted Slater. He didn't give her the satisfaction of doing more than blinking at her.

"I just got into town," Nina said, "and I couldn't wait to see my graduating baby. When did she get so old?"

While you were off chasing the wrong men up and down the west coast?

"Time flies when you're out of town," Slater dead-panned. The comment was meant as much for Nina as himself.

"Yeah, well, you should know," Nina fired back.

"No way," Rachel said. "If you guys are going to snipe, I'm out of here."

"I'm sorry, baby." Nina tried to kiss her cheek, but Rachel expertly twisted out of the loose hold and moved to stand by Derrick. Someone Nina finally noticed. "And who's this? One of your teachers?"

Derrick snorted loudly.

"That's Dad's boyfriend, Mom. His name is Derrick."

Nina's confused gaze shifted from Slater to Derrick and back again. "He's your *what?*"

"My boyfriend," Slater snapped, his temper sizzling hot and hard below the surface. "He's been a godsend since I busted my ankle, and he was gracious enough to come with me for Rachel's graduation. Derrick, this is my ex-wife, Nina...what's your last name right now?"

The dig worked because her eyes narrowed. "Austin. Nina Austin. And since when are you gay?"

"When did I ever tell you I was straight?"

"Nina, dear," Kim said, "can I get you something to drink? I have fresh iced tea."

"Yes, thank you," Nina said. She turned a familiar smile onto Derrick that made all of Slater's senses go on high alert. "So, how did you meet Ken?"

Derrick looked confused for a few seconds before he made the connection to Slater's legal name. "His place of work. We hit it off. Stayed in touch. Things progressed from there. And it's nice to meet you, Ms. Austin."

"Miss."

Slater knew this move. Flirt and tease and try to take away anything good in his life. But today, he didn't care. Derrick displayed no signs of being remotely interested in Nina; he was simply being polite in the presence of a new person.

Nina spotted the framed sampler on the table and picked it up. "My, my, Kim have you taken up embroidery? This is lovely."

Rachel gently eased it out of her hands. "It's cross-stitch and Dad made this. For me."

"Since when do you do women's crafts, Ken?"

"Crafts aren't gendered, Nina," Slater snapped. "When I busted my ankle, I needed something to keep me busy, and a friend taught me this. It's creative and challenging, and I have a lot of fun doing it. What hobbies have you taken up lately?" *Besides flirting with my boyfriend.*

"I'm too busy working to have hobbies."

"Oh? What is it this time? Personal masseuse? Grand Canyon tour guide? Yoga instructor?"

Rachel shot him a warning look.

Nina huffed. "I work the phones and front desk of a tattoo parlor owned by my good friend Rocco, and it's very steady work."

Good friend often equaled fuck buddy but Slater didn't want to risk Rachel's wrath by needling her mother much more. "If you're happy there, then I hope it works out."

His polite response left Nina grasping for something to say.

"Lunch was amazing," Slater said to both Dad and Rachel, "but Derrick and I need to check in to our hotel and get ready for the ceremony tonight."

"Your tickets," Rachel replied. "Let me go get them." She dashed out of the kitchen.

"She seems like an amazing young woman," Derrick said. "You should all be very proud."

Slater wasn't sure how much of an influence he'd had in Rachel's life, but he very much appreciated the compliment.

"She's always been an impressive student," Nina said with a smug grin. "I probably could have gotten college scholarships, but, well, life happened."

Annoyance flared hot and tight behind Slater's breastbone. As much as he wouldn't give up Rachel for anything in the world now, back when they were both seventeen-year-olds dealing with an unexpected pregnancy, he'd offered to pay for an abortion. So Nina could fulfill her dreams of college and a career as a physician's assistant. He'd been willing to go the adoption route, too. Nina had said no, too excited about being a wife and mother to care back then. And now she was tossing that choice in his face?

"It's never too late to go back to school," Slater said. "Be more than a receptionist."

"He's not wrong," Dad added. "Every college around here's got self-improvement courses of one kind or another. You could look into one of those."

Nina made a soft, scoffing sound, and she was only saved from Slater's sharp tongue by Rachel's return to the kitchen. She had a ticket for everyone, including Derrick. "You guys probably won't need them to get in, because the weather looks great and it'll be outside on the football field, but I figure it's a nice souvenir, right?"

"It's perfect." Slater studied the slip of paper, still dazzled that his little girl was graduating high school in a few hours. "I'll frame it and hang it on my cabin wall." He'd have no way to explain it to anyone who saw it, but the words made Rachel beam at him.

"It was very nice meeting everyone," Derrick said on their way out. He shook Dad's hand, hugged Kim, and gave Nina a polite nod from a distance. Then Rachel surprised the hell out of him by hugging Derrick and whispering something in his ear.

Jealousy burned hot and tight in his chest, because she didn't hug Slater. Only tossed him a smiling wave and promised to see him tonight. Slater pushed against that jealousy as he eased into the car and adjusted his leg. Derrick didn't bring up prison while he followed the GPS to their hotel. Regular chain hotel with basic rooms, but they'd only had two full beds available when Slater placed the reservation. Probably a lot of people coming into town for graduation and things.

Derrick didn't comment on the bed situation beyond asking if Slater wanted the one by the door or the window. Slater chose the window, undid the brace and stretched out on top of the coverlet. Derrick fussed with their toiletries for a few minutes spent in awkward silence, before Slater couldn't stand it anymore.

"Are you gonna ask me?" he said to the ceiling.

"Ask you what?" Derrick eased on the bed opposite him, his face annoyingly passive.

"Why I was in prison? When? For how long? The usual shit everyone wants to know."

"If you haven't brought it up before now, you have your reasons. Yes, I'm curious, and I admit I'm a little upset you didn't share this before you moved in."

Slater turned his head to glare at the other man. "Why? So you could take the offer back?"

"No, so I had all the facts about the guy moving into my building and getting his own front door key."

"I might be a felon, Derrick, but I'm no thief and I don't plan on ever going back. Not for any reason."

"Were you guilty?"

"Yes."

Derrick's face pinched once before smoothing out, and since they were having this conversation, Slater didn't want to do it on his back. He sat up—which still wasn't the easiest thing in the world because bruised ribs could take forever to heal right—and twisted to face Derrick.

"It happened eleven years ago," Slater said, his stomach a mess of acid. He hated remembering that night.

"Rachel was maybe a year old when Nina cheated on me the first time, and it pissed me off royally because I was working two jobs to take care of her and the baby, but she apparently had time to run around and find dick. I put up with it for a while for Rachel's sake, but we were both miserable, so when Rachel was five I filed for divorce. Got joint custody, but Nina took off and left me with Rachel.

"We moved in with Dad and Kim, and I wanted to be more for my daughter, so I tried a stint in basic training. Thought maybe an Army career was the path to go but I washed out. I was really bullheaded back then and didn't like taking orders. I also didn't have much of a censor, so I'd say what was on my mind, and it got me fired from more than one job. So when Nina came back around a year or so later with a new husband on her arm, wanting to take Rachel, I lost my temper.

"I was working at a lumberyard at the time, and they actually came to my place of work to say they wanted Rachel." Slater's fingers twitched with the phantom pain of split knuckles and the rough two-by-four he'd grabbed. "The guy's name was Pete, and he got in my face, saying he knew people who'd help him take Nina's kid away from—his words—trailer park trash like me. A few guys at the yard who saw the fight swore Pete put his hands on me first, but since Nina was standing right there, the jury seemed to believe her when she said I punched Pete first and started the fight."

"But Pete started the fight?" Derrick asked.

"He put his hands on me, to push or grab, I don't know, because I decked him. He stumbled and then came at me. We both landed a few good punches before the other guys got us apart. Then Pete decided to mouth off and said, 'If you fuck like you punch, no wonder she left your faggot ass.'"

"Oh, shit."

"Yeah." Slater clenched his hands in his lap as his worst moment came back in vivid detail. "I barely remember grabbing the two-by-four off the pile but I remember how it felt in my hand. The way the impact jarred all the way up my arms to shoulders when I slammed it into the back of Pete's head. The thud when he hit the ground. That was the main reason I got five years for assault. I attacked with a deadly weapon and put a man in the hospital."

"Five years?" Derrick seemed equal parts furious and horrified at everything he'd learned in the last ten minutes. "Damn, man."

"It sucked beyond explanation, but I kept my head down, tried not to make any enemies, and I did my time. Even took a few classes before they stopped the program. I wanted to be a better man when I got out, so I could make it up to Rachel, but she was so scared of me the first time she saw me again."

"She didn't visit you?"

"I didn't want her to see me in that place. I couldn't believe how much she'd grown. But even though she'd been mostly living with my parents, Nina had tried to poison her against me. Rachel wouldn't hug me, wouldn't come near me for weeks. I worked odd jobs for a while, until my parole was over. I got the gig with the shipping company that led me to Clean Slate. No one at the shipping company cared I was a felon and neither did Arthur Garrett when he hired me."

Slater's heart skipped with trepidation. "I know this is a huge thing to learn about a person, but no one outside my family except Arthur and Judson know I was in prison. I don't talk about it. But I am sorry if I broke your trust, Derrick, I mean that. I value our friendship."

"Me, too." Derrick picked the bed's coverlet. "And I get you wanting your privacy about the prison thing."

"But you're upset I moved in with you without telling you?"

"I don't know. Not upset. You haven't said or done a single thing to break my trust, and you were honest just now."

"Yeah, because my dad outed me at lunch." Slater definitely got his blunt nature from Philip Stamos.

"Still, you could have easily told me it was none of my business, but you trusted me to keep your secret. Thank you."

"You're welcome." Relief finally washed away some of Slater's anxiety over sharing this part of his past. "Thank you for taking it all so well."

"Everyone's got a past. Yours is just more colorful than some. I'm not standing in any place from which to judge you, man. But I think I see more clearly where you're coming from, so I'm grateful you shared Rachel with me today. She's beautiful and smart."

"Thank you." Slater beamed, because if he'd done anything right in his life, it was making that perfect young lady. "I was terrified she'd hate her gift, or she'd think I was, I don't know, less of a man for knowing cross-stitch."

"Nah, her generation is going to change the way we look at gender norms. Like you said to Nina, why do crafts need to be gendered? Why do sports or clothes or anything else?"

"I hope so. I just…really hope she'll give me a second chance, you know? I can't remember the last time she hugged me like that." *And then she hugged you, too, you lucky bastard.*

"What?" Derrick asked. "What just happened?"

"What do you mean?"

"Have you always been bad at hiding your tells, or am I just getting really good at spotting them? For one instant, you looked mad."

"I wasn't mad, just had a thought I didn't like."

"Care to share with the class?"

"It's childish."

Derrick leaned back on his hands, his posture open and reassuring, and he was definitely not going anywhere. And neither was Slater, with his crutch on the floor beside him.

"I was jealous Rachel hugged you goodbye but not me," Slater admitted. "Okay? She really engaged with you today, and then she hugged you, and it hurt that she reached out to a relative stranger instead of her own damned father." He hadn't meant to let his temper spin out but his voice definitely rose by the time he shut his mouth.

Derrick's face fell. "I'm sorry. Shit, I didn't even think about it."

"I know, and there's no reason you should. Decent dads get hugged by their kid."

"Hey, come on." Derrick moved to sit beside Slater and held one of his hands. "You are trying your best. That's all you can do. And Rachel strikes me as a smart girl. She'll come around."

"I hope so. She's the only thing in my life I've ever done right, and I even messed that up."

"I don't know." Derrick squeezed his hand briefly.

"I think you've got the friendship thing down pat, and you're an outstanding lay."

Slater snorted laughter that made his ribs twinge. "Yeah, fucking is something I know how to do well. Just wish I was a better people person."

"Man, you do like putting yourself down a lot, don't you? You *are* a people person, Slater, you're just guarded. Look how fast you befriended Dez and Morgan. Hell, you even got a conversation out of Orry Thompson upstairs. You were great today with Rachel and your parents. You'd probably have fifteen best friends at the ranch if you allowed yourself to open up and let them into your life like you let me in."

He probably wasn't wrong about that. Slater did his very best to avoid personal conversation with his fellow horsemen. The few times early on that Hugo tried to befriend him by sharing bits of himself, Slater usually grunted and found something else to do. He kept people at arm's length because he'd been disappointed by them so many fucking times, and he was tired of it.

Except for Derrick. Derrick hadn't disappointed him once since their…arrangement began.

He will, though, when we break up. And it will be my own damned fault for falling for the man in the first place.

But Slater didn't want to think about that right now. He wanted to get his mind off his confessions and mistakes and problems, and he had a hot guy beside him who could do just that. "We have three hours before we have to leave for the ceremony. Feel up to fooling around, Tiger?"

Derrick barked laughter. "Geez, segue much?"

"Why beat around the bush when being blunt gets things done faster?"

"Too true." Derrick leaned in and nuzzled at the pulse point that always got Slater's crank going. "I didn't pack anything."

"We can faux-fuck. Don't hotel rooms always have little bottles of lotion?"

"I like where your mind is at." As Derrick lurched off the bed, Slater smacked his ass once. Derrick flashed him a wolfish grin on his way to the bathroom.

Slater whipped off his shirt, grateful for the distraction and the amazing, attentive, forgiving man providing it.

Derrick had been to more graduation ceremonies than he could count, thanks to all his cousins, and they were all pretty boring in their own ways. But tonight, Derrick fed off Slater's excitement over seeing his baby girl graduate. They met and sat with Philip and Kim, as well as Rachel's best friend Jayla, who'd graduated last year and had completed her first year of college. Jayla had looked Derrick up and down like he was a popsicle she wanted to lick, even after Slater used the b-word to introduce him.

The guest speaker droned on about something Derrick tuned out, and the class's valedictorian was mercifully brief. With the last name Stamos, Rachel wouldn't be called until near the end. But when the principal said her name, Slater let out the loudest, proudest wolf whistle Derrick had ever heard. If Nina hadn't spotted their group in the bleachers, she knew where they were now.

Derrick applauded while Rachel strode across the small stage to collect her diploma, pause for a picture, and then walked back off. He'd known the girl for all of two hours, but his heart still surged with pride for her. He glanced at Slater, whose eyes were full of unshed tears. Kim discreetly handed Slater a tissue.

Finding Rachel again once the ceremony was over took a bit of doing, but she texted her location to Jayla once she got all of her stuff from wherever she'd left it in the school. Rachel and Jayla squealed and hugged, and then Rachel hugged everyone again—Slater included. She allowed Slater to cling for a moment, and he whispered something in her ear that made Rachel beam.

"Thanks, Dad," she said.

Nina ruined the beautiful moment by swooping in to hug her daughter. Philip and Kim excused themselves first, so they could head home and start putting out party snacks. Derrick wasn't sure how many people to expect, and when he and Slater arrived at the house, a few new faces were there. Philip had a bachelor brother who'd come by to support his only grand-niece. Three neighbors whose names Derrick forgot the minute he was introduced. Rachel's tenth grade social science teacher, who'd turned her onto government as a career.

They ate simple snacks of chips and dip, pizza bagels, and veggies with ranch. Drank cola and ginger ale, and Derrick did his best to keep Slater socializing, instead of alone in a chair. Trying to prove to Slater he could be a people person if he tried, especially around folks he'd known for years. No one was blatantly rude to either of them, even if Rachel's great-uncle gave Derrick funny looks a few times.

As one of only three black folks at his workplace, Derrick was used to standing out in a crowd.

Overall, they had a good time. Derrick truly enjoyed

getting to know Slater's family better, and he adored Rachel. She had a lot of her father's stubborn nature, which would serve her well if she did pursue a political career. President Rachel Stamos had a nice ring to it. She even held a lengthy conversation with Derrick and Slater about all the work Mack had put into keeping the tiny town of Garrett, California, alive and running with his investments. Rachel definitely had thoughts on the state investing in dying small towns in ways that made sense and brought true trade to those areas.

She and Jayla even made plans for a summer road trip south to see Bentley Ghost Town. Derrick wanted to text Wes about spreading the word but no one else knew about Rachel, and it wasn't his secret to share.

By the end of the evening, the guests trickled out and it was just the family left, plus Jayla, who was spending the night with Rachel. The uncle was also staying over in the guest room, which had been Slater's room once, according to Slater. Nina left first, and no one was sad to see her go. The woman was tolerable in small doses but something about her made Derrick's skin itch.

Rachel shocked the hell out of them both by inviting Derrick and Slater over for breakfast before they left town. Derrick thought Slater was going to cry again over the offer, but he graciously accepted, hugged his daughter goodnight, and they left.

Back in their room, Slater was so full of excited energy that Derrick barely had the door shut before Slater was wrangling him out of his pants. Things went happy places very quickly, and since Slater had used regular crutches tonight instead of the hands-free because of the bleachers, they didn't have to stop and fiddle with the brace. Clothes came off. Slater made a meal out of Derrick's nipples and navel before moving down to suck him hard.

This was the aggressive guy he'd wrestled with two months ago at the ranch, and holy damn, Derrick had missed this side of Slater. He'd never be able to pin Derrick with that cast on his foot, but the wrestling and pinching and rubbing was the best part. Giving and taking. Hands and lips and tongues and dicks. Derrick longed for a real kiss, to properly taste his boyfriend, but that was Slater's limit, and Derrick wouldn't break the trust between them by forcing one on Slater.

Trust that had been cracked slightly today with the prison confession. It had stunned Derrick to his very core, especially when he heard the charge was assault with a deadly weapon. But when he looked at Slater, he didn't see a criminal, or a guy who'd intentionally tried to kill another person. He saw a damaged soul working his ass off to do better and be better, every single day. He saw a kind man who loved his daughter and wanted the best for her.

Hours later, after they'd both come hard and Derrick had gotten them cleaned up, he watched Slater sleep in his bed, a little sad they weren't snuggled up together on one. But it also clearly spoke to their arrangement. At home, they only had one bed. Why share when they had two here? They weren't a couple, no matter what they said or did in front of others. No matter the chemistry that sizzled between them. No matter that Derrick had real feelings for the guy. But how could Derrick be honest about his feelings when the façade they were presenting to the world was a lie?

It was too intense a thought after such a lovely day. Still, he missed the closeness of sharing his bed with

Slater. Knowing he could reach out and touch Slater if he wanted. Knowing Slater had trusted him enough, especially during that first week or so of recovery, to share his bed every night and know he was safe. His bed would be too big, too empty when Slater left.

He'd leave a hole in Derrick's life Derrick wasn't sure he'd ever fill again.

Chapter Fourteen

"Are things between you and Derrick okay?"

Slater looked up from the bag of tortilla chips he was pouring into a bowl at the kitchen counter. Mack, Wes, Conrad and Sophie had come over the Saturday evening post-graduation to play board games and chill. Mia was staying the night at her grandparents' house to give her exhausted parents a break.

Mack hovered by Slater's elbow and he'd asked the question in a whisper.

"We're fine, why?" Slater replied, genuinely perplexed by the question. He also appreciated the fact that someone from his Clean Slate life came by every weekend to hang, and Slater was trying to be more interactive with his friends. To show his gratitude for the effort they made to include him in their lives.

"Dunno, you just seem different. Can't put my finger on it."

Slater had been walking on air since Rachel's graduation party and the lovely breakfast the following morning. They didn't call or text every day or anything, but it was a positive start. He'd finally made a real connection with his daughter. Maybe he could try to make a real connection with Mack.

"I'm not sure if content is the right word," Slater said softly. Everyone else was in the living room, parked around a paused game of Parcheesi while Slater had gone to fetch snacks and others took bathroom breaks. "But I had a real breakthrough in my personal life this week. Something really special, and I wanna say I'm grateful for your friendship, Mack. I mean it."

"Same, buddy, same." Mack shook his hand firmly. "I know we aren't the closest but you're family."

"Thank you. I, uh, I have a daughter who just graduated high school, and we were never close before but I think we're going to have a much better relationship going forward."

Mack's bushy eyebrows rose into his hairline. "Wow. Congrats. I had no idea."

"No one does because I don't talk about her. It's complicated."

"I know complicated family, believe me. And I'm not one for spreading private information around."

"I know. I told you because I trust you."

"Trust him with what?" Wes asked as he bounced up behind Mack.

"It's private, boss," Mack said to Wes.

"Okay. Come on, we're ready to keep playing." He plucked a chip out of the bowl and walked away on a loud crunch.

Slater grabbed the bowl of chips and crutched his way back to the game. Derrick had invested in a card table and a few folding chairs now that they had regular weekend guests, so people didn't always have to sit on the floor. Plus, the elevation meant Slater didn't have to unstrap the crutch every time he wanted to stand or sit.

He just made sure he stayed angled so no one tripped over the protruding crutch.

Wes was still nattering on about an upcoming gig down in Hollywood. Back during pilot season, he'd auditioned for a new medical drama and not gotten the part, but the producer had called him to audition for a two-episode guest spot that he'd nailed. He was packed up and ready to fly out tomorrow to start filming his scenes.

"Are you working on anything new, Slater?" Sophie asked while Conrad took his turn. "I love the stuff you've added to the apartment. It was always so colorless before."

"Gee, thanks, Soph," Derrick deadpanned.

"I'm serious. The frog rug is adorable. I kind of want one for Mia's room."

"I can make her a rug," Slater said. "I, uh, kind of did already make her a present."

"Really?"

"Yeah." His face heated now that he was the focus of every single person's attention. Derrick helped him out by fetching the small box from their bedroom and handing it to Sophie. She opened it and then peered inside.

"Oh, my gosh." Sophie lifted the baby bib out of the tissue. *"Uncle Derrick's My Favorite."*

Conrad snickered, while Wes harrumphed. Slater had found baby bibs online that could be embroidered and couldn't resist. "There's another one," Slater said.

Sophie moved a piece of tissue aside and started cackling with laughter. Conrad plucked the second bib out, then tossed it to Wes. Wes snatched it out of the air and huffed. *"Uncle Wes Is My Second Favorite.* Gee, thanks."

Slater shrugged. "Sorry, man, but Derrick's kind of

my favorite, too." The ease with which that slipped out shocked Slater as much as it seemed to surprise Derrick. Derrick's surprise quickly melted into a tender smile that Slater tried not to read too much into.

"Have you ever thought of doing this as a business?" Sophie asked. "You're really good at it, and there are tons of places online you could set up a storefront. Or you can do local craft fairs and stuff."

"Nah. Dez has posted some photos of my stuff on her blog, and I've gotten great responses to the really vulgar stuff, but I'm not sure the art world is for me. It's a fun hobby and it keeps me busy, but I doubt I'll have time to keep up with it when I'm back at work."

"You got an ETA on that?" Mack asked.

Slater's gut squirmed with unease. He didn't like *thinking* about leaving this apartment, much less discussing it. Ignoring was easier, but he'd gone and brought it up, hadn't he? "Not an exact one. I finally get this damned cast off next Friday, but the doc says I'll still need to use a walking boot and maybe a cane for at least four more weeks while I do physical therapy. Plus, I have to work back up to actually using the foot, never mind trying to swing up into a saddle."

"I hear you, and there's no rush. We miss your ugly mug at the ranch, but your job is still safe. Judson says so every time I talk to him."

"I appreciate it, Mack." As much as Slater longed for the wide-open spaces of the ranch, he was…comfortable here. He had friends and things to do, but he couldn't ask Judson to hold his job beyond what Slater reasonably needed for his recovery. And he had at least six to eight weeks left before he had to make that call.

Later that night while they took turns getting ready

for bed, Derrick said, "Maybe you should look deeper into selling some of your stuff online. Or offering commissions or something. You really are good and didn't you say someone asked on Dez's blog about buying a piece she featured?"

Slater took his time slipping a sleeveless tee on where he sat at the foot of the bed, grateful Derrick had waited to bring that up. "I guess I can. I mean, I love making stuff I can gift to people, but a little extra cash never hurt anyone."

"Dez turned her hobby into a thriving career. I'm sure she'd give you tips."

He looked up to where Derrick stood just inside the bedroom door, as if unsure about entering his own room. Derrick's expression was mild, his tone conversational, but this was also the most direct Derrick had ever been in insinuating Slater should consider a career change. Slater loved his job at Clean Slate; he also loved crafting with Dez during the day and being with Derrick at night.

No, there was no way he could establish a platform and enough business in less than eight weeks to make quitting Clean Slate financially reasonable. Except he did have a decent savings account, thanks to his lack of living expenses at the ranch. An account he'd dipped into a bit for his hobbies, but he'd be okay, even able to afford paying rent here if he chose to stay…

No. Nope. Unless Derrick freely asked Slater to stay, he wasn't going to start imagining a future beyond their agreed-upon time frame. Dreaming about that would just get his heart broken, and he'd had enough heartbreak for one lifetime.

"I'll talk to Dez on Monday," Slater hedged. He'd

obviously talk to her but hadn't promised what he'd talk to her about.

"Cool." Derrick finally entered the bedroom and slid under the covers on his side. "Tonight was fun."

"Yeah. And we get to see Conrad and Sophie again on Tuesday night." Wedding three was an oddly planned Tuesday night ceremony, but apparently that specific date was important to the couple. Derrick was taking off work an hour early so he had time to change and drive them to the venue.

"Yeah, we do." Derrick reached over and turned off his bedside lamp. "Night."

"Night."

Slater stared at the dark ceiling for a while, his thoughts tumbling all over the place and unable to settle. Once Derrick began snoring softly, he eased out of bed and used his regular crutches to leave the bedroom. But the living room was too small, so he quietly exited the apartment and eased into one of the foyer's sitting chairs. The main interior light was on a timer that dimmed halfway from midnight to six in the morning, and the murky space reminded him a bit of the woodier areas of the ranch lands, where he could wander under canopies of leaves and branches.

He'd forgotten his phone, so Slater simply stared. Thumbed through some of the books and magazines folks left out but found nothing of interest. He still had the wrestling magazine Derrick had given him in the hospital, tucked away inside his suitcase. A memento of this strange plan they were both hell-bent on seeing through to the end.

The front door opened, and Orry Thompson stepped inside. He jumped a mile when he spotted Slater sitting in the gloom. "Christ, dude, you scared the piss out of me," Orry said.

"Sorry," Slater said, mostly to be polite. "I figured everyone would be asleep."

"I'll sleep when I'm dead."

"That's not technically sleeping you know."

Orry stopped in his attempt to walk past him for the staircase. "Why are you out here? Did you and Derrick have a fight?"

"No, I just can't sleep. Before I busted my foot, I'd take long walks to wear myself out but I can't exactly do that here."

"Why don't you ask your boyfriend for a blow job?"

Because Derrick turned the light off and fell asleep.

They hadn't had sex since the hotel and Slater wasn't sure why. Derrick had been fairly hands-off the rest of this week, despite all the amazing sex they'd had on Tuesday. Then again, Slater hadn't initiated anything, either, but he had also never been the touchy-feely type. He came, made sure his partner came, and then he left.

"He's asleep," was the dumb response Slater came up with.

Orry didn't look impressed. He also didn't brush Slater off and go to his own place to do whatever. The kid was young, probably in his midtwenties. Cute with shaggy blond hair and big round eyes that reminded Slater of Japanese anime characters. But he had a deep voice that offset the boyish exterior. Slater hadn't yet met the elusive twin George, and he wondered if the pair was completely identical.

"You're the cowboy, right?" Orry asked.

"Well, not born and raised like some of the guys I

work with. I sort of landed in the job but I do love it. Working with horses and wide-open spaces."

"Does that mean you're going back when your foot's better?"

"That's always been the plan."

Orry cut his eyes at Derrick's apartment door. "But plans change."

"Sometimes."

"Well, whatever happens, I guess I hope it works out."

"Thanks. You know, if you or your brother ever need anything, you can always knock on our door."

Orry chewed on his bottom lip for a few seconds before nodding. "Thanks. Goodnight."

"See you around."

The staircase creaked as Orry ascended them, and about twenty seconds later, a creaky door opened and shut on the second floor. He was intensely curious about the twins' story but there was no law saying you had to befriend your neighbors. Slater had extended the proverbial olive branch tonight. Now it was up to Orry to ask if he needed help.

Eventually, fatigue stole over him and Slater returned to bed. He studied Derrick's sleeping face in the dim room and tried to imagine not having this anymore. Going to sleep in that small cabin with a guy he barely knew across the way. Working with the horses and tourists and not seeing Dez every day. Putting his beloved hobbies aside for a job that left him exhausted at the end of the workday.

Maybe Clean Slate Ranch wasn't Slater's final destination. But if not there, then where?

For all Slater was excited to finally get his leg out of that damned cast—how had it already been eight weeks

since his surgery?—and stop relying on crutches, walking in that boot was almost a bigger pain in the ass.
The good news was his ankle was healing nicely and
he could start light physical therapy next week. The
bad news?

The boot was heavy and awkward, and he walked
like he had a constant wedgie he couldn't dig out. When
he limped into the house Friday afternoon, Dez was
hand-stitching something in the foyer, and she immediately started laughing at him.

"You're walking like a guy doing a horrible John
Wayne impression," she said.

"My thighs are killing me." Slater eased down onto
the love seat beside her. "But the cast is gone, so that's
progress."

She put her needle down and side-eyed him. "Does
that mean your time here is drawing to a close?"

"I don't know." In the almost-week since his conversation with Derrick about selling his art, Slater hadn't
actually brought it up directly with Dez. He'd asked
vague questions about her blog, how she sold stuff, the
fees and things, without insinuating he was curious for
himself. But Dez was super smart and probably had a
clue or five. "When Derrick first offered me a place to
stay, I never imagined how much I'd enjoy living near
the city again. I thought the ranch was it for me."

"You thought you'd tend horses until you're old and
gray?"

"Arthur did."

"Yeah, but he's the ranch owner, right? He made
that place because he had a passion for what he does.
Just like I have a passion for creating new things out of

worn and broken things. Do you really think the ranch is your passion?"

"I have no fucking idea. Seriously, none."

"Do you love him?"

Slater didn't patronize her by asking "him who?" "I have strong feelings for him, for sure. I enjoy being around Derrick. He makes me feel good about myself, which I haven't done in a long damned time." And because he considered Dez his best personal friend right now, he decided to come clean. "I'm gonna tell you a secret, Dez, and you have to promise to keep it to yourself."

Dez mimicked turning a key in her lips.

"Derrick and I aren't really boyfriends," Slater said, admitting it out loud for the first time.

"Oh, I knew that."

Slater would have fallen over if he wasn't already sitting. "You knew?"

"Definitely."

"How?"

Dez angled to face him more fully and ticked each point off on a finger. "First of all, you are nothing like the men and women Derrick usually brings home to fool around with. Second, we'd never met you until he moved you into his place. Third, he was always going on about privacy, being content as a single guy, and not wanting the complications of a relationship. Morgan and I both knew it was a ruse so we played along. But now your feelings for him are real?"

"Yes. We told the truth about how we met at the ranch, but we didn't actually see each other again until that Friday in the hospital. I could tell he was genuinely glad to see I was okay, and I didn't understand why it mattered so much to him. Me living with him was kind of made up on the spot, because he needed a fake boyfriend for five weddings this summer to keep his relatives off his back."

"So you traded five dates for a place to stay."

"Yeah. I mean, we both knew we could live together, and we got along great. Get along great still. But the plan has always been for me to go back to Clean Slate when I can reasonably work again. I guess I could technically go back now but Judson won't allow me to be around the horses until the boot's off, and I'm closer to physical therapy here, anyway."

"Do you want to stay once you're healed?"

"Part of me does. But that wasn't our agreement. I can't just decide I want to remain in his place." Lucky jumped into his lap and started purring. Slater scratched the senior kitty between her shoulder blades as she settled.

"I think Lucky just voted for you staying." Dez reached out to pet Lucky, who swatted at Dez's fingers. "Fine, fine. Suck up to Slater, you little hussy."

He absently stroked the cat's soft fur. This was as close to owning a pet as he ever had in his life. "Since I'm confessing all over the place today, I have a daughter named Rachel who turns eighteen next month, and she adores Derrick. They actually text each other." Rachel had texted him twice since graduation, simple messages, and each one meant the world to Slater. He couldn't imagine returning to a life where months of silence went by between visits.

Dez stared at him blankly. "You have a daughter who's almost eighteen? How old are you?"

"Thirty-six soon. We had her way too young, and I

made a mistake that ruined my relationship with Rachel for a long damned time. But we're finding our way back to each other, and Derrick's part of that reason. Her seeing us together… I think it showed her people really can change and make true amends for our mistakes. That I'm not the bad man she used to be afraid of."

Questions danced in Dez's eyes but she didn't press about those mistakes or Rachel's fear. "So you're grateful to Derrick for that?"

"Grateful beyond words. And I adore Derrick's family. Conrad and Sophie and little Mia, and even his parents are amazing and accepting folks. I can see myself being around them far into the future and watching Mia get more siblings. But I can also see myself back at the ranch, damn it. And even if I wanted to stay here, what sort of job can an ex-con reasonably get that pays well?"

Shit. Oh, well, the ex-con thing is out there now.

"So do what I do," Dez said. "I get comments on the blog every day asking about your profane pieces. You make your own patterns so you could reasonably scan and sell the patterns to other crafters, if you don't want to sell the actual finished pieces. Start small and experiment. I can show you how to set up an online storefront. I've got a whole network of craft bloggers who can promote the hell out of you on their platforms."

Dez made the whole thing sound incredibly easy, so why not take a peek? "Okay, we can play around, but this is our secret, okay? Don't tell Derrick."

"Promise. Hang tight." Dez carefully folded the shirt she was working on and put it on the coffee table, then dashed to her apartment. She returned with a tablet that she attached to a small keyboard and started typing. "Let's get you started."

* * *

Derrick had texted Slater earlier that he was bringing home a surprise dinner to celebrate the cast removal, and the scent of the food filled his car on the short drive home from the restaurant. Curbside pickup was such a blessing after a long day at work, when all he wanted was to get home to his boyfriend.

My boyfriend of maybe six more weeks, if I'm lucky.

Fake. Boyfriend. It had always been fake.

Except it didn't feel fake anymore. At Tuesday's wedding, he and Slater had talked, laughed and joked with his family like Slater had become a permanent part of it. They'd flirted with each other, held hands a few times, and Slater even indulged in a single slow dance with him. They had amazing sex that night. Still no kissing or anal but what they did do was perfect and left Derrick exhausted in all the best ways.

But the wedding had also left him with a deep sense of…not melancholy, exactly. They only had two weddings left before Slater's part of their arrangement was over, and once his ankle was healed…what? The plan had always been for Slater to leave, because feelings were never supposed to get involved. Especially not the strong feelings Derrick now possessed for the man.

He kind of hoped to seduce Slater tonight, prove to him why being Derrick's real boyfriend was a very good idea.

Predictably, he found Dez and Slater in the foyer, Lucky on Slater's lap, both of them poring over her tablet. "Hey, guys," Derrick said.

"Hey." Slater grinned brightly at him before his blue gaze dropped to the takeout bag. "Whatever's in there, your timing is perfect, because I'm starving."

Derrick laughed. "Happy Cast Removal Day." He dropped a kiss on Slater's temple—a small gesture he'd been making more frequently because it made Slater blush. "Is it me or is the boot bigger than the cast was?"

"Definitely feels bigger, and it's a pain in the ass to walk in."

"Pain in the thighs, too," Dez added. "He walks like John Wayne."

"Oh, I need to see this," Derrick said. "Up and at 'em, cowboy."

Slater stood with absolutely no grace, but he was up and on his own steam. He did walk pretty funny but the boot had a thicker heel than Slater's sneaker.

"How's it feel putting weight on it again?" Derrick asked once they were in the apartment. He took the bag to the counter so he could plate their meals properly, while Slater fetched them both beers and got out flatware. Now that Slater was only popping the occasional ibuprofen, he indulged in beers with Derrick more frequently.

"Weird but also good. The doc says everything looks good and I start PT next week."

"Excellent." Slater tried peeking over his shoulder and Derrick shooed him off. "Go sit. Let me wait on you like I did the first night." The first night when nothing between them was as comfortable as their lives were now. So right and settled. And fleeting.

Derrick had indulged in medium-rare ribeye steaks, baked potatoes with garlic butter, sides of creamed spinach and steamed carrots, and a bag of the brown bread rolls the steakhouse was famous for. Dessert too but he'd save that for later. Slater's eyebrows shot up when

Derrick delivered their plates. Derrick also grabbed two steak knives out of the drawer.

"This looks amazing, thank you," Slater said, gratitude shining brightly in his eyes. "Can't remember the last time I had a proper steak. One thing I do miss about the ranch is Arthur's barbecue every Sunday night. The man makes a mean rib and his sauce is to die for."

"I remember." Derrick had enjoyed the ranch barbecue several times, and he'd even been cheeky enough to use a protein joke on Colt once, back when Derrick was trying to flirt the blond cowboy into a quickie. But Colt had been pining for his ex, who was now the man's husband, and Derrick was happy for them.

And the food at the ranch was yet another good reason for Slater to go back when he was healed up. Patrice's meals didn't compare to the basic dinners Slater cobbled together, or the frozen meals Derrick nuked when they were both too lazy to cook.

Slater cut into his perfectly cooked steak. "Yes, medium-rare all the way."

Derrick grinned and smeared a healthy dollop of garlic butter over his potato. The food was delicious, but he had more fun watching Slater enjoy the meal. Cutting careful bites of the steak and chewing each one so he really tasted it. He bypassed the garlic butter and covered his potato with salt and sour cream from the fridge. The garlic butter went onto a roll, though, and Slater looked like he was on the verge of orgasm when he bit into it.

"They have the best bread," Slater said around a mouthful of the stuff. "Yum."

"Guess I chose right, then."

"Spot on."

"Good." Derrick speared a piece of carrot. "So I still have those gift cards from my birthday, and once you're steadier in that boot, I'd like us to go out. Have dinner at a nice place, go see a movie. A real date. If you want to, obviously."

Slater watched him silently for a few seconds, his expression mild. Then his lips curved into a half smile. "You want to go on a date with me?"

"I do."

"Don't people usually do that before they live together?"

Derrick chuckled. "Since when has anything about our relationship been traditional?"

"True."

"So? You wanna?"

"Yes. Sure, let's go out on a real date. On one condition."

"Okay."

"I get to pick the movie."

"Deal."

They shook on it, which made both men laugh. And then, as Derrick continued eating, it left a strange feeling in his gut. Had they just made another arrangement? Or was this the potential first step toward making their previous arrangement more permanent?

Time would tell.

Chapter Fifteen

With Slater more mobile in the boot, his Saturday night visitors kidnapped him and Derrick to a sports bar for dinner, drinks and a few rounds of darts. Slater had always sucked at darts—and the boot didn't make his posture any better—so he mostly watched the guys play. Mack, Wes, Robin, Hugo, Colt and Reyes were there, and when Slater asked about their better halves, Reyes said that Miles, Shawn and Avery had made plans. It surprised him a bit that Miles had made plans without Wes, but Wes seemed perfectly happy here with Mack.

Slater couldn't remember the last time he'd hung out at a sports bar with guys he genuinely liked, eating greasy food, drinking pitchers of beer and bullshitting for a few hours. Being sociable and enjoying himself with people he trusted to have his back.

He was in such a good mood when Reyes dropped them off later that he wanted to share, so he blew Derrick where he stood in the living room. Took his time licking and sucking, pulling Derrick to the edge before backing off and playing with his balls. His taint. His hole. Slater had avoided anal sex because of the cast and his own tangled thoughts over the act. Quick fucks were one thing, but he wanted to make love to Derrick.

And if he did that, Slater wasn't sure he could ever let the man go.

So Slater sucked him until Derrick begged to come, and Slater swallowed the load. Derrick eagerly returned the favor after Slater stripped and spread out on the futon. He spent what felt like hours feasting on Slater's neck and collarbone. He knew how to kiss and lick without leaving hickeys, and it turned Slater's crank hard at how oral Derrick was. How much Derrick seemed to get off on playing Slater's body like a rock star.

How much Slater loved this and how much he'd miss it when their situation was over.

Ask me to stay. Ask me.

Derrick didn't ask him that night or any other night the following week. They planned their first real date for Friday, and Slater threw himself into his art projects. With the boot, getting to and from both craft and thrift stores—Dez was now turning him onto the magic of thrifting for cheap supplies—was a lot easier. With Dez's help, he set up an online storefront on her recommended site, and he uploaded the pattern he'd created for his "I Gave My Last Fuck Yesterday" cross-stitch and waited.

And he sold some. So he uploaded another pattern and sold some of those. It wasn't enough money to live on, but the sales did boost Slater's confidence by about a thousand percent. For all the odd jobs he'd had in his life, for all the choices he'd made and hobbies he'd tried, he was actually fucking good at this whole designing thing. And it was fun! He spent more time that week designing new vulgar patterns than he did creating anything—patterns for both cross-stitch and for latch hooking.

Dez encouraged him all week, and she vaguely intimated he should let Derrick in on this, but Slater refused. He didn't want to risk jinxing the whole thing before it could take off.

He didn't want to fail in front of Derrick.

Slater was a bundle of nerves waiting for Derrick to come home Friday night. The boot meant Slater could take it off briefly to change his pants, but instead he'd put on his rip-away wedding slacks with his nicest shirt. Again, his wedding shirt, but before this he'd lived in his ranch polos, so his wardrobe was fairly limited.

Didn't stop Derrick from eye-fucking Slater on his way to the bedroom to change. Derrick's job was pretty casual, so he usually wore jeans and a simple shirt to work. He emerged from the bedroom five minutes later in black slacks and a white shirt that offset his gorgeous complexion. The man was beautiful from top to bottom, and it often made Slater wonder what Derrick saw in a dusty cowboy from the middle of nowhere.

"Ready to go?" Derrick asked.

As if there was any question?

Derrick drove them to a restaurant near Santa Rosa that offered small plates at big prices, and they had a blast spending his gift card. Tasting amazing food and trying things they'd never eaten before. Slater genuinely did not get the appeal of black truffle, but okay. And he could now scratch "trying escargot" off his bucket list. A little chewy but not completely bad. The place was also near several wineries, so they shared a lovely bottle of cabernet sauvignon with the meal.

The gift card didn't cover the entire meal plus tip, but Derrick handed his debit card over to cover the rest and called it, "Money well spent." He also adamantly refused to let Slater help pay the balance, so Slater didn't worry too much about the extravagant food. They were on a date, as well as a belated celebration of Derrick's birthday, so Derrick could spend his money however he wanted.

Instead of a summer blockbuster, Slater chose a quiet drama he thought sounded good, and despite being full, they splurged on sodas, popcorn and candy. More than the movie itself, Slater enjoyed the novelty of watching one in a theater, with a date. Every time their fingers brushed in the popcorn bucket, Slater's skin heated. He anticipated and wanted and needed, and he didn't understand those reactions. Wasn't used to them.

I can't fall in love with him. I can't.

After the movie, they walked for a while to burn off some of the food they'd eaten, and to see more of Santa Rosa. Slater had never been, but Derrick seemed to know his way around. They didn't hold hands but their elbows brushed, and it was enough for now. Their evening truly had been perfect, and Slater didn't want it to ever end.

They drove home with the windows down, enjoying the late summer air. June was almost over with July teasing in only a few more days. Three weeks until the boot could come off at the earliest. Two weddings left to attend. Only a few more fragile weeks until this beautiful bubble he'd created with Derrick would burst, and Slater would have to make a decision.

Once Derrick parked by the house, he told Slater to wait and came around to open his car door. The sweet gesture melted even more of Slater's resistance, and he easily took Derrick's arm for the walk to the house. Then through the foyer to their door. Instead of unlocking it, Derrick turned Slater to face him, his expression so lusty Slater nearly came on the spot.

"I had an amazing time tonight," Derrick whispered. "Best date of my whole life, and I mean that."

"I know you do. You've never lied to me, Tiger." Slater brushed his knuckles across Derrick's cheek, undone by all that naked emotion. "It was the best date of my life, too. Only time anyone's ever truly treated me like that."

"Like what."

"Like I matter."

"You've always mattered, Slater. You just never let other people see how much you have to offer. More than a paycheck. More than a pair of hands to move a heavy object. More than a guy with a record." Derrick's hand rested over Slater's heart. "Tonight's been so amazing that I kind of hoped we could end it with a goodnight ki—"

A heavy thud directly overhead cut off the request before it could send Slater's belly flipping all over. They both looked up. The Thompson apartment was above theirs but the pair never made noise. A second heavy thud was followed by breaking glass.

Derrick turned and bolted for the stairs, and Slater did his best to follow with his damned boot.

The Thompson twins had only lived in the building for six months or so, but they were quiet. Incredibly quiet, barely creaking the ceiling overhead when they walked. All that noise on a Friday night worried Derrick enough to check it out, every instinct in his body on high alert. Adrenaline made his heart pound as he ascended the twisted staircase that ended at a small landing and door.

Derrick pounded his fist on the door. "Orry? George? You guys okay?"

"Stay out of this!" a strange, male voice shouted back, muffled by the door.

He tried the knob. It turned but the door was on a chain and only opened a few inches. Not enough to see much of the apartment but he did hear the stranger snarl, "Ungrateful piece of trash," to someone.

"Open this fucking door or I'll call the police," Derrick said.

Slater had joined him on the landing, his expression tense and alert. The door shoved shut, nearly taking one of Derrick's fingers. The chain slid back and the door flew open again. A tall, slender man with a thick beard and mean sneer filled the doorway. "This is none of your concern," he snapped. Without the door in the way, he had a vaguely Eastern European accent.

"Where are George and Orry?" Slater asked.

"Orry's probably out selling his useless ass like he used to. Their whole family is trash and ungrateful."

"Who the fuck are you to them?" Derrick asked, trying to get a look into the apartment. He heard what could have been muffled sobbing. "Where's George?"

"On the ground where he belongs."

"You guys okay up there?" Morgan's deep voice called from below. "You need backup?"

The stranger's menacing expression cracked as he seemed to realize he was strongly outnumbered and there were people here who had the Thompsons' backs.

"I think we should let the police sort this out," Derrick said.

"No," a soft voice, probably George, said somewhere in the apartment. "Please, let him go. It's over."

Unwilling to push away his neighbor by going
against his wishes, Derrick stepped aside so the bearded
man could stomp down the stairs. Derrick stepped inside the apartment, a little surprised by the lack of furniture, the place as bare bones as Derrick's had been
when he moved in. The futon had been knocked over
backwards, and he found George on the floor behind
it, cradling his left elbow in his right hand.

George looked up, his haunted eyes pleading with
Derrick but Derrick didn't know what they were asking. The boy was the spitting image of his brother, if
a bit skinnier, and he had a split lip that oozed blood.
"Fuck, did that asshole hit you?" Derrick asked.

George didn't respond, only stared at Derrick, and
then at Slater when he hobbled over with a paper napkin
for his lip. "Sorry to be a bother," George said. "You
don't have to stay."

"Who was that guy?" Slater asked.

"No one."

Derrick seriously regretted not calling the police before that asshole got away, but George had to know who
he was if he'd invited the man inside. Then his thoughts
swirled back to what the stranger had said about Orry
selling his ass, and he couldn't help wondering what
sort of operation these two secretive brothers had going
on up here.

George wasn't talking, so Derrick and Slater set
the futon to rights, and Derrick helped George stand.
Guided the kid to sit on the futon. The breaking sound
from earlier was a framed photo that had fallen off the
wall and shattered. Derrick peered down at the photo,
which had landed upright. The twins were easy to spot,

along with a smiling man and woman. Their parents, maybe?

Footsteps thundered up the stairs, and a few seconds later, Orry barreled into the apartment and went straight for his brother. "Jesus Christ, G, what happened? Morgan said some guy with a beard stormed out a few minutes ago. Why did you let him in?"

"I don't know, I'm so stupid," George said as he collapsed against Orry's chest and started crying.

"Hey, you're not stupid. I've got you." Orry wrapped his arms around George and rocked him gently. "I'm here." He looked over George's shoulder at Derrick and Slater, his eyes asking silent questions.

"We'd just got home from a date and heard two loud thumps and a crash," Derrick said. "We came upstairs to check on you guys, and a man with a beard told us to mind our own business. Said some nasty stuff about you two. When I said I wanted to let the police sort this out, George said no and to let the man leave, so I did."

And he really regretted that now, seeing how scared George was—and that he'd been hit at least once.

"Thank you for paying attention and caring," Orry said.

"Who was that asshole?" Slater asked, venom in his voice.

Orry whispered something to George, who sat up straighter. Wiped his runny nose and damp eyes on his already blood-flecked T-shirt. "He was my figure skating coach," George said. "I was good, until I quit right before I was supposed to skate for my first national title. Adrian was furious, and he's obviously still furious."

"Why did you quit like that?"

George dabbed at his cut lip with the bloody napkin.

"I guess I had a nervous breakdown of sorts. I refused to leave my hotel room and wouldn't let anyone in for hours, not until Orry got there. I just couldn't do it anymore. I was anorexic and bulimic, and Adrian encouraged that so I'd stay slim and light and skate faster, and I missed my high school friends and Orry, and it was just too much fucking pressure to be the best. I couldn't handle the pressure of winning, much less losing."

No wonder George is so reclusive.

"Our parents were furious," Orry said, taking over the story, and it was eerie how much they looked and sounded alike. "They treated George like an investment and not a son. It was all about the money they'd put into him over the years and not his feelings, or the fact that he could have died from his eating disorder. So we moved in with our grandparents until we were able to get solid jobs and live on our own."

George whispered something that made Orry groan. "And before you guys start wondering, I'm not a prostitute. Back in high school, I got so pissed about all the attention our parents showered on George and his skating that I ran away for a few months. Did what I had to do to survive until I got my head on straight and went home. Right in time to be there when George needed me most."

"We won't gossip about this," Slater said. "Thanks for trusting us, though."

"Thank you for caring," George replied. "It's nice having friends."

"Well, you definitely have two. Plus, Dez and Morgan from downstairs are pretty awesome, too. Us tenants need to stick together."

Us tenants. Does Slater even realize what he just said?

"I have to admit I'm curious what you guys do for a living," Derrick said. "Tell me to butt out, but I never see you coming or going, George."

"I don't." George blushed to the roots of his blond hair. "I, uh, transcribe closed-captions for online video content providers."

Nothing embarrassing about that, but okay. "Orry?"

"I do a couple of different part-time things right now that keep me busy, like delivering food for a phone app and bartending. It's why I'm all over the place with my hours. I like being flexible in case George needs me." Orry tugged at the curly ends of George's hair, the pair's affection for each other so clear in how they still sat with their arms around the other's waist. "I wish I'd been home tonight so you didn't let that jerkwad inside."

"I don't know why I did. When he used the intercom, he said he wanted to make amends and fix things, apologize for how he treated me. But when he got up here, all he did was start yelling about how our family had ruined his reputation and ruined his life, blah blah. Same shit, different year."

"Are you sure you don't want to get the police involved?" Slater asked. "Him hitting you is assault, period, and if he comes at you again, you'll have a record of his behavior."

Derrick tried to hide his surprise at Slater wanting to get someone else arrested for assault. Slater still looked keyed up and angry, but he was also being gentle with the twins. Derrick had no idea how old they were. At least twenty-one if Orry bartended.

He's a parent. Of course he's being protective of these guys.

Part of Derrick fell for Slater even harder.

After the twins conferred quietly for a few minutes, George agreed to call the police and report the assault. It wasn't how Derrick imagined spending his Friday night, talking to police officers and repeating what he'd seen and heard. But it was still time with Slater, and in the end, everyone felt safer.

They didn't return to their own apartment until close to midnight, each with Orry's number in their cells in case of another emergency, and Derrick was exhausted. It had already been a long week at work, and now this drama?

"This wasn't how I saw our night ending," Slater said as he hobbled right toward the bedroom. Derrick trailed after him, and they went through their familiar evening routines in the bathroom. Slater still usually showered at night but he was drooping around the edges, so they'd have to take turns in the morning.

It was Saturday, anyway. They could sleep in and be lazy, especially after tonight's excitement.

"On the plus side of things," Slater said as they settled in bed with the lights off. "We finally got to befriend the twins. I'm glad they talked to us."

"Same. Hopefully, that creepy coach doesn't become a bigger issue."

"Yeah. I feel so bad for George. For his parents to put so much pressure on him…they broke their own kid."

"Thank God we had good parents."

Slater let out a long sigh, and Derrick didn't have to ask why. He reached across the bed to brush his fingers against Slater's shoulder. "You're trying your best with Rachel. You can still be a good parent to her. Needing our parents doesn't stop when we turn eighteen."

"True. Thanks for tonight. I had a great time while we were out."

"So did I. I'd like to do it again. Maybe not spending a hundred dollars on dinner, but the dinner and a movie part."

Slater chuckled. "Me, too."

Every muscle in Derrick's body wanted to roll over, cover Slater's body with his and kiss the man breathless. To truly thank him for the wonderful date, and for being a wonderful human being. But he didn't. Derrick knew that if he had just one kiss, he'd need another and another, times infinity.

I am so screwed.

They'd both been too exhausted last night to get it up, so when Slater woke Saturday morning with a raging boner, he didn't try to hide it from Derrick. Derrick had matching wood, so Slater spread his legs for a long, sensual frotting session. He kind of loved this position best, Derrick heavy above him, moving with deliberate shifts and grinds while he mapped Slater's neck with his mouth.

Slater had been so close to breaking his no-mouth-kisses rule last night, while they stood outside the apartment door. Chatting on the stoop like any couple on a first date would, each probably hoping the other would initiate the kiss. He didn't regret the interruption, though, because they'd befriended the Thompsons and that was a huge win. Everyone needed a tribe around them, even grumpy loners like Slater, and he couldn't wait for the twins to get to know Dez.

And a shocking thing happened around noon, when he, Derrick, Dez and Morgan all settled in the foyer with pizza and board games—George and Orry came down and joined them. No one commented on George's bruised lip or what happened last night. George didn't talk much and mostly watched the rest of them play, until he complimented Dez's blouse, which she'd sewn herself, and then out came her phone. They even paused the game for ten minutes so Dez could show George her apartment and all her various projects.

When they returned to the group, Dez said, "I even turned Slater over there into a master cross-stitcher. He's really good and even designs his own patterns."

"Really?" George said. "That's cool. You don't look like someone who'd sew."

Slater laughed out loud, genuinely amused by the comment. "Trust me, I know, but I needed something to keep me busy while my ankle healed, and I surprised myself with how much I enjoy it."

"You just like stitching cuss words on things," Derrick teased.

"That's true." Slater showed the twins a few pictures of his work.

"I saw you're out of a cast and into a boot," Orry said. "How much longer before it's healed?"

"It'll take at least three more weeks in the boot, then more PT to get the muscles used to movement again. This boot is a pain in the thighs, but it's way easier than crutches."

"I bet."

"Oh!" This had been in the back of Slater's mind to mention all week, and he'd completely forgotten every time he was around Derrick. Might as well include his friends in the invitation. "So next Friday is July Fourth, and the ghost town attraction where some of my friends work is having its second annual celebration. They'll have live music, riding demos, crafters selling stuff and all kinds of food. I wasn't able to go last year, but I saw a lot of pictures and all the ranch guests who went had a blast. Anyone up for a road trip?"

"I'm in," Derrick said immediately. "I don't work because it's a holiday, and you know I love visiting the ranch and ghost town."

Will you visit me when I go back? If I go back?

"You have friends who work at a ghost town?" George asked.

Slater gave him a brief explanation of Clean Slate Ranch, Wes's discovery of the town's remains and Mack's restoration. "The ranch is where I busted my ankle two months ago."

"Wow."

"Busted his ankle saving a little kid's life," Derrick added, then told that story. Slater wasn't a fan, because he was no one's hero, but he enjoyed the pride in Derrick's voice.

"Anyway," Slater said, "unintentional heroics aside, anyone else want to come? It's about an hour's drive so it'll be an all-day trip."

"I make my own hours, so I'm in," Dez said. "Honey?"

"Sounds like fun, I'll work it out," Morgan replied. "Guys?"

The twins seemed absolutely flabbergasted they were being included. "Can we let you know?" Orry asked after several seconds of silent eye contact with George.

"Definitely," Slater said. "Derrick's car is big enough for all six of us to ride together."

"Cool."

"Perfect."

Slater settled in to keep playing, stupidly excited about this trip. He hadn't been back to the ranch since the day he got out of the hospital, and he missed it. He couldn't wait to see his fellow horsemen, who'd likely be up at the ghost town with that week's ranch guests, and to have Judson's barbecue again. And Shawn's cheddar biscuits. Shawn had cooked for the guesthouse for a few months last winter, and the guy might be quiet, but he was a great cook.

And two more people here knew about his needlepoint and they thought it was cool. People loved his patterns, and he was even considering posting a finished piece for sale next week. Just to see what happened. He felt kind of rotten for not telling Derrick about his online store, but it was just an experiment and could still fail. So he'd wait and see.

Like everything else about his life with Derrick, he would wait and see.

Chapter Sixteen

The first week of July passed too damned fast for Derrick, and he wasn't sure why. Was this what happened when couples found a simple, domestic routine and settled in? Days breezed by on the calendar? That's definitely what was happening lately. He slept with Slater every night, and they occasionally had sex. Breakfast and dinner together every day. Fun weekend routines with their friends. Slater's stockpile of craft stuff had grown to three full plastic tubs, and he'd even set up a small craft table in the corner of the living room by the big window.

Sometimes he'd work there in the evening if he was creating a pattern, or he'd cross-stitch a project on the futon beside Derrick while they watched TV. They were everything a committed couple could possibly be—except a committed couple.

Two more weeks until the boot came off. Two more weeks until Slater had to make a decision about staying here with him, or going back to his old life at Clean Slate. As much as Derrick wanted him to stay, he'd never ask. This had to be Slater's decision alone. He was the one uprooting his life, changing his career and to what? Sure, Dez made a living off her work but Slater was a hobbyist.

Two more weeks of bliss that could blow up in his face and leave Derrick heartbroken. So he refused to acknowledge the still, small voice inside him that kept whispering, "I love Slater." And he absolutely kept those words to himself.

By the day of their road trip, the twins had agreed to go. But they all realized that because of Morgan's size, they weren't all going to comfortably fit in one car. So the twins agreed to ride with Derrick and Slater, and Morgan and Dez would follow them. Derrick found the small town of Garrett with no fuss now that he'd been here enough times. Orry and George stared at the landscape the entire drive up the bumpy road to the ghost town. The lot was already packed, and they still had twenty minutes until the town officially opened for the day. A length of chain prevented folks from crossing the barrier from the parking lot yet, so guests stood around and waited, some dressed up in period costumes, but most not.

"This is so fucking cool," George said as their group waited in a small huddle. "I've never been to a ghost town before."

"It's crazy authentic to the time period," Derrick replied. "The man who restored it even hired a historian to get it right. Plus, the food is excellent."

"You know, I've never tried anything from the saloon," Slater said.

"Oh, then you are definitely ordering a buffalo burger. By now, the chef has a cult following for the sauce on that thing. Mi-m-m-Art Milo refuses to tell anyone the secret ingredient." Derrick was glad he'd caught himself. The saloon chef Miles had used a pseudonym initially to hide here from a stalker ex, but now that the ex was cooling his heels in state prison, Derrick wasn't sure what to call him.

Better to stick to what was still on the website.

Eventually, Mack Garrett himself appeared by the entrance and welcomed everyone to their second annual July Fourth celebration. The crowd cheered, and so did Derrick, and then Mack pulled the chain barrier away. Their group moved with the swarming crowd, and when Mack spotted them, he came over to shake hands and introduce himself to the Thompsons.

As they wandered, Derrick spotted more men in Clean Slate Ranch polos, and most of them came up to chat briefly with Slater about his recovery. When would he be back to work? Things that made Derrick uncomfortable, so he tuned them out and enjoyed the festiveness of the town. Patriotic bunting hung off buildings. The streets were lined with vendors. A mobile barbecue unit was set up near the saloon, and Judson already had the thing fired up with real wood. No charcoal for his meat.

And everyone was smiling. So many bright, cheerful faces this holiday weekend. Folks out in the heat to enjoy their day, eat good food and just have fun. Dez and Morgan split off to do their own thing, but the twins stuck close to Derrick and Slater as they wandered up and down Main Street.

"Maybe you should set up a table of salty samplers next year," Derrick teased Slater as they browsed the craft tables.

"Salty samplers, huh?" Slater pinched his ass and didn't seem to give a shit who saw. "Maybe I will. Who knows, right?"

Who knows where we'll both be in a year?

On their second time past the saloon, Judson waved

Slater over and their group chatted for a while. Judson was completely charmed by the Thompson twins, and he gave Derrick knowing smiles. "You're keeping our Slater out of trouble, yeah?" Judson asked.

"I'm doing my best," Derrick replied.

"Good, good." To Slater, he said, "You know you'll always have a job at the ranch, but if your heart takes you someplace else, you follow it there, you hear me?"

Slater opened and shut his mouth a few times before answering. "Okay. Thanks, Judson."

"You young ones go enjoy yourselves."

The saloon was packed, and they had to wait for a table. The young woman who took their order was bright and cheerful, and their buffalo burgers were eventually hand delivered by Miles himself. He didn't stay long, because he had a kitchen to tend, but Derrick loved the service and Slater seemed awed by the generosity of the people he'd never allowed himself to open up to before.

Their table was finishing up when the noon robbery occurred, and it was both cheesy and fun to watch the kids who weren't sure if it was real react. George seemed mildly spooked, but Orry stayed close and everything turned out fine. After settling the bill, they headed for the far end of town where a live band was playing music. Folks danced in a grassy area. This past spring, Mack had begun a new attraction that had live trick-riding demos, and they caught that around two o'clock. Robin was part of the act, and he shined up on his horse, riding alongside an old friend from his rodeo days.

Learning Robin had been part of a traveling rodeo show for years had shocked the hell out of Derrick, but it also fit what he knew about the man. After the demo, Robin and his riding partner Levi came over to chat with their group.

Robin seemed genuinely thrilled that Derrick and Slater were together and happy, and they were. Sort of. George, on the other hand, couldn't seem to make eye contact with anyone, and Levi watched him with open curiosity.

Interesting.

Derrick had no idea if the Thompson twins were straight or not, and he was starting to think not. He didn't know much about Levi himself, but Robin vouched for him, and that was good enough for Derrick. Or maybe Levi was just a figure skating fan and recognized George's name.

The pair came with their group to scrounge for barbecue at Judson's grill, and Derrick wolfed down a few sauced ribs. So fucking good. And since Robin was dating the saloon's sous chef, he led them around to the rear kitchen door to beg for scraps. Since Shawn had a final pan of cheddar biscuits fresh from the oven, he tossed them the last from the service line to share.

"Man, you know all the right people," Orry said as he munched on half a biscuit.

"Being sociable has its perks," Derrick replied, with a wink at Slater.

"I can't believe you live and work up here," George said to Slater directly. "It's so beautiful. The big sky and mountains. There must be a million stars at night."

"There are," Slater replied. "We do overnight camping trips with guests, and it's one of my favorite things, because we're far out into Mother Nature's territory with only the stars to see by at night. I only know a handful of constellations, but Mack? The ranch owner's grandson? He knows dozens of them. It's peaceful here at night."

"I agree," Levi spoke up. "I like to get up early and go running, and it's like you're in your own unique world."

Something in George's expression pinched and went flat, and Levi seemed at a loss as to what he'd said. Probably something to do with running and George's own history with ice skating and food. The kid wasn't as reclusive as before but he still didn't like talking about himself or his past. Or his present and whatever was or was not happening with Stalker Coach Adrian.

Slater complained about his foot hurting, so he and Derrick parked it at a picnic table while everyone else continued exploring the town. "You look like you're having fun," Derrick said.

"I am." Slater closed his eyes and tilted his face toward the sun. "Glad to be home. I missed this place so much."

Derrick's heart gave an unhappy lurch. "I bet. It's nice to be back. Get the full ghost town experience, instead of just being up here for weddings."

Slater chuckled. "Well, they did two other non-employee weddings up here last fall, and I bet Mack's got some others scheduled for this coming off-season. It's good business for Bentley and Garrett."

"Yeah. I guess Sophie and Conrad started a trend."

"Can you see yourself getting married up here?"

"Nah. Never really saw myself as the marrying type."

Even though Slater's eyes were closed and his face tilted up, Derrick swore the man flinched. "Same, I guess. Got married once and for all the wrong reasons, and it blew up in both of our faces. Lesson learned."

Derrick studied Slater's profile, a little confused. The man's tension didn't jibe with his words. Had Derrick said the wrong thing? He'd been honest, and hadn't Slater praised Derrick for having never lied to him? Weirded out by it, Derrick palmed his phone. "You about ready to call it a day? If we leave soon, we'll miss the mass exodus of guests and some of the rush hour traffic closer to home."

"Yeah, okay. I'm exhausted. Not used to this much sunshine anymore, I guess."

"Okay." Derrick texted Orry to meet them at the car in twenty minutes, and then let Morgan know their group was heading out soon. Morgan sent back a quick thumbs-up emoji.

He and Slater made it back to the car first, and Derrick watched the twins appear in the distance. If it wasn't for the faint scar on George's lip, the only real difference between the pair was George's slightly leaner build. Orry also walked with a bit more confidence, head up and watching the world for danger. Their story truly saddened Derrick. They were young with so much potential and he wanted them to be successful and happy.

By the time their quartet got home, Slater had a text from Dez. Video footage of the end-of-day fireworks display they watched in a huddle around Slater's phone. Afterward, the Thompsons excused themselves upstairs, so Derrick and Slater went into the apartment. Slater sprawled on one side of the futon, legs stretched out, hands over his belly.

"I am beyond stuffed and need a nap," he said. "Fuck me, but today was a great day."

"It was a lot of fun." Derrick sat beside him, putting a good foot of space between them on the wide cushion. "The land suits you."

"It suits you, too, you know. Fuck, it seems to suit everyone who goes there. Nature is precious and there isn't enough of it left in the world. If I learned anything from Arthur Garrett these past few years, it's that the natural world is too beautiful to let greedy men ruin it completely. If we can't stop and admire the simplicity of a tree, then what's the point?"

"I never really thought about it that way." Derrick loved that way of viewing the world. Through the lens of someone who sought to protect Mother Nature and her beauty, rather than dig her up and ruin her for money. "I can't wait until Mia is old enough to explore the wider world. See all it has to offer her."

"I felt that way about Rachel, until I realized I'd become a man who terrified her, instead of a dad she could admire and learn from." But Rachel had reached out to him, and Slater had renewed hope in their future as father and daughter.

"You still can and you will." Derrick reached over to squeeze Slater's thigh. "I have faith in that, Kendall Stamos. Even if you don't."

Slater met his gaze, something burning in those blue eyes. Eyes that dipped briefly to Derrick's lips. Derrick licked them, hoping to entice a nice, long kiss out of his boyfriend. Slater's own lips parted…and then he released a jaw-cracking yawn. "Shit, sorry," Slater said. "All that sunshine."

"Go take a shower and relax. I'm too full for dinner but I'll see if I can find a movie to watch or something."

"Sounds good." Slater groaned as he stood, and when he passed by Derrick, paused. Leaned down and kissed Derrick's forehead. "Thanks for a great day."

"You're welcome." His skin burned where Slater's lips had touched him, and Derrick stared at the blank TV for a long time after the water turned on in the shower. Stared and didn't think beyond the chilling reality that Slater had a foot in two worlds. He shined up at Garrett around his fellow horsemen and in the open sunshine. He also shined here in the city with his crafts and friends and with Derrick.

But no one could stand in two worlds for long without being consumed by indecision and doubt. Derrick absolutely wanted Slater here, but he also loved the buff cowboy too much to demand he stay. Whatever choice Slater made, it was his alone. Derrick would simply deal with the fallout.

Rachel's eighteenth birthday was on Wednesday, and Slater spent a good twenty minutes talking to her on the phone that day. He told her about the Bentley July Fourth day, and she told him about a day trip she and Jayla had taken to Folsom Lake last weekend. Casual conversations between parent and child, and it left him floaty for the rest of the day. Dez teased him about it, and he let her.

For dinner, Slater threw together a quick pasta dish with frozen meatballs and garlic bread, and he savored the big grin his meal got from Derrick the instant he walked in the door. "You talked to Rachel today, didn't you?" he asked.

"Yup." He popped a piece of garlic bread into Derrick's mouth. "Come eat, I'm starving."

Derrick pinched the top of his ass. "Hungry for anything besides food tonight?"

"Maaaybe." Slater was definitely on board with sex after dinner. He was learning how to maneuver the boot better so he didn't accidentally whack Derrick in the head with it when they switched positions. Definitely helped they had a big damn bed. Sex was also a great distraction from thinking about the boot possibly coming off in a week and a half.

"I like this sassy side of you," Derrick said as he sat

at what was becoming his side of the table. The chair nearest the door, while Slater sat with his back to the kitchen. "Don't see it very much."

"Honestly, I wasn't sure I had one. I guess you found it and brought it out of me." Slater scooped the mixed pasta, sauce and meatballs onto Derrick's plate, then did the same for himself. Shook a bunch of grated Parmesan on top, too.

"Thanks for cooking, this smells amazing."

He shrugged. "I boiled pasta and added a few spices to jarred sauce."

"Still, you made the effort." So much affection shined in Derrick's dark eyes that it left Slater breathless, and he had to look away. "Do you enjoy cooking?"

"I guess so. Not as much as I enjoy needlepoint or designing patterns, but it's another semi-creative outlet, I guess. And I never got to do it at the ranch, because Patrice fed us. I cooked a bit more when Rachel was young and we lived with Dad and Kim."

"How about after prison?"

Slater waited for irritation or shame to wash over him, like it always did when someone brought up prison. But not today. Not with Derrick. Because Derrick had never treated him like there was something wrong with Slater for having done time. "Nah, I mostly subsisted on bologna sandwiches and pickles for a while. With the shipping company, I was always on the road, so I ate at a lot of truck stops and fast food. I don't know a lot about much, but I can tell you the very best places for red-eye gravy on any California interstate."

"I bet. You probably saw a lot of the west coast with that job."

"I did. I also didn't like the nomadic part of the job.

Never standing still for too long. No roots. Maybe that's why the ranch and rescue appealed to me so much. I couldn't be around my own blood family, but I could live near a family. Maybe pretend I was part of it once in a while."

"You are part of it, Slater."

"I know. Now that I've been away for so long, I know I've got family there." Slater's heart thumped wildly. "I've also got family here. And in Sacramento. More family than I ever thought I deserved."

Derrick's tender smile nearly undid Slater's tenuous grip on his emotions, and when Derrick reached out, Slater clasped his hand. "There isn't a thing in your life that you've told me about that makes you undeserving of family. Or of love."

Slater swallowed hard against his sudden desire to admit his feelings to Derrick. That he was pretty sure he was falling in love with the man, but he was too scared to say so. Terrified to allow himself these feelings, only to leave it all behind in a few weeks. So he gave Derrick's hand a firm squeeze and let go. "Thank you for saying that."

"Anytime."

Sex was different that night. They took their clothes off more slowly, taking their time to admire each other's naked bodies. Slater trailed his fingers over swaths of smooth skin and toned muscle. Derrick never went to the gym that he told Slater about, but he somehow maintained a gorgeous form Slater couldn't wait to properly wrestle to the ground again. To turn Derrick over the back of the futon and fuck him properly, hard and fast and furious. But not tonight.

Tonight they pulled the covers back and slid together

onto the mattress. They kissed each other's cheeks and necks and shoulders, while hands never stopped moving. Their erections rubbed lazily against each other's belly, thigh, cock. A long, lazy exploration of skin on skin. Maybe Slater couldn't say "I love you" with words, but he could make love to Derrick with his body.

Time stopped existing. It was only them moving together. Stroking and rutting and loving each other. They barely spoke because they didn't have to. This thing they'd been creating between them for months spoke for them. Helped them find a synchronicity that scared Slater as much as it elated him.

Everything he'd ever needed was in this apartment with him. But unless Derrick asked him to stay, Slater would have to leave it all behind.

So he made tonight last, like he'd make every future, final encounter with Derrick last. They both came twice before collapsing, exhausted and sated, and Slater curled his front against Derrick's back. Spent cock pressed against Derrick's taut cheeks. Derrick drew one of Slater's hands up and kissed the knuckles.

"Damn," Derrick whispered.

"Yeah." He kissed the back of Derrick's neck, half expecting a joke about Slater needing phone calls with his daughter more often. But Derrick remained silent in this reverent moment. They'd said the same silent thing tonight.

I didn't want to fall in love with you, but I did. God help me now.

Saturday was a busy day of driving for Derrick. Wedding number four was in a town about an hour north of Sacramento and it started at one. He and Slater had negotiated the ceremony and leaving the reception by three, so they could get down to Rachel's birthday party that evening. Derrick didn't mind all the driving or cutting out of the reception early. He kind of wished he had a classic convertible like Robin, but oh, well. And Slater was so excited to see Rachel again he vibrated in his seat the entire way north.

Things between them had shifted again since Wednesday night. Everything was…easier. Almost a silent understanding that, despite their verbal agreement that this was a fake relationship, it was very much a real one now. They no longer had to pretend they liked touching each other, holding hands in public or sharing goofy smiles. Nothing was fake. But how much longer would it last? After today, there was only one wedding left.

Sophie had come down with a dreaded summer cold, so Conrad was staying home with his family. They did meet up with Mom and Dad at the church and they sat together. Slater seemed more confident now that he was seeing familiar faces and was off the crutches. No more worrying about tripping people with them. He was also confident in his place by Derrick's side, and it showed plainly during the reception. Family members remembered him and asked about his foot. Trevor and Trish found them for a chat.

Slater even agreed to two slow dances.

They made their excuses at three—the only thing they'd miss was blowing bubbles at the married couple on their way to their car—and hit the road again. Rachel's birthday present and an overnight bag were in the back seat. Now that Rachel was eighteen and the custody agreement no longer valid, they'd been invited to stay in the guest room.

The party didn't officially begin until five thirty, but they'd arranged to arrive early and help with setup. Kim welcomed them at the door with big hugs. Rachel was out with Jayla, which disappointed Slater, but they were quickly tasked with hanging streamers in the living room because they could reach high without a stepladder. Philip was fussing with food in the kitchen, but the house was small enough that they all conversed without trouble.

They both had fun talking about last week's trip to Bentley, as well as today's wedding. Slater had brought Kim a small framed sampler he'd designed that said "Queen of the House." She adored it and immediately asked Philip to find a place to hang it so their guests could admire Slater's hard work.

After the streamers, they were tasked with blowing up matching balloons, which he and Slater turned into a game of "who can blow up the most in the least amount of time." Derrick was winning until his current balloon escaped his lips and sailed across the room.

"You two just look happier every time I see you together," Kim said on a peal of laughter. "I would love to meet your parents one day, Derrick. They must be lovely people to have raised such a good man."

Derrick smiled, a little embarrassed by the compliment. "I'm sure they'd be thrilled to meet you and Philip, as well." Not that he expected the meeting to ever happen, especially if he no longer had a boyfriend in a few weeks.

"Good, good. Now finish those balloons so we can get them tacked up before the girls get back."

"Where are they, anyway?" Slater asked before sticking another limp balloon between his lips.

"They went to pick out Rachel's cake."

"She's buying her own cake?" Derrick said, because Slater was mid-puff.

"She has my debit card, but the only thing she wanted to pick out herself for this party was her cake. I gave her a budget and said have fun. Besides—" she flashed them both a charming smile "—it means I got free rein to decorate."

They had the balloons and a wide "Happy Birthday!" banner hung when Rachel and Jayla returned with a bright pink cake box. Rachel hugged Derrick, then her dad, and then proudly announced, "I got a cookies-and-cream ice cream cake."

"Sounds amazing," Slater said. "Is cookies and cream your favorite?"

"Depends on my mood. Sometimes I want mint chocolate chip, or maybe chocolate peanut butter."

"I'm sensing a trend with the chocolate part."

"She always picks on me because I don't like chocolate," Jayla said. "Give me cherry vanilla any day."

"I'm with you," Slater replied to Jayla. "Chocolate dessert is okay in moderation, but I'm a fan of fruity ice cream like classic strawberry."

The conversation shifted into an argument about the best ice cream flavors, and Derrick soaked it in. Slater fit in here so well now that he'd figured out how to navigate social situations and banal conversations. How to listen and answer. How to be part of his own family again.

I helped give him that.

Guests began arriving shortly after they'd filled all

the bowls with chips and snack mixes. Mostly high school friends and neighbors, but also a few out-of-town relatives here to celebrate Rachel's accomplishments. Cards piled up in a basket next to Slater's wrapped gift, as well as a few other packages. Delivery pizza arrived at five thirty on the dot. Slater introduced Derrick to everyone who asked about him with a bright smile that never seemed to go away.

Tonight, Slater was a proud dad and he shined like the fucking sun.

Slater couldn't remember the last time he'd had a truly great evening in this house. Last month, the graduation party had been good but also had lingering tension. Tonight, Slater and Rachel chatted without that tension. Nothing was magically perfect between them but they had a relationship, and that was everything.

Derrick stuck close to him or to Kim most of the evening, smiling and joking with whoever was nearby. More than once, Slater caught him talking about work and chatting up the Dream Boxes program. Sneaky bastard. Then again, Slater loved telling anyone who asked about his work at Clean Slate and the nearby ghost town. He had to sit a few times to rest his ankle, which was getting stronger every week he attended PT, but he didn't want to push himself. One wrong move could delay his recovery.

Not that he was eager for this beautiful dream with Derrick to end, but life went on and he couldn't live on pause forever.

No, no more thoughts about that. Slater watched his daughter work the room, talking to adults with as much poise as anyone twice her age and experience. When she sat down to open the handful of gifts, Slater's belly swooped with nervous anticipation. He'd wanted to give her something practical, but also fun, so he'd gone on-line in search of ideas, and he had been working on this project off and on for weeks, desperate to get it exactly right.

Rachel glanced his way with an eager smile before she opened the box. Below the tissue was an embroidery hoop he'd painted green. On the canvas, he'd stitched twelve different flowers around the border, spaced exactly like a clock face. Hidden inside each flower—and Dez had helped him a lot patterning those—was the vague shape of the number it represented. She'd also helped him attach clock parts to the center. Rachel found the battery he'd put in the box and inserted it.

It started ticking.

"Holy crap, you made this?" Rachel asked, eyes shining with tears.

"Designed it with a friend's help, yup," Slater said, keenly aware all the eyes in the room were on him. Some of the older men didn't look impressed, but Rachel's girlfriends fell all over themselves trying to get a look at the clock. "Kim said you love visiting the McKinley Rose Garden, so I figured you must love flowers."

"I do. I love this, thank you." She gently placed the clock back in the box, and Slater rose to accept her warm, tight hug. "Thank you, Dad."

"You are so welcome, baby girl."

She sniffled once, and it didn't do much to help the tears stinging the corners of Slater's eyes. Thankfully, Dad announced it was time for cake, which gave Slater a moment to recover. He excused himself to the bath-

room so he could wipe his eyes and pull himself together. Every time he didn't think he could love Rachel
more, his heart just got bigger and bigger.

He studied his reflection in the mirror and someone
he almost didn't recognize looked back at him. The
only visible sign of his fall down the mountain was a
small scar on his left cheek, low by the jawline. His eyes
seemed brighter. Even his skin seemed to glow with the
inner peace and joy he could barely contain.

*Derrick gave this to me. He drew me out of the shell I
existed in and showed me how to be a real person again.*

Slater returned to the party. Derrick handed him a
piece of cake. He was about to ask if he should eat it
with a spoon or fork when Kim handed him a plastic spork. Perfect. The cake was overly sweet for him
but worth it for how much joy it put on Rachel's face
as she ate and chatted with her friends. A decent mix
of boys and girls, and she didn't seem to overtly flirt
with anyone.

That was fine. She had goals and ambitions, and right
now those goals didn't seem to include dating.

Dad approached and asked Derrick, "Mind if I steal
Ken away for a few minutes?"

"Steal away," Derrick replied. "I see his ugly mug
every day."

Slater flipped him off before following Dad through
the kitchen to the back door. Outside into the hot July
evening. The yard was small with only a few bushes
to speak of, and Dad led him to the rickety old picnic
table near the rear fence.

"I'm proud of you," Dad said. "Really, truly proud
of you, son."

His eyes filled with unwanted tears for the second

time that night. Slater couldn't remember the last time his father said he was proud of him. "I know I fucked up. Big time. But I'm not that guy anymore. I've got too damned much to live for now."

"I know. I see how you've changed. Rachel sees it, too. And I think she also sees the ways Nina hasn't even tried, which is why she wasn't invited tonight. Rachel wants to surround herself with positive people. She told me that herself when we sat down to plan this party. First person on her invite list was you."

Slater pinched the bridge of his nose to keep those damned tears at bay. "Thank you for telling me this. And I know it's been a long time since I've said it, but I love you, Dad."

"I love you, too, son."

They hugged, long and hard, and it was everything Slater had ever needed in a hug from his dad. The Kendall Stamos who'd fucked up his own life was gone, blown away like ash, and a brand-new man stood in his place. Slater had truly redeemed himself and fixed his relationships with the most important people in his life—his daughter and parents.

And in that precious moment in time, nothing else mattered.

Derrick and Slater had no specific plans on Sunday, so when Rachel asked to take them to the McKinley Rose Garden, Slater couldn't possibly say no. They went as a family, all five of them, and the garden was absolutely beautiful. Rachel showed off her favorites, and then they simply walked the neighborhood. Slater bought everyone lunch at a quirky little restaurant they all agreed on, which gave him a chance to rest his foot.

By midafternoon, though, they were all hot and tired from the wandering, so they went back to the house. Kim mixed up a pitcher of lemonade for everyone to share, and they gathered around the kitchen table to play Rummy. It wasn't Slater's best card game, and he lost every round but that was okay. He was here, spending time with his family and his boyfriend. They even busted out leftover chips and dip from last night's party.

After an hour of losing, Slater suggested Hearts. Derrick wasn't familiar with that one, and it was a four-player game, so he sat close to Slater and tried to learn. Eventually, Slater let Derrick play a hand and he did pretty well on his own, with the occasional pointer from Slater. Around five, Kim heated up the rest of last night's pizza for supper, along with whatever other party leftovers she could find in the fridge.

At six thirty, it was time to leave. Slater hated going, but he didn't want to overstay his welcome. It had been an amazing weekend, and he couldn't wait to see them all again. "Maybe before school starts," Rachel said by the car, "Jayla and I can drive down to your area for a day. Hang out."

"I'd love that," Slater replied. "I am so proud of you, Rachel. I can never tell you how much. And I love you."

"I love you, too, Dad."

Those words broke the dam, and Slater wasn't ashamed of the few tears he cried as he hugged his little girl. This beautiful young woman he'd helped create. She clung to him and kissed his cheek before stepping back, her own eyes bright and red-rimmed.

"I'll see you soon," Slater said.

"Count on it." She stepped back from the curb to stand on the sidewalk with Dad and Kim.

Slater hated it to his core, but he got into Derrick's car and buckled up. "You did good," Derrick said as he pulled away from the curb. "The change in her attitude toward you in one month is astonishing."

"She's the best thing I ever did." He looked behind them to watch his family slowly disappear in the distance. "And she wants me in her life."

"She'd be crazy not to." Derrick squeezed his thigh; Slater covered that hand with his own and turned to face the front.

They didn't talk much on the drive south, mostly commenting on other idiot drivers or the scenery, and that was okay. The silences between them were comfortable and familiar now. As familiar as that old futon and the way Derrick snored. The scent of his body wash. The way Derrick always let Slater have the last few bits of popcorn when they watched a movie.

They got home late, both exhausted from the long, fun weekend, so after quick business in the bathroom, they went to bed. Instead of keeping to separate sides, though, they snuggled up together near the middle, hands clasped, noses nearly touching on the two pillows they'd pushed together.

"Best weekend ever?" Derrick whispered in the dark.

"Yeah." Slater leaned in and brushed a kiss over Derrick's cheek. "Best. Weekend. Ever."

Chapter Seventeen

Life resumed as if a strange shroud of doom *wasn't* hanging over Slater's Friday appointment with his doctor. His head had been cleared weeks ago, but many things hinged upon the boot removal. Did he have to wear it longer? Could he now go without? Would he need some other assistance device? He tried to focus his nervous energy into pattern design, actual stitching and making love to Derrick as often as possible. Ever since the amazing weekend in Sacramento, they'd gotten off together almost every day, usually after dinner, and it was awesome.

It was also a reminder of what Slater would be leaving behind.

Dez distracted him as much as she could as his online business continued to grow by small degrees. Twice that week, George came downstairs at lunchtime to chill with them in the foyer, but he rarely stayed long. Even though the father/daughter duo in the other apartment were still pretty standoffish, this house felt like home to Slater.

And so did Clean Slate Ranch. He had no idea what to do other than push forward, so he did. Living one day at a time. Enjoying every moment he had with Derrick, whether it was sucking his dick or challenging him to a racing game on his system. He chilled with Dez and texted with Rachel, and life was good. Simple. Fun. Full.

Dez basically demanded she take him to his appointment on Friday, so he let her. Cheaper than paying for a car, and he could not wait to be able to drive again. Not only a car, but his own motorcycle, which was gathering dust in the Clean Slate garage.

His doctor was thrilled with Slater's progress and range of motion with his foot. The scar didn't look too awful, and he could bear weight without much discomfort. He still had to ease back into things and it would be a while before he could mount a horse without help, but Slater was free of the boot. Free of crutches. He had a cane for extra assistance until his ankle was back to normal—or as normal as it would get, the doc warned—but he was free. His foot was in a sock and shoe again for the first time in three months.

Slater kind of wanted to weep for joy, but he hugged Dez instead. They swung by a place for celebratory milkshakes before going home. Slater called Judson with the news, and Judson asked the mother of all questions: "When do you think you'll be coming home, son?"

"I'm not sure." Truth. He still owed Derrick a fifth and final wedding date a week from tomorrow. After that their agreement was fulfilled. Slater could go home, and Derrick could return to his solitary, clubbing existence. "I'll let you know as soon as I'm sure my ankle is strong enough for me to return to my regular duties."

"Good enough. You take care."

"Thanks, Judson."

That night, their sextet of friends—Slater, Derrick, Dez, Morgan, George and Orry—shared a celebratory dinner of Chinese takeout in the foyer. George stuck to the steamed white rice and veggies, while Slater pigged out on egg rolls, crab Rangoon and Mongolian beef. He ate until his stomach hurt, so happy to have his right foot finally free. Not perfectly healed, but at least free.

Derrick was subdued, and Slater didn't have to ask why. They made love that night with the same care and tenderness as other nights, but also with hints of sadness. Sadness for this thing they'd agreed was about to end.

Slater didn't start on it that weekend, but on Monday, he began a new pattern for a project his heart wouldn't let him avoid. One particular piece of art that could say what his own words had not yet voiced. Dez thought he was nuts and should just fucking say it, but Slater didn't have the words. So he stitched them.

But that week…something was different. Slater couldn't put his finger on the change in Derrick. It was that subtle, but he knew Derrick well enough to see that something was off. Derrick was sweet, attentive and definitely game whenever Slater initiated sex. But Slater felt a distance, too. As if Derrick saw the inevitable end and was trying to create a barrier between them so it wouldn't hurt as much. That barrier hurt, too, but Slater persevered with his design and final gift. It probably wouldn't make a difference, but he had to try, damn it.

Wedding five was on Saturday, the final weekend in July. Since Mia was sick this time around, Sophie stayed home and Conrad hitched a ride with them to a town about two hours south. As much as Slater loved the tear-away slacks Dez had sewn for him, he was happy to dress in regular pants for the day. His cane was simply for additional support as his ankle continued to strengthen, but at this point he'd met most of Derrick and Conrad's extended family at least once and didn't have to explain his limp.

The family had witnessed his recovery from the earliest days to the end.

It was an indoor wedding, thank God, because the weekend was sweltering hot. Another unique venue, this time a 1920s-era mansion with a gorgeous ballroom and all kinds of authentic antiques. At least, Slater assumed they were authentic, since he didn't know crap about antique clocks or chandeliers. It was also much more formal than the previous four weddings, which made for an interesting switch. Slater simply went where Derrick and Conrad led him, and he did his duties as Derrick's doting boyfriend.

A title he wished he could keep after tonight but that wasn't their deal.

At the reception, they were seated at a table with Trevor, Trish and little Gus, and Slater realized this was the last time he'd see the young family. He was truly fond of them, like he was fond of Conrad and Sophie, and of Robert and Sharon. He'd been embraced by the people who mattered most to Derrick, and that meant the world to Slater.

"So," Trevor said after appetizer plates were served to their table, "how long have you guys been together now?"

"Three or four months, depending on when we were technically together," Derrick said. "We've lived together for about three."

"And you haven't had a single fight?" Trish asked.

"Nope."

"That's kind of amazing. When I moved in with Trevor we couldn't agree on anything for months."

"Your kitchen cabinets were set up weirdly," Trevor retorted with a teasing grin. "But seriously, Derrick, if Slater there's a keeper you need to put a ring on it fast."

Slater nearly choked on his soup. When Derrick didn't say anything, Slater said, "Derrick's made it clear he's not the marrying type, and to be honest, neither am I. We like things the way they are."

Derrick flashed him a look that was unreadable—not something Slater was used to. As if the man wanted to argue with him, but hadn't Derrick admitted as much to Slater on July Fourth? He'd used the exact words "not the marrying type." So why did Derrick look as if he wanted to amend his statement. Or start a fight so their eventual breakup was more believable?

Instead, Derrick said, "Pretty much, yeah," and ate his soup.

Trish changed the subject after that. The food was delicious and probably expensive per plate, but Slater barely tasted the potato leek soup, or the prime rib that came after. The Belgian chocolate mousse that was served for dessert. Each course, each speech, drew their agreement to a close. After today, Slater had no reason to stay unless Derrick asked him to. Asked not to break up but maybe try long distance? Do something besides accept the inevitable and quietly move on from each other.

That's always been the plan. I wasn't supposed to fall in love.

They danced two slow numbers together, Derrick incredibly careful of his right foot. Slater memorized the feeling of Derrick in his arms like this, moving gently to romantic music for the last time. When Slater said goodbye to Trish and Trevor later, it was a real goodbye on his part.

It was late when they dropped Conrad at his house. "You guys wanna come over for dinner some night this week?" he asked as he opened the rear passenger door. "I bet Uncle Derrick needs some Mia time."

Slater's heart skipped, and he glanced over at Derrick. Derrick twisted around to speak to his brother. "We'll let you know, okay? Not sure of our plans this week."

True enough.

"Sure thing. Later, guys." Conrad shut the door.

They sat in silence for a few seconds, before Derrick pulled away from the curb. Neither of them spoke on the drive back to their place. No, Derrick's place. No one was chilling in the foyer, thank God, because Slater was too depressed to make nice with his friends tonight. Usually, the silences between him and Derrick were easy. Tonight, it was tense. Uncertain.

Sad.

Slater finished in the bathroom first and was waiting in bed when Derrick came in. "So we both fulfilled our ends of the arrangement," Slater said.

Derrick flinched. "Yeah, we did. Your foot is better and wedding season is over."

Ask me to stay.

Derrick got into bed and turned off the light. "Night, Slater."

"Yeah."

Slater stared at the ceiling, his thoughts and emotions tumbling all akimbo. Derrick hadn't asked him to stay, but he also hadn't asked Slater when he planned to leave. That meant something, right? He didn't sleep well that night, his dreams full of nebulous, unpleasant things, and he was glad for the first rays of morning light. They had standing plans for brunch with Dez and Morgan at ten, but that was hours from now.

Derrick was still lightly snoring away, so Slater got up, dressed and went out to the living room. Eyeballed his craft corner. He had no idea what to do with all that stuff when he went back to Clean Slate. He could stack the three tubs in the cabin's living space but didn't want to crowd out Hugo without asking first. The table he'd leave here for Derrick; it wouldn't fit in the small cabin. He'd accumulated some new T-shirts over the past few months, but all his other belongings should still fit in his single suitcase.

His box of personal items had grown by a few things: his ticket to Rachel's graduation and event cards for all five weddings. He'd treasure those memories always.

Slater also wasn't leaving today, so he settled down to work on a pattern. Eventually, the water in the shower turned on. Derrick emerged smiling and dressed about thirty minutes later, and Slater couldn't help but return that familiar, handsome smile. "Sleep okay?"

"Yup," Slater lied. "I don't have to ask if you did, judging by the snoring."

"I don't snore."

Brunch had been Dez's idea, and Slater imagined it was because she knew about the arrangement. Morgan drove their quartet to a popular place one neighborhood over, so they had to wait a while for a table. But they did make a fabulous brunch buffet and the wait was worth it. Slater's stomach was still a bit of a nervous mess, so he stuck to less-greasy things like a waffle and some cut fruit. Derrick used an omelet station to create some sort of piled-high concoction.

Once they were all seated, Dez asked how the wedding had been. Derrick did most of the talking, his smile almost always in place. The whole thing was so fucking normal Slater wanted to scream that it was all an act. But he didn't. He nibbled his waffle, ate his fruit, and tried to imprint this meal into his memory for later. In case he never had it again.

Oh, he'd stay in contact with Dez for sure. She was his best friend besides Derrick, and he treasured their friendship.

"You okay, dude?" Morgan asked him. "Not hungry?"

"Not really." Slater didn't want to lie and say he'd eaten a bagel before coming, so he left his answer there.

"Then can I have half before you mangle it to death?" Morgan pointed at the waffle.

That got a genuine belt of laughter out of Slater. He cut off the portion he'd been picking at and pushed his plate toward Morgan. Morgan speared it with a big grin. He'd already packed away a plate of food, but Morgan was an eater. He could probably do those food challenges if he needed a new hobby to go with his body-building lifestyle.

Slater had been a bit nervous about coming out of his ankle ordeal with a pooch and weak muscles, but he'd used the free weights and done crunches while in the boot, and he didn't think he'd gained all that much, despite his fairly steady diet of takeout. Not that Slater was all that vain about his body, but he needed to be in shape to properly muck a horse stall and haul around bales of hay. Once his ankle was up to par, he'd be good as new.

Morgan and Derrick got up together to hit the buffet a second time. Dez immediately leaned across the booth and whispered, "You obviously didn't give it to him yet. You look like you've been kicked in the nuts. Just tell him."

"I can't. If he wants me to stay, it has to be because it's what he wants, not him feeling sorry for the sad sap who fell in love with him when he wasn't supposed to. I don't want an invitation out of pity."

"God, men are so stupid sometimes. Why can't you two just sit your stubborn asses down and talk to each other?"

"I'm not even sure what I want yet, Dez. I don't want to leave, but I'm not sure I want to quit Clean Slate. Maybe breaking up is the best thing for us both. We can figure out what we want."

Dez frowned. "I don't agree with you, but it's your decision. I won't meddle."

"Thank you." He loved her even more for not having to be asked to keep this between them. Some things between friends were simply understood.

Their guys returned and Dez picked a slice of watermelon off Morgan's piled-high plate. Derrick had rounded out his earlier omelet with hash browns and a bowl of yogurt with granola in it. "When did you start eating healthy on your own?" Slater asked.

"Since we started eating vegan shit at their place." Derrick pointed his spoon at Dez and Morgan. "I can make healthy choices on my own, thank you."

Good to know.

Not that Slater had ever been the poster child for healthy eating, but he liked knowing Derrick would take care of himself once Slater was gone.

The day's painful attempt at normalcy continued when Morgan suggested they drive into Alameda and check out the Pacific Pinball Museum. It was such an oddball suggestion that Slater couldn't say no. He'd spent hours in arcades as a teen, trying to master various pinball games with a roll of quarters in his pocket. Some of the arcades had given away tickets for points scored, but Slater always gave those away. For him, it wasn't about collecting enough tickets for a cheap pair of knockoff sunglasses at the trade-in counter. It was beating the game.

The museum was pretty cool. Brightly painted murals on the walls perfectly accented a huge variety of working machines, from the 1940s to present day, and you could even play on them free all day with the price of admission. There were other arcade games like Pac-Man as well as jukeboxes, and even a small gift shop.

Slater had a blast playing some of the older, restored games he'd never seen before. Derrick mostly watched, but he did hover close, while Dez and Morgan wandered around to different machines. Slater felt like a teenager again, young for the first time since that pregnancy test came back positive, and it was the best feeling in the world.

One last amazing date with my boyfriend.

Even that thought didn't put a damper on Slater's good mood over the arcade trip, and he played until he'd definitely been on his ankle too long. He found a spot to rest so the others didn't have to quit playing, until Dez suggested they go get coffee. Slater didn't have much use for those fancy drinks but let Dez order him an iced soy drink with too many words in its name that was actually pretty good.

Not that Slater was ever going to ask Patrice to keep soy milk in the guesthouse refrigerator—he'd get laughed right out of the kitchen by his fellow horsemen—but maybe he could keep a small carton in his cabin's mini-fridge. He never used to keep much in there besides the occasional six-pack and string cheese, and Hugo didn't stock a lot of snacks.

His foot was sore from the day's activity by the time they got home. Derrick ordered him to the futon, pushed over the green stool, and then fetched Slater an ice pack—just like he used to during those first few weeks post-surgery.

"Thank you," Slater said. "For the ice pack and for today. It was a lot of fun."

"It was all Morgan and Dez, but you're welcome. I had a great time. That arcade museum was nuts."

"I don't know how I never knew that was there, but I also never spent a lot of time exploring the Bay Area. The other guys like the clubs, but it was never my scene, so I had no real reason to drive that far from Garrett every weekend."

Derrick's hands were resting on his thighs, and the fingers of both curled slightly at Slater's words. "Yeah. Right."

"Again, not knocking your old clubbing habits or any future clubbing you'll do."

"Just not your thing."

"Exactly." For some reason, Slater got the impression they weren't just talking about clubbing specifically anymore.

"You know, you can stay as long as you want, right?"

"I know. Thank you." *But do* you *want me to stay?* Slater was so turned around he wasn't sure what to say, so he let his body say it for him again. If this was their last night, it sure as hell was going to be a memorable one. He scooted closer, body angled toward Derrick, who watched him with open curiosity and barely contained desire. Positive this was the right thing, Slater curled his left hand around the back of Derrick's neck and urged him forward. Closed his eyes and brushed his lips over Derrick's. Derrick inhaled a sharp breath, followed by a low moan that sent arousal zinging down Slater's spine.

Derrick's hot mouth crashed over his, and Slater gave in. He hadn't been properly kissed in so long he'd nearly forgotten how, but Derrick showed him again. Derrick made love to his mouth in small nips and sips, his tongue gently probing Slater's teeth and lips, until Slater allowed him inside. Derrick hauled Slater forward, practically onto his lap and kissed him harder, deeper. His entire body ached with need for this man. To share one more rare thing with him.

Slater reluctantly broke their first, dazzling kiss and held Derrick's dark gaze. "I want you to make love to me tonight, Derrick. I want you inside me."

Derrick nearly fell right off the futon from Slater's two statements. His brain was already short-circuiting from the sensation overload that was kissing Slater, so he couldn't have heard that right. "You want what?"

"Please. I trust you implicitly, Derrick. I want this so badly." Slater's eyes burned with need and Derrick saw no lie. Only a man giving in to lust and taking steps Derrick had been jerking off to for months. It wouldn't be a hard, sweaty fuck on gym mats.

"Yes. I'll make love to you, Slater."

"Thank fuck."

Derrick chuckled, then kissed him gently. "You're absolutely sure? Have you bottomed before?"

"No. Never met someone I trusted enough to go there. Until you."

Until you.

Two little words that meant the world to Derrick. He couldn't contain the impulse to hug Slater tight, and Slater hugged him back. And because kissing was now on the table, Derrick made love to his mouth again while they slowly peeled away layers of clothes. Shoes and socks. T-shirts and shorts. By some silent agreement, they left their underwear on for now, and simply played. Kissed and licked and teased. Fingers stroked bare skin, tweaked nipples, and memorized dips and valleys of muscles.

Eventually, the futon was too small for the scope of their lovemaking, so they went into the bedroom. Then the underwear came off. Derrick got a condom and lube and put them on a pillow. Slater eyed the condom, seeming as nervous as he was eager to do this. To share this experience with Derrick.

No matter what happened tomorrow, they would always have this moment.

And Derrick planned to make it last. Make it so good Slater wouldn't want to leave. "Hands and knees, middle of the bed."

Slater complied, showing off a taut, muscled ass Derrick wanted to bite all over. It was a new view he stood back and enjoyed a beat before climbing onto the bed behind Slater. "You ever been rimmed, cowboy?"

"It's not really my thing. Are you sure you want to— holy shit."

Derrick hadn't let him finish answering the question before he pulled Slater's cheeks apart and licked at his hole. This wasn't something he did often, so Derrick wanted to make it last. And make Slater fall apart for him. He listened to the noises and words Slater dropped as he savored the man's entrance with both fingers and his tongue. The scent and taste made Derrick harder and he resisted stroking himself. This was about pleasing Slater.

Slater bucked and jerked his hips, fingers clawed at the sheet, and a fine sheen of perspiration dotted his back. Derrick snagged the lube with his right hand while his left index finger rubbed at the wet muscle. Snapped the cap and drizzled lube over Slater's entrance. Pushed it slowly inside while Slater panted and moaned.

"You doing okay?" Derrick asked.

"Great, oh, fuck. Go slow."

"I've got you, babe. Relax and feel it."

"Trust me, Tiger, I fucking feel it." The laughter prompted Derrick to nudge in deeper. A gentle glide so Slater could adapt to the new sensations battering his body from his most sensitive places.

Derrick squeezed Slater's balls, then the root of his cock. "It's okay if you lose this during penetration. Not all guys can keep it up."

"I know. More."

Derrick gave him more but took his time, using his thumb instead of his index. Giving Slater a little more stretch, more sensation. "You ever finger yourself?"

"No."

"Ever had a prostate massage?"

Slater glanced over his shoulder with wide eyes the

instant Derrick curled his thumb down. Pressed on Slater's gland. Slater threw back his head and moaned, over and over, and Derrick worked his prostate. He tormented Slater until a line of clear fluid oozed from the tip of his straining cock.

"You're going to make me come," Slater warned. Derrick pulled out so Slater didn't blast off before the main event, and he wasn't prepared for the way Slater rolled and lunged, knocking Derrick over onto his back. Derrick stilled and let Slater take over, incredibly curious what the older man would do.

Slater adjusted until he was kneeling over Derrick's groin, knees on either side of his hips, and he peered down like Derrick was an ice cream sundae he wasn't sure how to attack first. The cherry? The whipped cream? Dig right in and get a taste of it all? He lazily jacked Derrick's dick as he pondered his next move.

"Whatever you want," Derrick said.

Those words seemed to unstick Slater's gears. He reached for the condom and rolled it down Derrick's length, then smeared on lube. Derrick put a steadying hand on his hip. "You sure you're ready?" he asked.

"Yes." Slater inched his knees forward to line up his hole with Derrick's dick, which he held tight at the base. "I need you in me, Tiger. Now."

"Oh, yeah."

Derrick gripped both of Slater's hips to help balance him as Slater lowered himself with agonizing slowness. Pressure against his cockhead. So tight and hot, and holy shit he wasn't going to go in. Up and down, Slater worked his body, his face a study of serenity and lust. And of absolute trust. This was often the best position for first-timers, so they could control the penetration, but a flash of pain in Slater's eyes had Derrick moving him up and off, so they were both sitting on the bed.

"Sorry, it wasn't my ass," Slater said. "My ankle didn't like that position."

"Okay. Well, we can try doggie-style if you keep your ankle bent the right way."

"Can we try on our sides?"

"Definitely." Derrick took his mouth's proximity and kissed Slater again, loving that simple thing so much. "I just want you to feel good."

"It did feel good. Intense but good."

"I'm glad." So glad to give his boyfriend the pleasure he desired.

They rolled onto their right sides and Derrick spooned up behind Slater. Lifted Slater's left leg up and draped it around Derrick's legs, opening Slater up to him. Giving Derrick more room to move. He lined up again and pushed. Slater bore against him, and again, the intensity of it worried Derrick he hadn't stretched Slater enough. And then his cockhead popped inside on a blast of pleasure, and Slater let out an impressive string of cuss words.

"Holy fucking hell, wow," Slater panted. "Oh, God, more. I think."

"Take a second, cowboy, not everyone rides fast the first time."

Slater snorted and reached back to pinch Derrick's ass. "Said like a true Clean Slate horseman."

"You trying to get me to apply for a job there?"

"Well, the horse rescue is nonprofit and that's your specialty, but what I'd really like right now is more of your dick in me."

"Yes, sir." Inch by torturous inch, Derrick's cock

disappeared inside Slater's ass. He'd pull back before pressing in, teasing Slater's entrance, revving him up for when Derrick was ready to go faster. This wasn't going to be a fast, hard fuck. Oh, no, Derrick planned to take his time and truly make love to Slater's body.

He stroked Slater's stomach and thighs, bypassing his groin simply to tease, and he'd never felt closer to the man he'd fallen for. Never been more sure of their place in each other's lives.

Please, tell me this means you'll stay.

As Slater's body adjusted to the glide of Derrick's cock, Derrick set a steady pace, rocking his hips, giving them both pleasure without either of them taking off. He wasn't in a good position to nail Slater's prostate like this, and that was okay. Meant he'd last longer. Derrick bit and licked what he could of Slater's neck and shoulder, loving the way Slater bucked and shivered every single time.

"Fuck, Tiger, feels good," Slater slurred, a bit drunk on the sensations buffeting his body. "So fucking good. Unf."

"Good. You are so gorgeous. So responsive." *So mine.*

They moved together, existing beyond time in a place where only their two bodies existed. The slip and slide of this dance as old as the earth, moving as one to a shared climax Derrick wanted and feared. He didn't want this existence to end. Everything was too much, too wonderful and too fucking fragile. But nothing perfect could last forever. His orgasm winked too damned close, and Derrick stopped moving. He reached around to jack Slater's cock, needing Slater to go over first.

And he did on a long shout, his body clenching tight around Derrick's dick, and that was it. Derrick snapped his hips and pumped into the condom, his entire body trembling from the force of his release. Slater was shaking, too. Derrick pulled his cock out and tugged Slater close to his chest, arms tight around his boyfriend's waist. Nose pressed into his neck, tickled by his too-long hair.

They breathed and held tight, and Derrick had no idea what to say. He'd never experienced anything like this before, and he hoped Slater was having similar thoughts. They had truly, passionately made love, and Derrick had never been more content or sated in his life. More eager to have this always.

I love you. Stay with me.

The words danced on the tip of his tongue, but sweaty and tired after sex was never the best time to utter them. Slater was completely boneless so Derrick got up, fetched a washcloth and towel, and cleaned him up. He washed himself in the bathroom before returning to bed and curling up around Slater. Covering them with the sheet and blanket. They shared a single pillow for the first time, and Derrick fell asleep positive everything would be okay.

Slater was still asleep when his Monday morning alarm went off, so he kissed his boyfriend's cheek once before going about his day. The two texts he sent went unanswered, and as quitting time drew near, Derrick's anxiety rose. A call went unanswered. He drove home in a state of agitation, only to find the lobby empty. Their apartment was dark and quiet.

Slater's totes were gone, as were his clothes and suitcase. All traces of the man, besides the ugly green stool and folding table, were gone.

Slater was gone.

Chapter Eighteen

Derrick searched the entire apartment a second time, but all he found were empty drawers and hangers, and space where the art supplies should have been. As he stared around, a hole opened inside Derrick's heart and his chest began to ache. Another call to Slater's phone went directly to voice mail.

Someone knocked, and he flew to the door, stupidly hoping Slater had forgotten his key. Dez stood on the fuzzy frog rug with a sad expression and an envelope in her hands. "He asked me to give you this," she said.

Derrick took the envelope with trembling fingers and wandered to the dinette set. Sat before his knees gave out, vaguely aware of Dez hovering near the doorway. It wasn't sealed, and he felt the shape of two keys before they tumbled onto the table. Apartment and main house keys. A folded letter came out, too, written on a page of that grid paper Slater used for his patterns.

Dear Derrick—

Now that our arrangement has come to an end, it's time we both move on with a fresh start. I have no regrets about the time we spent together this summer, and they will always be among my fondest memories. I've also loved getting to know your family, and I regret any pain our "breakup" will cause them. Feel free to tell them any story you want for why I left. I'll go along with it.

I'm going to be traveling for a while, so I can figure out what I truly want. If it's the ranch or something else. In the meantime, I left you one final gift under your pillow. If you don't find it useful, please pass it along to someone else who might.

Be well, Tiger.

—Slater

"I can't believe he left." Derrick dropped the letter onto the table. "Do you know where he went?"

"No." Dez inched closer, as sad as he'd ever seen her. "He came over a few hours ago and asked if I'd give you that letter, and if I'd store his supplies for him. I tried to get him to talk to me, to talk to you, but he was determined to bug out and do it his way."

"Why didn't you call me?"

"He asked me not to."

"I'm your friend, Dez."

"He's my friend, too. I didn't want to get in the middle of whatever happened between you two. He said you guys didn't fight, but that was it."

We did the exact opposite of fight last night.

"I love him," Derrick said, the words finally falling from his tongue and to the wrong damned person. "I love him and he left."

"Did you ever tell Slater that?"

"No." Slater hadn't said it, either, and the fact that he

walked away showed he didn't feel the same. That he could simply pack up his shit and leave without talking to Derrick first spoke volumes. And yet... Derrick had seen the emotions in Slater's eyes. Felt it in every single action and kiss and touch last night.

The note said he'd left a final gift.

Derrick bolted into the bedroom and threw his pillow across the room. A piece of folded tissue lay on the sheet. He unwrapped a cloth bookmark with a carefully stitched border done in pink, lavender and blue. The bisexual flag colors. And stitched in the center in blue were the words "I Fucking Love You."

His heart squeezed. "I don't understand."

Dez appeared by his elbow. "He wouldn't tell me that was for you, but I had an idea. It was the only way he knew how to say it, I think."

"Then why didn't he wait and give it to me himself? If he'd stayed and we'd both admitted our feelings, he wouldn't have had to leave."

"Are you sure?" She tugged at his arm until they sat together on the bed, and she kept tight hold of his hand. "I didn't read the letter, but I got the sense that wherever he went, it's what he truly needs right now. He doesn't say it a lot, but he's conflicted about where he's supposed to be." She bit her bottom lip. "I also have a confession to make."

"Oh, God."

"It's nothing bad. I helped Slater set up an online storefront, and he's been selling not only his patterns, but also a few finished pieces. It isn't enough to pay rent or anything, but he's actively growing a business. Or he was. After he left, I checked and everything is delisted right now."

Derrick gaped at Dez, shocked by the secret Slater had been keeping from him, but also so fucking proud of Slater he couldn't stand it. Slater had turned a hobby into something that made him actual money? "Why? Why the storefront?"

"I think he was trying to see if there's another path for him in life. A path that allows him to stay here, rather than going back to Clean Slate. He told me about his status as a felon and how hard it can be to get good, legit jobs with that millstone around your neck. And I think he likes being his own boss. I know I do."

He rubbed a finger over the word *Love* on the bookmark. *If you don't find it useful, please pass it along to someone else who might.*

If you don't love me, you don't have to keep this gift.

His eyes prickled with bitter tears. He loved the bookmark, loved the man who'd made it, and he wasn't giving it away. Ever. He also wasn't going to chase a man who was hell-bent on running away to find himself. Derrick had more pride than that. If Slater called or came back, they'd talk. Figure shit out like the adults they were.

He tugged his phone out of his pocket and sent Slater another text: Wherever you are, please be safe. I'm here when you're ready to talk.

Part of him wanted to sign off with *I love you* but he wouldn't say it for the first time in text. One day he'd say it to Slater's face.

He hoped.

As much as Slater had wanted to feel the wind on his face and the vibrations through his body by riding his motorcycle north, his foot wasn't strong enough and the thing was still at the ranch. Plus, his suitcase. So he'd hopped on a bus to Sacramento with plans for Kim to pick him up at the station. She and Dad were happy to have him for as long as he needed to stay. He was somewhat disappointed Rachel wasn't home. She was spending a few days at the beach with some high school friends and would be home Wednesday afternoon. Her last chance to "chill out" as Kim put it, before the craze of college life.

He couldn't begrudge her one more vacation before orientation began on Friday.

Kim helped him settle into the guest room, then asked if he wanted anything special for dinner. He didn't. Mostly he wanted to wallow, so he went into the backyard and sat in an ancient folding chair with a glass of lemonade.

Leaving the way he had would hurt Derrick's feelings, and he regretted that, but it had to be done. This was what they'd agreed upon months ago, and Slater was seeing it through. Leaving like he said he would when his foot was better. And maybe he wasn't one hundred percent yet, but he was getting there. His body was almost fully healed. Now he had to deal with his heart.

Last night...he had no words to describe how it had felt. To be so loved and adored and taken care of, in both body and spirit, by another person. They had well and truly made love, and Slater missed the sensation of Derrick moving inside of him. Filling him so completely. Drawing him to the most incredible climax of his life.

Was Derrick truly his future, though? Was the ranch? Somewhere else?

When Dad got home from work, he didn't press Slater for details. Slater simply said they'd needed some time apart, and his parents accepted it. Derrick's eve-

ning text made him smile. He'd found the bookmark.
Slater had debated long and hard over leaving it or not,
but he'd made it for Derrick and no one else. Hopefully,
Derrick understood that while Slater had to leave, he
wasn't giving up on them. He was doing this *for* them.

Tuesday passed slowly. Slater was too used to working alongside Dez, and the quiet house was too empty.
He kept the TV on as a distraction, but he'd lost some
of his creative spark, and his grid paper stayed blank.

He needed to talk to someone about this, but he hated
the idea of admitting his relationship with Derrick had
started as a sham. That they'd put on a show and then
real feelings got in the way of a simple ending.

Sophie texted him that night: Derrick said you guys are
taking a break. If you need to talk, call me, okay? Hugs.

The message was sweet but he didn't want to talk
about this with Sophie. Dez was who he usually talked
to about things that were bothering him, but she was
also too invested in his and Derrick's relationship.
When Mack called him Wednesday morning about
making Saturday evening plans, Slater found himself
in the position to either lie to his friend, or tell the truth.

He picked a half-truth. "I can't this weekend, I'm out
of town visiting my family," Slater said.

"Ah, no problem. How's your ankle?"

"Almost like new. Won't be long now."

"Good to hear it. You and Derrick have fun with
your family."

"Thanks. Bye, Mack." He hadn't really lied, he simply hadn't corrected Mack's assumption that Derrick
was with him.

Rachel was surprised and delighted to see him when
she came home that afternoon. She was also an astute ob-

server and asked if he wanted to go someplace and talk. They were home alone, but Slater needed out of the house for a while, so they ended up in a nearby park with soft drinks they'd picked up at a convenience store on the way over. She led him to a bench under a tree and they sat.

"How come Derrick isn't here?" she asked.

"Because the terms of our deal were up and it was time for me to go." He couldn't lie to her. Not ever. Not about this.

"Deal? What deal?"

Slater explained it all, from the truth of how he met Derrick to the agreement they'd made in the hospital. How much chemistry they'd shared and how they'd become the perfect platonic couple. And then not so platonic. That last weekend had been his final appearance as the doting boyfriend, and how conflicted he was about his feelings for Derrick.

Rachel listened without interrupting, absorbing the information with a gentle smile.

"We were never in a real relationship, and I am so sorry for how we fooled you and everyone else," he said. "It was selfish. We were both selfish."

"It was a little selfish," she said after a moment of silence. "But I also understand both of your motivations. You weren't trying to hurt anyone."

"Right."

"I do, however, disagree you weren't in a real relationship. When I first met Derrick, I could see he had feelings for you. Everyone in the room could, except you two, apparently. Nothing about how you two act around each other is fake. Saying it was just an arrangement is a cop-out so you could run away, instead of facing your feelings for the guy."

"I love him. But my living there was always meant to be temporary. I have a job waiting for me at the ranch. Judson's held it for me for months. I can't repay his generosity by quitting."

She tilted her head in an assessing way. "So you're going to dump Derrick and go back to your job out of loyalty to your boss?"

"I…" Slater hadn't consciously made that choice, no.

"I can tell how much you love the ranch when you talk about it. But I can also tell how much you love Derrick. Why do you have to choose? Can't you guys do long distance?"

"We never really discussed it as an option for us. We've both been cheated on in the past, and being apart from your partner for so long isn't easy. I mean, I work with a guy who makes long distance work and he's married, but I don't know if I could handle only being able to see Derrick one night a week. I already miss him so much, and it's only been three days since I last saw him."

Saw him, hugged him, kissed him, made love to him.

Slater did not regret his choice to give his mouth and body to Derrick. Not one bit. But it had also given him a taste of the other man he craved and wanted back.

"Do you want to go back to the ranch, Dad?" she asked. "Like, truly want and desire to return to that life?"

"I don't know, and that's the truth. That's why I'm here. The ranch gave me something I needed." He sipped his soda without tasting it. "I was pretty messed up when I got out of prison. I saw stuff in there that gave me nightmares, and I spent a lot of time trying not to be noticed. Made choices I had to live with. And I was angry at myself when you wouldn't come near me, because my choices made that happen."

"I'm sorry about that."

"No, don't apologize." He angled to face her better, hating the sadness he'd put in her eyes. "I own what I did. You were just a kid when I went in, and five years is a long time not to see someone. I was angry and bitter when I got out, and I didn't know how to act around you. I hated that I scared you, which is why I left. I knew I needed to get my act together, become a man you'd be proud to call your dad. Clean Slate gave me that.

"That ranch gave me a stable job, a chance to work with other men like me who'd burned up their other chances. To be around horses and nature. Walking those trails helped me forget the walls of that prison cell and gave me space to exist. I lived around people who couldn't judge me for my mistakes because they didn't know. It was a safe place."

"Do you still need that safe place?" Rachel asked. "Because you are someone I'm proud of. You're nothing like the man I met when I was eleven. You've stepped out of your comfort zone. You fell in love, you learned needlepoint, and you have friends who care about you. If that life is what you want, don't give it up because you feel like you owe the ranch some sort of debt."

He studied the face of his little girl who spoke with so much wisdom his heart ached. He'd missed five years of her life, and he was grateful they now had their entire future to spend getting to know each other again. She'd forgiven him and wanted him in her life. Slater had to forgive himself and let go of his past. To look into the future and decide what he wanted.

I want to be happy. I deserve that.

But where was happy? Here, close to Rachel? Back in that big house with Derrick? The ranch?

"When did you get to be so smart?" Slater asked.

"After-school academic programs," she quipped. "Seriously, though, do you feel any better about this?"

"I do. You've given me a lot to think about, so thank you."

"You're welcome."

Slater hadn't made up his mind yet, but he sat there and enjoyed the simplicity of an afternoon in the park with his daughter.

Derrick was going out of his goddamn mind missing Slater. Missing the man's smile, his voice, his crafts, his limp, the warmth of his body in bed next to Derrick. He missed coming home and seeing Slater in the foyer with Dez. Missed them eating vegan meals with Dez and Morgan. His body ached for one more hug. So when Conrad called Wednesday evening to ask if he and Slater had worked things out yet, Derrick let it all go.

He told his brother everything, and maybe over the phone wasn't fair, but he couldn't seem to stop his verbal diarrhea. The whole story from start to finish, with certain sexy bits left out, and he ended with a groan of frustration. Conrad's end of the line was silent.

"Bro?" Derrick said.

"I'll be right over with beer. Stay put."

"Not going anywhere."

Derrick ate a few pieces of Slater's leftover roast beef while he waited, because he hadn't eaten dinner and beer was about to get involved. The front doorbell buzzed, so Derrick hit the button to unlock it. Conrad didn't bother knocking on the apartment door, he barged right inside with a twelve-pack of longnecks and a bag of barbecue pork rinds. He deposited both on the green stool Derrick was using as a small coffee table, then wrapped Derrick up in a big hug.

The kind of hug Derrick desperately needed right now because nothing in his life made any sense. He squeezed Conrad's waist, and his baby brother let go.

Conrad's face was a study in surprise, worry and irritation. "Okay, first of all." Conrad smacked him upside the back of his head. "That's for lying to me about dating Slater when all this started."

Derrick flinched but he'd deserved it. "I'm sorry. I honestly figured on telling you the truth, because I didn't think you'd buy us dating."

"Yeah, well, you two obviously never saw how you each looked at the other. Sit and have a beer."

He followed orders, glad this brand was the twist-off kind because he wasn't in the mood to search for the bottle opener. Conrad allowed him a few long pulls of a beer and a handful of pork rinds—a rare treat because fried pork skin wasn't exactly good for his abs—before he said, "So your fake relationship became real, you fell for the guy, and he left you."

"In a nutshell, yup."

"Did you want him to leave?"

"No."

"Did you ask him to stay?"

"No."

Conrad head-smacked him again. "You are such an idiot."

"Thank you, that's helpful." He gulped down more beer. "Staying had to be Slater's choice, and he obviously wanted to go, but…" Derrick pulled his wallet out of his back pocket and removed the slightly bent bookmark from his billfold. "He made this for me and left it here."

Conrad snorted as he studied the bookmark. "Okay, so you're both in love with each other. Congrats, by the way. So why aren't you together?"

"I don't know. In his note, he said he needed to figure out what he really wanted, so I'm giving him the space to do that."

"Why do you think he's doing that?"

"Because he's conflicted, duh. He loves Clean Slate but I also think he loves it here, too, and he isn't sure about the right next step."

"Can he go back to work and you guys do things long-distance? It works for Colt and Avery at Clean Slate."

"I don't know if I could. I was already in one long-distance relationship and got cheated on."

"Slater doesn't strike me as that kind of guy."

Derrick finished his first beer and reached for another. "Same. It's just fear, I guess. My own personal issue."

"You, big brother, have never been afraid of anything in my life. You run headfirst toward what you want, and if what you want is Slater, don't let him get away. If he wants the ranch and you want him? You'll make long distance work. If he decides he wants to break up for real and done? You'll grieve and then you'll move on. You'll fall in love again."

I don't want to fall in love with anyone else. I want Slater. I choose him.

And that wouldn't matter if Slater didn't choose him back.

They ate and drank in silence for a while, until Conrad said, "Let me put another perspective on this for you."

"Go for it." Derrick's own wasn't doing him any good.

"You said Slater left so he could figure out what he truly wants. Well, think about how you guys got together. You lived together right from the start, when most people date first. What if Slater needs to get away for a while so that coming back is his choice, and not simply that he was already here and just stayed put. Does that make sense?"

"Yeah." It made perfect sense, actually. Slater liked having choices. He'd made the choice to enter into their fake boyfriend arrangement, and he'd made the choice to walk away. If his next choice was to come home to Derrick, he'd welcome the big cowboy with open arms. If not... Derrick didn't want to think about "if not."

"Okay, good. He's got a good reason for wanting space. But as your brother, can I give him a hard time about how much he's stressing you out right now?"

"Be my guest. After we've made up and everything is good again."

It has to be good again, please.

After having Kendall "Slater" Stamos in his life for the last four months, Derrick couldn't imagine his future without the man in it.

Dropping Rachel off at the CSUS campus for late registration and orientation was an incredibly bittersweet moment for Slater and his parents. Sure, it wasn't as huge as dropping her off at a dorm five states away but whatever. She was living at home to save money, so registration was his moment. Rachel drove with Slater in the front seat, and Dad and Kim in the back, because she wanted it that way.

The campus was busy and sprawling but she found

the right building and double-parked. "Call me when you're ready to be picked up," Slater said.

"I will, I promise." She leaned over the console to hug him. "See you in a while."

"Be safe."

Dad replaced Rachel in the driver's seat, and Slater watched his girl disappear into the crowd. College. She was starting college in just a few more weeks.

"Makes you feel old, doesn't it?" Dad asked as he eased back into traffic. "Watching her go off like that."

"It really does. You guys did a hell of a job raising her."

"It was our pleasure," Kim said. "I was never able to have kids of my own, so Rachel was always a blessing to us. So were you, Ken, even during the hard times."

"Thank you."

He watched the city go by as Dad drove them back to the house, at war with himself and his own next steps. Derrick hadn't tried calling or texting since Monday, and while it hurt a little, he appreciated that Derrick was giving him space. But if Derrick truly wanted Slater there, wouldn't he have tried to reach out? Convince him to come home?

No, that life had been a beautiful dream he'd treasure forever. But it was time to move on. Hang up his needle and thread, and go back to the life he knew at the ranch. The job that had been so thoughtfully saved for him, the familiar open spaces, new tourists every week, and the men he'd gotten to know so well during these last few months of Saturday outings.

As soon as Slater got back to the house, he went into the guest room and called Judson.

Chapter Nineteen

Slater tried easing back into life at Clean Slate Ranch. He truly did try. Judson had insisted on light duty for a few more weeks, which meant tacking horses but no riding, and no strenuous labor that could damage the progress he'd made with his ankle. That didn't bother him. He liked rooming with Hugo again. He enjoyed Patrice's amazing cooking.

But he missed Derrick. And Dez and Morgan and the Thompson twins, and Derrick's family. Few people questioned him being back, and when someone did he just said that he and Derrick were working on things. Which was a flat lie because they weren't working on anything. But Derrick obviously hadn't told anyone they'd broken up, or Wes would have spread it all over Garrett and Bentley by now.

It had to mean something.

The ranch, though? It didn't mean as much to Slater as it once had. He still loved the views and the quiet and the people here, doing good work. But the land had also lost the magic it once held. Magic he now found in designing something with Dez, or in sharing a simple, home-cooked meal with Derrick. Playing cards with George. Holding little Mia.

How had his entire view of life changed in only a few months?

When he wondered that, Rachel's words came back to him. Did he still need this safe place, or could he be brave and try living a new life? Could he reach for what he truly wanted?

He'd only been back for five full days and was in the barn, polishing saddles in the tack room, when Mack walked in. Slater startled, surprised to see the guy on a Saturday afternoon. "Shouldn't you be at the ghost town?" Slater asked.

"They can handle things without me for an hour or two." Mack perched his butt on the edge of the work table. "So Derrick said something to Sophie, who said something to Wes, who told it all to me, and everyone wanted me to play the middleman here."

Slater groaned. "Great." He put down the rag he was using and folded his arms. "What?"

"First off, no one's mad you two lied about dating when you first moved into Derrick's place. Your reasons are your business. But man, you two have something. The more time me, Reyes, Colt and the other guys spent with you two? Something real is there. And Reyes doesn't think you're happy here."

"He doesn't?"

"No. He's head cowboy, and it's his job to pay attention to you guys. And as much as I know Judson would hate to lose a good employee, it's okay to move on. Find what does make you happy. Find it and hold on tight."

"Derrick makes me happy." Slater closed his eyes briefly. "He makes me so happy, but damn it, Mack, he didn't ask me to stay. I left him a fucking bookmark

I made that said I love you, and he didn't even call to say it back. I just… I don't know."

"You know, you guys remind me a bit of me and Wes. We were supposed to be a fling, nothing serious, and then feelings got involved. I avoided him so I didn't get hurt, and we both got hurt anyway. A big misunderstanding kept us apart for three weeks before our friends intervened, and I have never been happier in my life than I am right now. And grateful to Colt and Sophie for interfering."

"So what's this? You interfering?"

"Nope. Just a concerned friend making a few observations. Feel free to take 'em to heart or ignore 'em. But I guess you gotta ask yourself why are you really here? Because it's where you truly want to be? Or because you're afraid of trying something new?" With a tip of his hat, Mack left the tack room.

Slater stared at the empty doorway, tangled up and confused. Mack had given him a similar version of Rachel's comments and observations. Had Slater truly come back here to hide? He hadn't been asked to stay but that didn't mean Derrick didn't want him there, right? Was it really as simple as a misunderstanding because they couldn't just fucking say the right thing to each other?

Maybe.

It was two o'clock on Saturday, and when the guests departed at three, he was technically off the clock until tomorrow. His bike could get him to Derrick's place in under an hour if he gunned it. He should probably call first, but Slater liked the idea of showing up on Derrick's doorstep. Hell, he could even buzz Dez to let him in and sweeten the surprise.

Slater still loved the ranch, but it wasn't his home anymore. Home was with Derrick Massey. Time to go say as much and take his chances.

His ankle ached a bit by the time Slater parked his motorcycle on the street outside the house, but he didn't care. Well worth it to be home again. He trod up the familiar path and hit the buzzer for Dez and Morgan's unit. Silence. He tried again to no answer. On a wing and a prayer, he buzzed the Thompson place upstairs.

"Hello?" one of the twins said.

"Hey, it's Slater from downstairs. Can't find my key. Can you buzz me in?"

"Yeah."

The front door unlocked, and Slater went inside, surprised by the thundering of feet down the right staircase. George appeared, his expression wary and upset. "Where have you been, dude? You just up and disappeared."

"I'm sorry, I had to deal with some things."

George shocked the hell out of him by hugging Slater briefly. "Well, I'm glad you're back. The house isn't the same without you."

Regret squeezed Slater's chest tight. He hadn't gone upstairs and said goodbye to the Thompsons, and he'd hurt George's feelings without meaning to. "I'm sorry I didn't talk to you guys before I left. But I'm here now, and I really want to surprise Derrick."

"Good luck with that."

"Huh?"

"He isn't here. I was taking the trash out earlier when I saw him getting into a car with Morgan and Dez. Not sure where they went."

Well shit, there goes my grand plan.

"Don't you have your key?" George asked.

"Misplaced it. Damn it."

"Maybe the owner can let you into the apartment?"

"Nah, it's fine. I'll just hang here in the foyer for a while. They probably went out for an early dinner or something."

"Probably. Cool. Well, I'm glad you're home."

"Thanks, George."

George smiled and went back upstairs. Slater watched him go, his mind wandering a bit toward Rachel. Wondering if the pair would get along or not. George was a nice guy, but Slater also wasn't about to be the dad who tried to set his daughter up with nice guys. Or nice girls, if she swung that way. Slater didn't care, as long as she achieved the happy life she deserved. Without a project to work on, he played a word game on his phone for a while to pass time. Five o'clock came and went, and his own stomach began aching for dinner. He'd had a roast beef sandwich and big dill pickle for lunch, but that had been hours ago.

Text him and tell him you're here. Find out where he is.

Good old Stamos stubbornness set in, and he ordered a pizza for delivery instead. When it arrived, George came downstairs sniffing for food, so Slater shared with the kid. He only ate one slice and picked off everything but the veggies, but the skinny kid still ate. Slater was truly glad George had a brother to look out for him. He also gave the rest of the pizza to George, in case Orry wanted some whenever he got back from his current job.

The time was closing in on seven when Slater began regretting this plan. Derrick was obviously out for the evening. Coming here without announcing his arrival had been a stupid idea, and all he'd really done was waste his own time. Annoyed and defeated, he left the house and headed for his bike. Unlocked the helmet and put it on. The street was busy enough that he didn't pay attention to the occasional rumble of a car engine as it passed or parked.

Time to go back to the life he should have stayed in.

"Slater?"

Surprise and delight shot up his spine, and Slater twisted his upper body around. Derrick stood on the sidewalk a few dozen feet away, near Morgan's parked car. His own look of shock melted into delight. "Fuck, you're here," Derrick said.

Slater tugged off the helmet and climbed off his bike, but he didn't approach. "Hey."

"I went to find you."

Well, knock him over with a goddamn feather. "You did what?"

Derrick took three long strides forward. "We drove to Clean Slate so I could find you, but you weren't in your cabin, and Reyes said he saw you take off on your bike. I didn't think you'd come here."

"This is my home." The instant the words passed Slater's lips, he felt the truth of them deep in his bones. "I missed this place. I missed you, too. A lot."

Three more long strides left only the motorcycle and a bit of sidewalk between them. "I love you." Derrick's brown eyes were watery but his expression was firm. "I love you and I'm sorry I didn't say it sooner. I want you in my home, Kendall Stamos. My home, my life, my bed, my everything. I fucking love you."

Slater's heart trilled with joy. "I fucking love you, too, Derrick Massey. I have for a while, I just…"

"I know. Same."

The last of his restraint broke, and Slater circled the bike so he could throw himself into Derrick's strong, capable arms. To kiss the man who'd stolen his heart. The man who was his future. Period. They kissed and laughed, and after a few minutes, Dez and Morgan joined them. Their quartet eventually made it into the house foyer. Derrick and Slater cuddled together on the love seat, while their two friends sat in opposite chairs.

"Did you find what you were looking for?" Derrick asked.

"I wasn't really looking for a specific thing," Slater replied. "I had a great talk with Rachel about a lot of stuff. The past. Looking forward. But I was too scared of another big change, so I went back to the ranch. But it was different. I'm different. It wasn't the comfortable fit it used to be. And I missed you like crazy, Tiger. I'm ready to take a chance on us."

"Me, too." Derrick nuzzled Slater's nose with his. "I wanted to give you the space you asked for, but I can't live without you. I totally get that you had to make living here your choice, not just a random circumstance you landed in, but I missed you so fucking bad. Dez and Morgan basically kidnapped me into driving to the ranch to find you."

"And I was here, looking for you." Slater laughed against Derrick's neck. "What a pair we are, huh?"

"You're both adorable," Dez said. "And I am so damned happy you're back together. You are back together, right?"

"Not back together, not exactly," Derrick said. "This is us starting over. From scratch. No arrangements, no rules, just two guys who love each other and want to be in each other's life."

"Sounds good to me," Slater replied. "And if it helps, Rachel knows the whole truth, and she's totally rooting for us."

"Good. I'm rooting for us, too. And I know I'm leery about long distance but if you want to keep working at the ranch, I'll deal. I won't ever make you quit a job you love for me."

"I haven't really decided about that. Yes, I'd feel rotten leaving a job that Judson held for me for months, but like I said before, the ranch feels different now. I don't know if I could make a career out of selling needlepoint patterns, but I do love it." Slater stiffened when he realized what he'd said.

"It's okay," Dez said. "I told Derrick all about it. It's not huge money yet, but it could be. You are talented."

"Thank you." To Derrick, he added, "I'm sorry I didn't tell you about the storefront sooner. I was scared of failing in front of you."

"You don't have to be scared of that ever again." Derrick kissed his forehead. "Flaws and all, failures and all, you're perfect in my eyes. I was jaded and you made me believe. I was lonely and you made me whole. I resisted but you broke through. I love you and I want you to stay. Please, stay."

"Okay." Slater did not want to be anywhere else in the world right now. Everything wasn't magically made perfect, and they still had a lot of things to discuss, but in this moment, he was at peace. He'd chosen to come back and stay. Derrick wanted him and loved him.

Everything else was details.

Exactly three weeks later, Derrick made the bumpy drive up the long path to Clean Slate Ranch to pick up his boyfriend's stuff. Not seeing Slater in person every day had been an exercise in restraint, but they'd had phone calls, texts and Skype to help pass the time apart. And now, Slater was coming home to stay. After some soul-searching and long conversations with Derrick and Mack, Slater had put in his two weeks' notice.

Today had been Slater's last day as an employee of the ranch.

Derrick parked near the guesthouse a little after four, and he wasn't surprised to find a bunch of the hands lounging on its wide front porch, Slater included. Patrice was hosting a small going away party for Slater at four-thirty. Slater hadn't wanted the fuss, but no one could say no to Patrice when she made up her mind about something.

Mack was there, sans Wes, who was off filming a TV guest spot again. Derrick couldn't remember the show. Reyes, Robin, Colt and Avery were there, too, as well as Hugo, Ernie and Quentin. Judson and Arthur exited the main house at almost the same time Derrick got out of his car.

Slater trotted right down the porch stairs and kissed him soundly. "Hey, Tiger."

"Hey back. You excited?"

"Yup. A little nervous, too, but this is the right decision. Besides, it's not like we'll never be back to visit."

"True."

Judson approached and shook Derrick's hand. "Not sure if I should hug you for your happiness or throttle you for taking away one of my best horsemen."

"Does it help if I promise to take good care of him?" Derrick replied with a grin. "I promise no more falling off mountains."

"Hard to find a decent mountain out there in the city."

"Good point."

Their group went into the guesthouse, straight to the dining room where Patrice had a white-frosted sheet cake decorated with one of those edible photos of Mischief, the horse Slater preferred to ride on. Derrick imagined he'd already spent some time in the barn saying goodbye to the mare.

Derrick also felt perfectly at ease here with these men, plus Patrice. Maybe it was from all those Saturday night visits this past summer, but Derrick had been folded into the group, despite not being all that great with a horse. He was part of the Clean Slate family, too, just like Slater was part of the Massey family. For someone who'd been a loner five months ago, Slater had more family than he knew what to do with.

He met Slater's eyes and smiled. Slater grinned right back, then winked.

Slater hadn't wanted the fuss of a party, but he was mighty glad his friends here cared enough to send him off properly. Today had been bittersweet as he watched the final crop of guests load up onto the wagon for delivery to their cars. As he sorted blankets and saddles in the tack room and visited with the horses one more time. Packed up his things in the cabin. Walked the dusty trail from cabin row with his suitcase in hand for the very last time as an employee of the ranch.

Bittersweet and also scarily exciting.

"Well, we all know why we're here," Judson said, which quieted down the room. "Slater is moving on to the next stage of his life, and we're all here to wish him well. We'll miss you, Slater, but we're happy that you've found something new and exciting for your future."

"Thank you," Slater said. His throat swelled with emotion and made it hard to talk. "It's been a true pleasure working here these last couple of years. I love this land, and I've loved working with everyone in this room." He looked directly at Arthur. "Thank you for taking a chance on me when you heard my story. I can never repay that kindness."

"Psh." Arthur waved a gnarled hand in the air. "You repay my kindness by living your very best life, you hear me?"

"I will, I promise." Starting his life over again at thirty-five wasn't going to be easy for him, but he had a dedicated boyfriend, and he had Rachel. With them by his side, he could do anything.

Judson led the room in a round of "For He's a Jolly Good Fellow," which made Slater blush, and then Patrice started slicing up the cake.

"So you're really going all-in with this crafting thing, huh?" Hugo asked Slater while they stood around and ate cake.

"Yup, going all in." Slater had reopened his storefront and was still selling patterns. He'd worked on a few projects in his evenings, but he was excited to get back to his normal routine with his own craft spaces, and his afternoons spent with Dez. "I don't expect to make thousands right away, but I've got a good amount in my savings account, so I can help with expenses. And I'm looking at some part-time work."

Orry had helped him out quite a bit with that, researching the kinds of jobs that gave Slater flexible hours and wouldn't hold his record against him. Until

Orry told him, Slater hadn't realized California had strict laws about employers not asking for direct conviction information on applications. Even if Slater marked down he'd been convicted of a felony, the person interviewing him could not, by law, ask what he'd been convicted for. It was complex and kind of made Slater's head hurt, but it made him hopeful for future employment—especially with the glowing recommendations Judson and Mack had already written for him.

He'd been honest with the Thompson twins last weekend about his record, and while George had been briefly spooked by it, they knew the man he was today. Not the man who'd gone to prison for a crime he was very much guilty of committing.

"I think it's super cool," Colt said. "Finding a new passion for something and creating your own business. Plus, someone finally took that guy off the market." He jacked his thumb at Derrick.

Derrick swatted at Colt's shoulder. "Ha ha. You had your chance and you blew it."

"Or didn't blow it, so to speak," Slater joked.

Next to Colt, Avery nearly choked on a bite of cake. Hugo saved the day by handing Avery a glass of soda to sip. "Please don't kill my husband," Colt said to Slater. "I'd like to at least make it to our one-year anniversary."

"I couldn't help it, the joke was too perfect."

"So." Colt scanned the room with an impish smile. "Who do you think's the next one here to find true love?"

"Not a clue, but I'm pretty sure none of us were looking for it when we found it." Slater reached out to squeeze Derrick's hand. "Life just put us in the right place at the right time."

"Like a garage gym at three in the morning?" Derrick replied.

"Exactly."

They talked and ate for a while longer, until some of the guys headed out for their evening off and whatever plans they had. Judson, Arthur and Patrice both wished him well on their way to other duties. Mack shook his hand before heading back up to close down the ghost town. Colt and Avery returned to cabin row. Reyes and Hugo followed Derrick and Slater out to the porch. Derrick collected Slater's suitcase and put it in the trunk.

"You were a great roommate," Hugo said, his eyes bright, and if the kid started to cry, Slater would, too. "I'm glad we got to be friends, Slater."

"Same on both counts, kid." Slater allowed a brief hug, then ruffled Hugo's hair. "You take good care of Mischief for me, yeah?"

"I will." Hugo wiped his eyes and headed for the barn.

With a lump in his throat, Slater turned to Reyes. While they weren't the best of friends, their experiences at the summit this spring had bonded them, and Slater would genuinely miss the man. "You keep this place running, or you'll answer to me."

Reyes nodded. "Don't be a stranger. You'll always have a place to stay here at Clean Slate. You're family."

"Thank you." He hugged Reyes tight. "Brother."

"Yeah."

Slater wiped at his own eyes as he walked to Derrick's car, which was already running for the AC, emotions pinballing all over the place. He was stoked for this new chapter of his life to begin, even while he was sad for the old life he was leaving behind. But he'd be back to see his friends. And they'd likely show up in the city for beer and darts.

It had been a long, hard ride to get here, and Slater had overcome some huge obstacles, but this was the right decision. This was the life he was meant to live. He was happy, he had his daughter back, and he was in love.

And with Derrick by his side, nothing was impossible.

* * * * *

Reviews are an invaluable tool when it comes to spreading the word about great reads. Please consider leaving an honest review for this or any of Carina Press's other titles that you've read on your favorite retailer or review site.

For more information about A.M. Arthur's books, please visit her website here: amarthur.blogspot.com.

Or like her on Facebook: www.Facebook.com/a.m.arthur.m.a.

Acknowledgments

First and foremost, a huge thank-you to my long-time editor Alissa Davis. It's hard to believe this is book number fourteen! I have been so blessed to work with you over the years. I have learned so much and grown as a writer because of you. *heart eyes*

Another big thank-you to all the readers who've enjoyed the Clean Slate Ranch books and have asked for more. Your dedication to these characters is why this book exists. Thanks to the entire Carina Press team for your support and constant professionalism. And special thanks to Brandilyn and Erin for answering my bazillion questions about broken ankles, casts and walking boots (Slater thanks you, too).

About the Author

A.M. Arthur was born and raised in the same kind of small town that she likes to write about, a stone's throw from both beach resorts and generational farmland. She's been creating stories in her head since she was a child and scribbling them down nearly as long, in a losing battle to make the fictional voices stop. She credits an early fascination with male friendships (bromance hadn't been coined yet back then) with her later discovery of and subsequent love affair with m/m romance stories. A.M. Arthur's work is available from Carina Press, SMP Swerve and Briggs-King Books.

When not exorcising the voices in her head, she toils away in a retail job that tests her patience and gives her lots of story fodder. She can also be found in her kitchen, pretending she's an amateur chef and trying to not poison herself or others with her cuisine experiments.

Contact her at am_arthur@yahoo.com with your cooking tips (or book comments). For updates, info and the occasional freebie, sign up for her free newsletter: vr2.verticalresponse.com/s/signupformynewsletter1649267441690.

Chapter One

The last time Jonas Ashcroft had taken money from someone and made change had been during a drunken game of Monopoly at the Delta Theta house sophomore year. Everyone was wasted enough that they didn't care Jonas was probably giving the wrong bills back half the time, and eventually they'd abandoned the game in favor of beer pong and more tequila shots.

Staring down the ancient cash register behind the main counter at All Saints Thrift Store was like facing off against an old enemy. Jonas and math did not get along. Never had.

The teenage girl with spiky hair who'd handed him a ten-dollar bill to pay for three T-shirts glared at him over the top of her cell phone, waiting for him to make change. The register told him that three shirts at two-fifty each was seven dollars and fifty cents. It didn't tell him what to give her back.

He knew this. He wasn't a total idiot, no matter what his father seemed to think. Two quarters made it eight. Two dollars made ten. Right?

The girl took the change he offered without remark, then fled the store with her bag, the overhead bell announcing her departure.

Jonas slammed the register drawer shut with clammy hands. First transaction down. He could survive a few more, until Aunt Doris got back and took over running the till. She'd shown him how to use it yesterday, and while it seemed pretty simple, he flat out sucked at math. Thank God his father hadn't insisted Jonas go for a business degree, because he'd have flunked out the first semester.

Not that it mattered. Junior year was less than a month old and instead of living it up with his frat buddies and getting the Communication Arts degree he desperately needed so he could get a real job and be independent, he was stuck working at his aunt and uncle's thrift store on a run-down side of Wilmington, Delaware. A shitty fate, and exactly what he deserved.

"I can't have your recklessness interfere with my chances at Congress," his father had said last week. "You need to learn some responsibility for once in your life." Angry words lobbed at him from behind his father's walnut desk, moments before Jonas was stuffed in a car and stranded here for the next nine months.

Jonas poked at the cash register. He had another hour until Aunt Doris returned. She and Uncle Raymond had driven out to some person's house to pick up a load of shit for the shop.

Or something. She might have mentioned books.

He had no idea how people made an actual living running a thrift store, much less one that donated some of its money to charity, but they'd been at it all Jonas's life. Probably why Jonas's own parents had little to do with them.

Appearances and all that crap.

The store itself was clean and organized and smelled

like some kind of floral incense. The merchandise was sectioned into departments. A pretty typical thrift store.

Like you know what a typical thrift store looks like. Yesterday was your first time in one, asshole.

His mother hadn't come from money, but his father had, and Jonas had never worked a day in his life until today.

They'd opened twenty minutes ago and so far he'd had one customer. Good thing he had his iPhone.

He pulled his earbuds out of his pocket and was about to turn up some music when a shadow fell over the front door. It opened with the ding of a metal bell, and his second ever customer stepped inside.

"Good morning—" The guy faltered, eyes going wide behind a pair of round, black-framed glasses. "Um, hi, person I don't know."

Jonas grunted a greeting, then decided Aunt Doris would give him that sad puppy look if she found out he was being rude to her customers. "Hi."

About Jonas's age and a few inches shorter, the maybe-customer let the door fall shut and slid his hands into the pockets of very loose, very worn jeans that hung low on narrow hips. "Doris isn't in this morning?"

Does it look like she's here? "No, she's out picking something up."

"Oh, okay. Did she happen to mention a basket of sheets for Tate?"

Jonas had no idea what any of that meant. "No."

"Okay, let's try this again. Hi, I'm Tate Dawson." He held out a hand.

"Jonas Ashcroft." Jonas took the guy's hand briefly. "I'm Doris's nephew."

"Oh, hey, cool. I've never seen you around before."

"That's because I've never been here before."

Tate opened and closed his mouth a few times, probably unsure how to proceed. Yeah, Jonas was kind of being a dick. He wanted the guy to do whatever he needed to do and leave so Jonas could turn on his music and hope this day ended as quickly as possible.

"Yeah, okay," Tate said. "Listen, I help run the homeless shelter across the street, and Doris was supposed to bring in a basket of sheets for me today."

Jonas stared.

Tate's hands went from his pockets to his hips. A line creased his forehead, and his cheeks pinked up. "Could you check the back room, maybe? Or should I look myself?"

"I'll check. Jesus."

"Tate, not Jesus, and thank you."

Jonas resisted rolling his eyes. He took his time strolling to the back of the shop, and then ducked through a beaded curtain doorway. The back room was neatly organized with dated shelves for new stock, empty hangers for clothes, cleaning supplies and a recycle bin for things they simply couldn't sell. He found a plastic laundry basket of folded sheets on one of the shelves with a piece of paper taped to it that said "Tate" in Aunt Doris's careful handwriting.

"Found it," he announced upon his return to the main room.

"Hope you didn't hurt yourself." Tate's words were soft, but they carried in the quiet store.

Jonas liked the snark. Made needling the guy more fun, and it gave him something more entertaining to do than stare at racks of used women's clothing. He carried the sheets to the counter and set the basket down. "Do you need some kind of receipt for these?"

"Nah, Doris was just doing me a favor."

"Why do you work at a homeless shelter?"

I need to get my brain-to-mouth filter checked.

Tate tilted his head, apparently not offended in the least. "Why *not* work at a homeless shelter? There are a lot of people these days with nowhere to go, especially teenagers."

Jonas glanced out the front window at the brick building across the street. "You get a lot of teens there?"

"I would hope so." Tate arched one eyebrow impressively high. "We're a homeless shelter for LGBT teenagers." Jonas's confusion must have been all over his face, because Tate sighed. "Gay teens. Gay, lesbian, trans, whatever end of the spectrum they identify on."

"I know what LGBT stands for. I didn't know there were enough of them that they needed their own homeless shelter."

"Where the hell did you crawl out of, a rock in Siberia? Gay teens make up almost forty percent of the homeless youth population in this country. Their asshole parents kick them out and a lot of them have nowhere to go except the streets. We may not be a big operation but we help as much as we can."

Jonas made a time-out gesture. "Okay, sorry, Christ. I just…" *I don't think about those issues because they don't directly affect my life.*

So, did working in an LGBT shelter mean Tate was gay?

Tate crossed his arms and settled his weight on one foot, his gaze roving over Jonas like he was studying him for a quiz later. "Let me guess. Rich boy. Privileged life. Great future ahead of you until you... What? Crashed your BMW into a tree while driving drunk? Knocked up a sorority girl and you're being punished?"

Jonas stared, both impressed by and annoyed with Tate for reading him so easily. "You have no right to my life story."

"Ha, I got close. You don't want to be here, do you? Not even a little bit."

Nope. Well, maybe a little bit. Even though expulsion hadn't been at the top on his list of ways to remove himself from the role he'd played at college—the horny frat boy who would eventually find a girl, get a great job, settle down, make babies and maybe make his father proud of him.

He'd pledged the fraternity because his father had demanded it. Here, no one expected anything from him except that he do his job and respect his curfew. "It's not so bad here."

Tate's brow furrowed. "Where are you from?"

"Lake Bluff, Illinois. It's near Chicago."

"Ah. City boy."

"So? You some grass-fed country boy?"

"Hardly. I grew up in Wilmington. Been in or around it my entire life."

"All eighteen years of it?"

"Twenty-three."

Tate was older than him. Why the hell did that matter?

"And you're what?" Tate smirked. "Thirty?"

Ouch. "Ha ha. Twenty-one."

"Out of college?"

Time to change the subject, like, now.

Except he answered, instead. "I have two years left. I'm, uh, taking a break."

"You're twenty-one and still a junior?"

"Yes." No way was Jonas admitting he'd been kept back in fourth grade because he sucked so badly at math.

"Uh-huh. You're going to be around the rest of the year?"

"Probably until next summer, yes. Why?"

"Then, as it seems we'll be seeing more of each other, we should grab lunch or something one day. I can show you around the neighborhood. Maybe you'll realize it's not the slum you seem to think it is, that there are some great people here." Tate flashed him a cocky smile that irritated him to no end. "Believe it or not, there's a fantastic coffee shop two blocks from here."

"I'm, uh, pretty busy here most days." He also had no intention of letting Tate find out how close to the mark some of his comments were.

"Come on, man, even thrift store employees get days off."

He had to give Tate something so he would go away. "Maybe. We'll see."

"*Maybe* is not *no*." He pulled out a clunky flip phone that was probably on a monthly minutes plan. "Give me your number."

Jonas had no good reason to do that, but he did. And he put Tate's number in his own phone, a little embarrassed by his top-of-the-line model and unsure why.

"I've gotta get these back to the shelter," Tate said as he picked up the basket of sheets. "It was nice meeting you, Jonas. I'll see you around."

"Yes, um, you, too." That didn't make a whole lot of sense as a response, but something about Tate made him fumble around even though he usually had no problem talking his way through a social situation. That kind of pissed him off.

He tracked Tate's easy stroll across the street. He had just enough sway to his hips to make Jonas wonder...

Didn't matter. He and Tate were not now, nor were they ever going to be friends. If Tate actually called about coffee, he'd find a way to get out of it. Eventually Tate would get the message and back off.

He hoped.

Tate punched the lock code into the shelter's back door harder than necessary, taking his confusion over the last ten minutes out on the keypad with trembling fingers. Holy fucking hell, Jonas Ashcroft was gorgeous. Like, model gorgeous with a perfectly contoured face, high cheekbones, thick brown hair, the prettiest hazel eyes he'd ever seen on a human being. And the faint "I forgot to shave today" scruff?

Yeah, scruff always did it for Tate. Just enough to feel it when they kissed or to tickle between his—nope. Pointless fantasy. Tate was interested, but everything about Jonas—from his perfect posture to his pointed stares—screamed "straight."

Except for the handful of times he'd caught Jonas holding eye contact longer than most straight guys would with a gay one. Not that Jonas had any reason to guess Tate was gay. Tate wasn't obvious about it, and it wasn't like he'd gone in with any serious flirting. And a lot of straight people were staunch allies. Hell, they'd actually exchanged phone numbers, even though Tate had figured the coffee shop thing to be a long shot. Especially after he'd kind of insulted Jonas while delivering the invitation.

Tate was too busy with the shelter and his sisters to bother dating, but if Jonas could smooth out some of his prickly edges, Tate wouldn't mind being friends.

A friend you want to lick from top to bottom.

"Tate? You back?" Marc's shout echoed down the corridor from the direction of the kitchen, and he followed the sound.

When he and Marc had decided to go all in on the shelter two years ago, it was through determination—and maybe a tiny bit of luck—they'd landed this location. Not only because it helped tie them to the thrift store, but because the building had once been a restaurant and it came with a full kitchen. He found Marc in there with a clipboard in hand, going over the racks of metal shelves that stored their food donations. Their budget for purchasing food wasn't what Tate wanted it to be, so they relied heavily on the generosity of a few frequent donors.

"Oh good, you got the sheets," Marc said after a quick glance in his direction.

"Yep."

"How's Doris? Gout any better?"

"Not sure. She wasn't there."

"Yeah? She left Raymond in the store alone?" Marc chuckled.

Raymond Burke was good people, but Tate had witnessed him fussing with the registers—and customers—enough to know why he stuck to the back room and donation pickups. He'd been a construction foreman in his early life, until a back injury forced him to find new work. Doris had already been working for the owners of All Saints Thrift Store, and they'd wanted to sell and move to Florida. Doris possessed, according to herself, all of the business sense, so they'd taken a chance.

Money wasn't always free-flowing in the Burke house but they both seemed to enjoy the challenge. The store was open Wednesday through Sunday so she could supervise almost all business hours, unless their daughter, Claire, volunteered to help. But Claire was pretty busy lately surviving her senior year of high school, so Tate hadn't seen her around much.

"Her nephew is staying here for the year." The memory of Jonas's beautiful face made Tate smile. "I can't decide if he's an asshole or not."

"Uh-oh." Marc turned around to face him, lips twisted in a familiar smirk. "Don't tell me you're crushing on him already."

"You would too if you saw him. He could give Matt Bomer a run for his money in the drop-dead-stunning department."

"Oh yeah?" Marc straightened. "When you're done, can I have him?"

"You wish."

"He'd be so lucky. Unless…"

Tate stared at Marc's amused face until he finally gave in and asked, "Unless what?"

"Unless you think this one's gonna be more than your usual habit of pump and dump. You thinking about getting serious for a change?"

"Asshole. No. He's probably straight anyway."

"Doesn't mean you can't admire the goods."

"So true. Did Lilah strip the beds yet?"

"Yeah."

"Cool."

Tate used his elbow to push open the door from the

kitchen to the main area of the shelter. With planning help from Raymond and the design expertise of their third partner, Dave, they'd redesigned the open floor plan to make five smaller rooms with three sets of bunk beds each. Thirty beds that allowed them to create safe spaces for girls, boys and everyone in between, depending on who showed up for the night. They also had two separate bathrooms with showers, and a large living area with donated couches and picnic tables for eating breakfast.

They didn't have the resources yet to offer more than one meal, but they always had snacks available at night. The doors opened at eight and closed at nine, and everyone had to be out by eight the next morning, until the weather turned. Once the cold set in, they'd open the doors at six. In the two and a half months since they'd officially opened their doors, all thirty beds had been full every night.

All it had taken was word of mouth.

As much as Tate loved helping these kids, his heart also broke for each and every one of them. He knew what it was like to work the streets for meal money. He knew what it felt like to offer up your mouth for a twenty-dollar bill, and how dirty that money was in your pocket. So did Marc.

They both had their own reasons for doing this every day.

Lilah had stripped the beds, as promised, and they smelled faintly of lemon disinfectant. The mattresses were thin, college dorm style, and each one was encased in a rubber cover to protect against lice, scabies and anything else the kids might bring in with them. Cleanliness standards were huge, especially when it came to a nonprofit like All Saints House. Even the smallest violation could get them shut down.

Tate remade the beds with the freshly laundered sheets. They couldn't afford their own washer and dryer yet, so Doris had very generously offered to let them use her set at home. Sometimes Tate did them himself, sometimes another person in the Burke household helped out, but every single morning the shelter had clean sheets for the beds.

He bumped into Lilah in the main area, where she was wiping down the picnic tables with disinfectant. A retired school counselor with a husband who made good money working for the city, Lilah had plenty of free time to help with the shelter.

She'd also been friends with Doris forever.

"Did you know Doris and Raymond have a nephew?" he asked.

She paused in her work and looked up, her wire glasses halfway down her nose. "Yes, Raymond's sister's son. He's about your age, I think."

Jonas had seemed genuinely affronted when Tate teased him about being thirty, and Tate kind of liked that he was older than Jonas. "I met him today at the shop."

"I'd heard something about him staying with the Burkes for a while. Some kind of trouble at college."

"Oh yeah?" Tate's instincts had been spot-on, then. "He knock up some mayor's daughter?"

Lilah laughed. "No, nothing like that. Doris isn't one to gossip, especially about family. You'd have to ask her for the details. Or her nephew, I suppose."

"I tried. Jonas didn't seem keen on talking about it."

"Oh, Jonas, that's right. You two get along well?"

"He's a little rude, but he agreed to let me show him around. Get to know the neighborhood."

"That was generous of you."

"Well, he's easy on the eyes, so it's not a hardship, trust me."

"So you do have an ulterior motive."

"Don't I always?"

Tate went off to finish making the beds, the sound of Lilah's laughter trailing behind him. Tate had always had a plan, ever since he was fourteen years old and had become the man of the household. It had helped him and his two sisters survive their father's death, and two years later, their mother's.

First step in Tate's new plan: figure out just how straight Jonas Ashcroft really was.

Don't miss Come What May *by A.M. Arthur,*
available now wherever
Carina Press ebooks are sold.
www.CarinaPress.com